RED WIDOW

THE CHRONICLES OF JESSE AMES
BOOK ONE

LUANNE BENNETT

*Age like a fine wine and
kick butt every step of the way.*

1

THERE ARE PERKS TO STUFFING A CIGARETTE BETWEEN YOUR lips and not lighting it up. No ravaging of your lungs for starters. In my line of work, stopping to catch my breath after falling into a run could get me killed. I also didn't miss the way my clothes smelled like an ashtray twenty-four seven. But unlit tobacco is harmless, and I liked the way the butt felt against my lips. Just the thought of firing it up gave me a rush. Quitting is definitely one of the hardest things I've ever done, and I've done *a lot* of hard things in my forty-five years.

I pulled into a convenience store to pick up a pack and parked directly in front of the entrance so I could keep an eye on my bike. Taking your eyes off a vintage Harley in this part of town would be stupid. There was a single car parked a few spaces down and no one at the gas pumps, which meant a quick in and out.

Thor stuck his head out of my leather jacket as I climbed off the seat. He preferred to burrow in my inside pocket where he could have a little privacy as well as protection from the wind on the road.

"You need to take a leak?" I set him down on the asphalt and walked toward the door. "Hurry up. If you're not done by the time I come back out, I'm leaving your ass." My patience was wearing thin tonight, and I needed a cold beer. I didn't even like the stuff that much, but in the heat of Atlanta, a frosty bottle of hops was downright tantalizing.

As Thor padded off to the side of the building, I went inside and headed for the least healthy section of the store. The one with the most sugar. After grabbing a candy bar and a bag of chips, I made my way down the aisle toward the checkout window. The guy standing behind the plexiglass barrier was looking at me funny, his eyes stretched wide and his mouth agape like he'd been up for days or had just gotten high in the back room.

"What the hell's your problem?" I set the snacks on the counter and pointed to the cigarettes. "Give me a pack of those." I reached into my pocket to grab some cash, but he didn't move. "Did you hear me?" I was about to bark at him when I felt the Marine Corps–emblem tattoo on my wrist start to move.

Uncle Ames's words suddenly filled my head. *We got trouble, Jesse.*

"Yeah, I figured," I muttered out loud, making the guy behind the counter look even more like he was about to fall apart. He was a bag of nerves.

My dead relatives had a way of hijacking my thoughts whenever they damn well pleased, but it came in handy at times, like right now.

Mr. Nervous darted his eyes over my shoulder, but before I could turn around to see who was standing behind me, I heard a click. It was a sound I was all too familiar with. Eleven years at the Federal Bureau of Investigation had taught me a little bit about how to handle such situations, but even for a seasoned ex-fed, a gun pointed at the back of your head usually ends badly.

He nudged me with the barrel. "Get your hand out of your pocket and get over there against the counter!"

I slowly pulled my hand away from my jacket and raised them both in the air. As I turned around and started to back up, I noticed he was shaking. There was nothing worse than a shaky hand pressed against the trigger of a gun pointed at your face.

"You want the money in my pocket?" I raised a questioning brow and tried not to sweat as the gun shook in his hand.

His eyes shifted to the store clerk. "Empty the fucking register onto the counter!" Then he glanced at my nice shiny bike parked out front, and I nearly lost it.

Shoot me in the leg or something, but don't take my bike.

Uncle Ames seemed to agree and took control of the situation. I shifted sideways as my right leg kicked out, hitting the guy in the hip. He flew backward, slamming into an endcap that was loaded with junk food.

The gun flew and landed several feet away. We both lunged for it, but he beat me to it. As he tried to steady it in his trembling hand, it went off. The bullet shattered the plexiglass barrier, sending the clerk running around the counter toward the front door, squealing like a pig. As he yanked it open and ran out, Thor came in and let out a vicious growl.

Finally getting control of the gun, the robber pointed it at Thor.

"I wouldn't do that if I were you." I grabbed the chips from the counter and tore the bag open, popping a few in my mouth. "His bite is worse than his bark."

The guy snorted. "It's a damn rat in a fur coat."

"Poodle, actually." He was right about Thor's size though. He was barely bigger than a guinea pig. "But hey, take your best shot."

He turned back to Thor and pulled the trigger. As the gun discharged, Thor jumped, shifting into a sizable gray wolf. The bullet burrowed into his thick coat, and a small spot of blood appeared on his fur as he sailed through the air and landed on top of the guy, taking him down hard.

After walking behind the counter to fetch the pack of cigarettes, I grabbed the snacks and tossed a bill at the register. "Don't kill him," I said without looking back as I headed outside.

While I watched Thor teach the thug a stern lesson, I kick-started my bike and stuffed a handful of potato chips in my mouth. By the time I finished the bag, crumpled it up, and tossed it like Jordan into the trash can next to the door, Thor was still going at it inside. I didn't have time for this shit. Nor did I care to have a chat with the police.

The guy went still on the floor, and the door flew open. Thor came bounding out, and the bullet that had barely pierced his skin fell from his thick fur and hit the sidewalk with a ping. I caught him as he jumped and shifted, the tiny wound already healed. He landed in my arms in a compact package of curly white fur without so much as a bloodstain on it.

After stuffing him in my pocket, I waited to see if the guy inside the store was going to move or if I'd wake up to a news report about a man getting mauled to death by a wild animal in a convenience store just outside Cabbagetown. Wouldn't that set all the hipsters invading the area into a tizzy? The neighborhood watch group would be armed with pitchforks by noon.

The man lifted his head slightly and glanced around, saving me from having to lecture Thor about moderation when we got home. Hearing sirens in the distance, I pulled my helmet on and stuffed the candy bar in my pocket. Then I got out of there before I found myself with some explaining to do.

Six blocks later, I drove up to the house I was renting and pulled around back. Ma wouldn't like it, but I'd like it even less if someone took a shine to my bike, so I preferred to park next to the back patio.

Why invite trouble?

After parking, I headed over to Speaks to get that cold beer I'd been dreaming about. Speaks—short for speakeasy—was an interesting establishment owned by Rhona Wallace, better known as Ma. She'd been a resident of Cabbagetown all her life, refusing to sell her property even when investors offered her a ridiculous amount of money for it. Her family had been some of the first to come down from the mountains of North Georgia to work at the cotton mill, so this was her home. Speaks would live on until she drew her last breath. Even then, you didn't just close a place like Speaks. It had a life of its own, and you'd probably have to burn the place to the ground to destroy it. Yeah, good luck with that.

As I crossed the street, I spotted a group of youngsters strolling down the sidewalk. Your typical college students that flooded the area on the weekends, looking for hole-in-the-wall establishments to ruin. Speaks had managed to remain an unsullied local treasure, but that was starting to change. Good thing it had a unique way of hiding under the radar.

"Excuse me, ma'am."

I turned around and resisted the urge to growl when one of them trotted over. "Yeah?"

He had a cocky look in his eyes as he sized me up and came dangerously close. Dangerous for him. Based on the overwhelming stench of beer on his breath, I gathered this wasn't their first stop for the evening.

"We're looking for a place called Spanks or Speakys." He glanced at his friends and laughed. Then he turned back to me, his bloodshot eyes wandering down the front of my jacket. "Want to join us?"

What I really wanted to do was point him to another street, but I felt generous tonight. "I'm heading over there, so you can follow me if you want." I walked toward the unassuming entrance at the end of the block. Speaks didn't make itself obvious, so unless you knew where you were going, you'd walk right past the entrance and have no idea that a dive bar was just beyond the door. It kept a lot of undesirables out.

As I reached the place, I pointed to the sign over the door that said PEAK, the first and last letters on the weathered board faded beyond recognition. The tinted windows didn't help either. Then I kept going toward the corner of the building.

"Hey! Aren't you coming inside?" He got that grin on his face again. "Ma'am."

Thor stuck his head out from under my jacket and let out a wolf-sized growl, but I stopped him before he could jump out of my pocket and take a bite out of the guy's scrotum. No need to disfigure the boy for trying to pull a Mrs. Robinson.

The guy glanced at him and chuckled. "What the hell is that?"

"Someone else who doesn't like the word *ma'am*." I stuffed Thor's head back inside my jacket and turned the corner, hoping the guy wasn't stupid enough to follow me.

He wisely didn't, and I walked around to the back of the building to an unmarked door. The entrance to the real Speaks. The only thing that separated the mundane restaurant front from the more colorful establishment in the rear was the kitchen, which also happened to be an energy hedge.

You could hear a pin drop outside, but the second I pulled the door open, the night air was filled with raucous laughter. Normally Ma would put an end to all the noise, preferring a more civilized crowd in the place, but it was Saturday night. Axe-throwing night. The one night a week when Rhona Wallace allowed her clientele to act like a bunch of rowdy fools. It also meant someone had bagged a specter, and bagging a specter wasn't easy. Usually one that caused trouble and wouldn't leave when asked nicely. It was harmless though. Ever tried to nail an apparition with an axe? Before the night was up, the spell holding it to the target would weaken and send it on its way, no worse for wear.

I'd met Ma shortly after moving to Atlanta from New Orleans. Actually, she found me. My Uncle Ames, who'd died three days before I was born, was protective of me. Even more so than the other ancestors who manifested as tattoos on my body. He led her straight to me when I was holed up in some roach trap on the south side of town. Ma and her mother, a hedge witch who'd opened Speaks in the fifties, had known him well.

After making my way through the crowd, I tossed the candy bar down and took a seat.

Ma came through the swinging doors and eyed the chocolate before grabbing a glass and filling it from the tap.

I glanced at the frothy drink when she set it down in front of me. "Did I ask for a beer?"

"It's ninety-three degrees outside at ten p.m. Of course you want a cold beer." Although she was born and raised on American soil, her Scottish-Appalachian temper was showing. She glanced at the candy bar again and shook her head. "I guess I'm not going to find the rent money tucked underneath it, am I?" Her right brow cocked as she looked at my jacket. "Unless that's a wad of cash bulging in there." Thor squirmed in my pocket. "I didn't think so."

"Come on, Ma. You know I'm good for it." If I didn't drum up some business soon, JT Investigations would be nothing more than a name on a business card, which I'd conveniently left in neat little stacks all over town. I'd slipped my calling cards just about everywhere, including in the ladies' room of the Ritz Carlton downtown. I even tacked a few to the wall in the men's room. The one thing I knew for sure was I'd sleep in my car if I had one before I'd go back to the bureau. That Harley seat would get awfully crowded with me and Thor both bunking down on it.

LUANNE BENNETT

She grabbed the candy bar and tore the wrapper open. "Next time get me some cookies."

"You're a lifesaver, Ma." I reached over the bar and pulled her closer, planting a kiss on her forehead.

She pushed me away and walked back to the kitchen. A few minutes later, she returned with two bowls of beef stew and a hefty piece of freshly baked bread. "No eating on top of the bar."

I set the other bowl on the floor and opened my jacket so Thor could hop out and eat his dinner. Then I glanced at mine and twirled my index finger over it. "There's nothing funny in here, is there?"

Speaks was known for its Southern cuisine, but the food in the back sometimes came with a little extra dose of funny business. To Ma's horror, a local magazine had written a glowing review of the place that resulted in an influx of curious outsiders to the more public front side of Speaks, including that group I'd come across on my way in. Thankfully, what they didn't know was that the real culinary magic took place back here.

Ma shook her head and walked away, and I dug in. I hadn't even swallowed my first bite when the place went unusually quiet. You could hear a pin drop when the front door creaked open.

"There you are."

When I glanced over my shoulder, the guy who'd insisted on calling me ma'am was walking toward me.

"Fuck," I muttered as I set my spoon down and looked at Thor, who was growling near my feet. "Don't do it."

Did he listen? Hell no.

He took off toward the group of young men who must have followed me and gotten curious about that back door. He was about to leap when something came whirling through the air. An axe embedded itself into the wooden floor with a thud, blocking his path to give his voice of reason some time to kick in.

8

I glanced at Hector, Speaks's resident axe-throwing champ. Then I glared at the noisy idiots who'd come to a halt by the door. "You guys shouldn't be in here."

Mr. Ma'am gawked at the axe and started to back up. "Yeah, we were just leaving."

Hector grinned, and I got a sickening feeling those boys were about to regret walking around the building. In fact, they were probably going to regret waking up that morning.

"Let it go, Hector. They're just a bunch of stupid kids."

The one with rusty-orange hair huffed. "Kids? Who you calling a kid?"

It was the alcohol talking, but he was about to sober up quickly.

Before I could intervene, Hector had him by the back of his shirt and was manhandling him across the room. "Double or nothing I can land the blade right here." He pushed the guy against the target and planted his index finger on the wall a mere inch above his head. Then he pointed it at the kid's face. "I wouldn't move if I were you."

I got up to put an end to it, but something stopped me. The tattoo on my wrist undulated, and I heard a voice in my head.

Stay out of it!

You didn't question Uncle Ames unless you wanted to find yourself on the floor. And Ma didn't seem the slightest bit concerned about the bloodbath about to take place in the middle of her establishment. The others stood frozen near the door with their mouths gaping as their friend faced his mortality. I don't think it was of their own volition. By the grin on Ma's face, I suspected she'd thrown a little incantation their way to make them stay put. Same with the kid facing the axe.

Hector walked back over to the door and yanked the axe out of the floor. Then he took a few steps toward the target and looked at the petrified young man, drawing a bead of blood from the tip of his finger when he ran it along the sharp edge. "Watch this." With a maniacal grin that would chill Charles Manson to the bone, he pulled his arm back and took aim.

I glanced at Ma. "You can't take this back if it ends badly."

She continued to wipe the glass in her hand and said, "Then let's hope it doesn't end badly."

Hector let out a war cry and released the axe, sending it somersaulting across the room. A collective gasp filled the air as the edge of the sharp blade hit the guy's forehead and came to an abrupt stop, leaving a surface cut no deeper than a scratch on his skin. The axe fell toward his feet but never hit the floor, picking up momentum as it reversed. With the speed of a rocket, it whizzed past his stunned buddies and embedded itself in the wall next to the door.

Hector looked at their stunned faces and lost his grin. "Git!"

Ma released her hold on the young men, and they wasted no time skedaddling out the door. But the one with the target on his forehead just stood there against the wall with a wet crotch.

"You!" Hector barked. "Out. And don't come back!"

When they were gone, I shook my head at him. "Was that really necessary? The kid's going to be traumatized for life."

Ma set the glass under the bar and locked eyes with me. "They came in here uninvited."

"And you think they won't mention this little stunt to their friends? Not to mention the authorities." I took a swallow of my beer. "I think you just advertised the place."

"They're going to wake up with a nasty headache and an unexplainable aversion to the place." Then she walked toward the kitchen. "Get me that rent money when you can."

2

A STREAM OF ANNOYING SUNLIGHT HIT ME SQUARE IN THE eyes when I rolled over. The clock on the nightstand said ten fifteen, so I'd overslept by… oh… three hours.

Glancing at the warm body lying next to me, I slipped out of bed and threw on a T-shirt and underwear before stumbling into the kitchen. I'd barely finished my beer the night before, but my head was saying I drank a six-pack. I needed water and food. Lots of spicy food.

I scratched my head as I stared at the refrigerator shelves. There were three eggs, a container of takeout that was probably a festering science experiment, and a bag of wilted salad greens I swear I was planning on eating this time. It all looked very unappetizing, but the protein was calling my name.

As I grabbed the eggs, an arm slipped around my waist. Then a set of lips trailed up my neck and stopped at my ear.

He murmured in a husky voice, "You were a beast last night."

"And you were still in my bed this morning." I shoved him away with an irritated look. "Why?"

He stepped back and slapped me on the ass. "What's the matter? Getting a little too close to actual intimacy?"

"Is that what you think last night was? Don't flatter yourself." I turned away before he could see the grin on my face. Letting it fizzle, I nodded to the loaf of bread on the counter. "See if it's moldy."

I really needed to get to the grocery store, but that required funds.

As I grabbed a pan from the cabinet, there was a knock on the door. No one knocked on my door. Ever.

"Are you expecting someone?" he asked.

I shook my head, acutely aware of my dead relatives jabbering away in the background of my mind. And not just Uncle Ames—all of them. "Fuck."

Before answering it, I went into the bedroom to grab my gun. Call me paranoid, but when you're low on acquaintances and on the run from a dangerous vampire, a knock on the door could get you killed.

The knocking got more persistent as I came back out and peeked through the front window. "It's a woman." By the way she was dressed, she looked like she was in the wrong neighborhood. I also noticed a large black SUV with tinted windows parked out front. Not to mention a tall guy leaning against it with a cigarette hanging out of his mouth.

"You better answer it," he said. "I don't think she's going away."

Holding the revolver behind me, I took Thor's advice and cracked the door open as he shifted and dropped to the floor behind me.

The woman gave me a thorough once-over, looking like she was on the verge of turning around and walking back to her car. I got that sometimes. People usually expected a man to open the door. "Are you Jesse Ames?"

"That depends. Who are you?" I glanced down at her feet and

decided she wasn't much of a threat. Not in those shoes. She wasn't a cop either unless they'd upped a detective's pay grade since I was in law enforcement. My old FBI salary wouldn't have covered her expensive manicure. And the large rubies hanging from her ears didn't look cheap. Who wears ruby earrings at ten a.m.?

With a disarming smile, she held her hand out. "My name is Kiko Fraser. I'd like to hire you, Ms. Ames."

Well, if that wasn't music to my ears. A paying customer was just what the doctor ordered, and she looked like she could afford me. As I swung the door open, I realized I was still wearing nothing but a T-shirt and underwear. "Shit. Sorry about the outfit."

"Don't worry. It's just us girls."

Yeah, and that guy with the dark sunglasses standing next to the SUV eyeing me. I leaned against the doorframe and waved at him.

Her face lit up when she saw Thor on the floor behind me. "What an adorable little dog. May I?" Without waiting for an invitation, she walked inside and scooped him off the floor.

"I'll just..." I pointed to the bedroom and went to throw on a pair of jeans. When I came back out, she was in the living room, standing next to the couch. The thing was pretty worn out, but it had come with the place along with all the other sparse furnishings. Ma's rental might have been little more than a shack, but it was clean, and she expected me to keep it that way. Despite the moldy food in the refrigerator, I was fairly neat. It was Thor who needed a nudge to pick up after himself.

He wiggled in her arms and started to lick her face, staring at me while he did it. When he slipped his tongue in her mouth, she grimaced. "He's a friendly little guy, isn't he?"

"Yeah, he's friendly all right. You might want to hand him over before he starts humping your arm." I took him from her and unceremoniously dumped him on the floor. "Lick her ass for all I care," I muttered as he trotted away.

Her forehead creased as she gave me a funny look. "Excuse me?"

I skated over the remark by offering her a seat. "I don't have anything but water to offer you, but I can make some coffee if you'd like. I might have a tea bag lying around." God, I hated entertaining.

"Thank you, but this won't take very long. I have another meeting I'm already late for." She took a seat on the couch and set her handbag on the cushion next to her. It had a few metal charms that spelled out DIOR dangling from the handle, announcing that she could afford to drop 5K on a purse. There wasn't a shiny black hair out of place, and her makeup was ridiculously impeccable. I had a feeling the woman didn't leave her house without a few hours of prep. Must be exhausting.

I sat down in the chair across from her. "What can I do for you?"

She reached inside her bag and pulled out an envelope. "It's my husband. He's missing, and it's imperative that I find him." She hesitated for a moment as if trying to decide how to broach the conversation. Then she opened the envelope and handed me two pictures.

The first one was a photo of a man I assumed was her husband. He looked like an average guy. A little nerdy. Not bad-looking, but I wouldn't look twice at him if I passed him on the street. With her expensive clothes and perfect makeup, it kind of made me wonder what she saw in him. Women like her usually went for men in flashy suits.

"I know what you're thinking, Ms. Ames."

"And what would that be?"

"You're wondering what I see in Charles."

She had me there.

"There's more to a man than his looks. My husband is quite charming."

No shit, but I didn't like what she was inferring even if that was exactly what I was thinking. Aside from how mismatched they seemed, it appeared to all boil down to a typical case of a wife looking for her philandering husband. But as much as I was up for some easy money, something didn't smell right. My dead relatives didn't seem to think so either, as evidenced by all the chattering in my head when she'd knocked on my door.

"If he's missing, why don't you just go to the police?"

She got a funny little smile on her face. "My family is very wealthy, Ms. Ames. The slightest indiscretion could be used against us. I'd prefer to handle this matter privately."

More bullshit.

"I'm not cheap, Mrs. Fraser. Even for something as typical as finding a missing spouse."

"Yes, I know. But you're discreet, and that's what I'm really paying for. I also hear you're the best at what you do, so I'm sure you'll get the job done."

I sat deeper into the chair and cut through the crap. "Why don't you tell me the truth. Then I'll decide if I'll take the case." She gave me that condescending smile again, and I almost got up to politely throw her out. Assholes tried my patience, and anyone who thought I was stupid qualified as one. "You have ten seconds. Make that five."

"We're newlyweds," she blurted out. "Charles and I have only been married for a few months." She turned her eyes to the floor for a moment before continuing. "I'm afraid he played me for a fool. Married me for my money." She handed me the envelope that was gripped tightly in her hand. "In addition to cleaning out one of our bank accounts, he stole something very precious to me. A ring. It's a family heirloom that's worth a lot of money, but more importantly, it can't be replaced."

The second picture was of an ornate ring with a large stone in the center.

"It looks like silver, so I'm assuming it's the stone that's valuable." At first I thought it was a ruby, but when I looked closer at the photograph, the stone appeared to be much lighter. Almost pink. "What kind of stone is it?"

"It's a very rare form of ruby." She quickly changed the subject, which made me even more suspicious about the ring and what she wasn't telling me. "We met at his favorite club. He used to go there every Friday night, so you might want to start there and ask around. He's also very close to his sister, so perhaps she'd be a good lead." She nodded to the envelope. "It's all in there. Pictures, background information. Whatever you need to find him and the ring."

"Would you settle for the ring alone if I can find it?"

Her eyes flashed with a look I'd seen a hundred times on the faces of scorned spouses. A combination of pain and anger with a little humiliation thrown in. "It's a package deal, Ms. Ames. I want them both."

Keep an eye on this one, Uncle Ames warned.

He was right to be wary. Kiko Fraser's motives were more than just to find her gold-digging husband and a ring. I could smell it. She was out for revenge, and vengeful women are dangerous.

Something told me to listen to my uncle and show her the door. Cases like this seem easy, but in reality, they're messy. I'd sworn I'd never make my living by tracking down cheaters. I preferred to hunt down bad guys for *other* bad guys. But Ma would eventually need a paying renter, and Thor and I needed to eat. "I'll talk to my partner and see if he's interested in taking the case."

"Partner? I thought you worked alone?" She was having second thoughts, and so was I.

"The T in JT Investigations. Don't worry. He's just as discreet."

"Perhaps I should meet with him myself to convince him."

I glanced at Thor, who was whining at me. "That won't be necessary. We'll take the case, but we'll need half our fee up front."

She stood up and reached into her bag for another envelope. "This should be sufficient. There's extra for expenses as well."

I looked inside but didn't need to count it to know it was more than enough. Looked like we'd be eating steak for dinner. "You got a number where I can reach you?"

She handed me a black business card with DRAGON ENTER-PRISES written in red letters across the front. I'd be checking out her company as soon as she left.

"Well," I said, standing up to follow her to the door, "it was a pleasure to meet you. I'll get on it this afternoon and let you know what I find out."

On her way out the door, she looked back at me. "For what I'm paying you, Ms. Ames, I expect swift results."

"Of course." As she headed for the SUV, I called out to her. "By the way, where did you hear about me?" And how the hell did you get my address, I wanted to add.

She stopped for a moment but didn't turn around. "An old acquaintance at the FBI recommended you."

"Oh yeah? Who?"

The driver held the door open, and she climbed in without answering me. My skin was crawling with questions, or maybe it was just the ancestors warning me to tread lightly around Kiko Fraser.

After watching the SUV pull away, I shut the door and walked to the living room where Thor was pacing back and forth naked.

"Put some pants on," I said before sitting down to rip into

the envelope containing her husband's information.

I watched him walk toward the bedroom, taking in his lovely ass. Thor—aka Theodore—and I had a convenient relationship. No messy strings. Just an occasional distraction that never went beyond the bedroom. He was a shifter after all, and shifters weren't boyfriend material, let alone marriage material. Not that I ever intended to dive into holy matrimony again. I tried that once and it didn't agree with me. The single life was more my cup of tea.

But Theodore wasn't your garden-variety shifter. He was a wolf who'd evolved into something unique out of necessity. In order to save his ass from a master vampire named Lucius, whom he'd swindled, he'd become a shifter within a shifter. His inner wolf adapted to shifting into a tiny little dog the size of a tin can. Why? Because the Roman vampires who were still hunting him to this day were looking for a wolf. Unless they got lucky, they'd never find him hiding under a coat of curly white fur.

Jesse Ames Investigations was born right before we met. I'd just left the FBI, and one of my first clients was a demigod named Gabriel. He hired me to find Thor, who'd been contracted by the Romans to kill him. To make a long story short, I got to Thor before he got to Gabriel, thwarting the hit, but Thor never gave the money back to the vampires. I couldn't blame him. Lucius would have killed him just to tie up loose ends. And since a wolf was useful to my business, we partnered up and formed JT Investigations.

So Thor was born. When we first met, I made the mistake of calling him Teddy for short. He nearly ripped my throat out. Now I only call him that when I'm feeling brave and want to really piss him off.

Thor came back into the living room as I was reading through the information in the envelope. "It says he's from upstate New York."

"Are you telling me we're going on a road trip?"

I chuckled. "Not if I can help it."

Thor picked up the business card I'd laid on the coffee table and read it. "What is she into? Dragon Con and RenFest?"

"Hey, don't knock it. There's good money in that shit."

He went to grab my laptop from the kitchen counter. "Not enough to buy Dior bags and a steady supply of cocaine."

"Coke? How do you know she does coke?"

He glanced at me with a deadpan gaze. "Because I could taste it."

"Oh, that's right. You had your tongue rammed up her nose. You're disgusting." I didn't care who he licked as long as he brushed his teeth and disinfected his mouth before climbing into my bed.

"I could smell it all over her. Either our new client has a drug problem or she's a dealer." His fingers tapped at the keyboard. "Dragon Enterprises doesn't seem to exist according to the internet. No website or anything."

I slid the laptop over to search for myself. Digging a little deeper, I came up with an address and a registered agent's name. I knew it was the right company because there was a picture of her distinct business card in the search results. "It looks like a shell company registered in Panama."

He shook his head in disbelief. "How did you figure that out?"

"Dark web, baby. You need to brush up on your skills."

"That's not what you said last night."

"Stop. You're making an old woman blush."

His lips quirked. "Old? Your words, not mine."

The dark web was a candy store of illicit information. Pornography, where to buy drugs. But there was perfectly legit information out there as well. It was the unfiltered sea of the internet. But the fact that there was no information through a

Google search, yet Dragon Enterprises showed up in the dark underbelly of the web, reeked of impropriety.

I shut the laptop and swung my feet up on the coffee table, mulling over the brief meeting I'd just had with our new client. Uncle Ames had picked up on something, and now the crescent moon on my biceps was vibrating. Someone named Sam or Samantha had manifested the tattoo recently, but I still hadn't been able to pinpoint who she was on the old family tree. "What are you hiding, Mrs. Fraser?" If I wasn't so hard up for cash, I would have called the number on the card and told her to come get her retainer. But I was desperate, so that money wasn't going anywhere.

Thor started digging deeper into the information Kiko had given me. "It says here his sister lives in New Orleans."

Swinging my feet back to the floor, I grabbed the envelope full of cash and confirmed that she'd added enough for travel expenses. "Then I guess I might be going to New Orleans this week."

"You mean *we're* going to New Orleans."

I stared at him like he was off his rocker. "Well, it is your funeral." The Romans were in New Orleans. Biggest and meanest house of vampires in the South. The very bloodsuckers who had a perpetual bounty on his head. They'd smell him out the moment he crossed the Louisiana state line. Then I'd have to go through the hassle of changing the company name back to Jesse Ames Investigations.

"Hmm. Good point," he said, pulling his brows together. "I guess I'll have to miss all the fun."

"Don't worry. I'll bring you some beignets."

I went to get dressed because I needed to go pay Ma what I owed her for the rent. Then I planned to make a stop to see a guy about a rock.

3

SPEAKS DIDN'T OPEN UNTIL NOON, SO I DROVE A FEW blocks north to a place I'd dubbed Jurassic Bark. Thor wisely passed on joining me because he wasn't in the mood for a fight, which was exactly what he got every time he walked into the place. He seemed to bring out the worst in certain people, and that included the four-legged type as well.

I pulled up to the ten-foot-tall orange dinosaur and climbed off my bike, making sure it was parked close enough to keep my eye on it but far enough away from the wall enclosing the studio to avoid any flying objects. Zeb had a reputation for getting a little overzealous when he got into the zone, and hunks of scrap metal were known to come flying out of the window, among other things.

"Damn piece of—"

I heard some colorful expletives the second I walked through the door, and a hammer came hurtling across the room, barely missing me. "Whoa! Hold your fire! It's Jesse!"

A distinct groan came from the studio after I announced myself.

"I don't have time for a visit. I'm working." Still wearing his welder's cap, he walked past me and grabbed a sheet of metal from a table at the other end of the converted machine shop. As if suddenly finding his manners, he laid it back down and turned around with a wide grin. "Hey, Jesse!"

Zeb was like a light switch. He could flip himself from dark and bitter to sunny and sweet in an instant. I didn't take it personally. It was just the way he was wired.

Before I could open my mouth to return the pleasantries, two large beasts came bounding around the corner. I stumbled against the wall as the gentle giants plowed into me, sniffing my jacket when they picked up Thor's scent.

"Off!" Zeb ordered.

Lula, the merle Great Dane, fell down on all fours, but the black one ignored him and stuck her snout in my face.

"Jesus, Raven! Get off me!" I covered my mouth before she could stick her tongue down my throat.

These two were the reason Thor had looked at me like I'd invited him to the proctologist when I asked if he wanted to tag along. Even in his human form, they could smell his alter ego, and both the wolf and the poodle brought out the worst in the gentle giants.

Zeb snapped his fingers, and the two dogs planted their asses on the ground obediently.

"I wish I could do that with Thor." I straightened my jacket and grimaced when my hand grazed a drop of slobber.

"Yeah, good luck with that. Where is the mutt?"

"At home where he can avoid them." I nodded to the dogs waiting for their master to release them from their sitting position.

Zeb gave them a hand command that sent them trotting across the room where they settled on a pair of papasan chair cushions in the corner.

"Moon chair cushions? Those dogs have it made."

He chuckled. "Ever tried to find a bed big enough for a Great Dane? Those cushions are a hell of a lot cheaper too."

Finally removing his welder's shield, he let his long white hair fall free. It had a crown of black streaks running through it, hence his name. Zeb, short for zebra, because that's exactly what his hair looked like. In his midsixties, Zeb was a well-known artist in the South. He could have made a lot of money off his work, but he refused to sell most of it, preferring to donate his pieces to institutions of his choice. His studio drew a lot of attention and often caused traffic jams outside due to all the colorful sculptures that lined the property.

I followed him into the adjoining studio where he was working on his latest creation: a seven-foot-tall something or other. On closer inspection, it looked like some kind of plant. Well, it was green, but the weird things coming out of it were a mystery. "What is it?"

His brow twisted. "What the hell does it look like?"

"If I knew that, I wouldn't be asking."

He walked over to the green metal structure, grumbling something under his breath. Then he kicked it hard. It toppled over and hit the ground, making the dogs jump to their feet when the loud noise echoed through the cavernous room.

"What did you do that for?"

Artists. They were temperamental creatures.

He snorted and pulled off his welding gloves. "It's supposed to be a Venus flytrap. A commission for the botanical garden. But it isn't gonna do any good if no one knows what it is."

I cocked my head and studied the heap of metal. "Oh yeah. I guess I can see it now."

"Why are you here, Jesse?"

I was starting to outwear my welcome, and I didn't want to piss him off. His hair began to take on a life of its own, growing a little longer and darker. That was just one of the signs that his temper was brewing. Wizards were like that. Unpredictable. And a wizard who also happened to be an artist was a powder keg when pushed too far.

"Put a lid on it, Zeb. I just stopped by to show you something. Then I'll leave you to your Venus flytrap."

That seemed to pique his interest. "Show me what?"

I reached into my pocket for the picture of that ring. "Ever seen a stone like this before?" Rare form of ruby, my ass. Kiko Fraser was lying through her teeth.

On top of being a sculptor and a wizard, Zeb was also knowledgeable about stones and minerals. He used a lot of them in his line of work. He took the photo from my hand and examined it. "Hmm. It's hard to tell for sure from a picture, but I guess it could be some kind of ruby."

"I was hired by a woman this morning to find it, along with her missing husband who stole it. She said it's a rare form of ruby, but look at the color."

He walked over to the desk against the wall and started rustling through the top drawer. After finding a magnifying glass, he took a closer look. "It is interesting. I've never seen a ruby this pale. Without having it in my hand, I can't say for sure what it is."

"Well, it was worth a shot. She said it's a family heirloom."

He handed the picture back, then grabbed his welder's cap and started to put it back on. "So find the damn thing and collect your fee. Sounds like you're making a whole lot of something out of nothing."

I hadn't known Zeb very long, but he sure had me pegged. "You're probably right, but I still want to know what it is."

As I climbed on my bike and backed it up, I glanced in my mirror at the car that had been following me since I left the house.

Rule number one when tailing someone—don't be so damn

obvious. Unless that's the whole point. I was supposed to know. After pulling onto the road, I took my time so he could catch up. Then I drove toward Speaks to pay my rent and to see if my new friend was stupid enough to follow me inside. Or at least try.

***

As I PULLED up to the house and parked, I noticed the car following me had disappeared. I figured he'd be back and we'd come face-to-face eventually.

I walked over to Speaks and sat at the bar. The place catered to night owls, so even at the height of lunchtime, it was pretty empty. The public or front side of the restaurant was another story.

An all-too-familiar face came up behind me and its owner took a seat on the stool next to mine.

"Not now," I groaned under my breath.

"Afternoon, Jesse. Looks like I'm just in time to buy you lunch."

"Randy, Randy, Randy." I shook my head. "Why do you always have to make me into one of those women?"

The goofy grin on his face grew wider as he leaned closer. "What kind of woman is that?"

"The kind that always has to tell you *no*." I glanced around the room at the few occupied tables. "You've got all these people in here thinking I'm some stuck-up bitch who thinks she's too good for a local guy like you when all I want to do is walk in here without worrying about getting hit on." He'd regret it if I ever took him up on his offer. I'd break him like a twig.

"That's because you *are* too good for him." Ma came up to us and gave him a warning look. "Go on. Leave the woman alone."

After he got the message for the hundredth time and left, I pulled out a wad of cash and handed it to her. "I got next month's rent in there, too." I figured I'd pay her now before Thor got his hands on some of that money. The word *budget* didn't exist in his vocabulary.

She leaned onto the bar and eyed it for a moment. "Either you got yourself a new case or you robbed a bank this morning." Then she took it from my hand. "Doesn't matter to me. Just let me know if the police are going to come and haul you off so I can start looking for a new tenant."

"Don't worry. JT Investigations is back in business. Some rich woman hired us to find her missing husband."

Her eyes popped. "Hell, I'll find him myself for that kind of money."

"You ever heard of a club called Sanguine?"

She gave me a funny look like she was trying to read between the lines. "Don't tell me you're into that kind of thing."

"Into what? My new client said she met her husband there. Said he was a regular, so I need to go over there and start asking around."

Ma let out a quiet laugh as she wiped down the bar. "Vampires. The place caters to them. From what I hear, you can go into one of the back rooms and take care of your needs."

"Needs? What kind of needs?"

She shrugged. "You know. Get yourself bitten."

"You mean like a fetish?"

"Yep. You know who owns that place? The Bastians."

The name rang a bell, and then it hit me. "You mean the vampires who run drugs through the Southeast?"

"That's right. If I were you, I'd stay clear of the place." She glanced at the cash in her hand. "As much as I hate to give up good money, you might want to return this and tell your new client you're not interested."

Vampires. I shuddered. The one thing I preferred not to mess with. But as much as I hated bloodsuckers, I needed the business.

"I'll be in and out of the place in less than an hour." Nothing about this case felt good, but if I played my cards right, I'd recover that ring and have Charles Fraser answering to his wife by the end of the week. All I had to do was walk into that club, ask a few questions, and leave. If it didn't pan out, I'd pay a visit to his sister. But the idea of setting foot in New Orleans, kingdom of vampires, the place I'd run from when the Romans showed up at my door looking for Thor, made me feel queasy. It was safer to walk into that club and hope for a strong lead.

"Keep the money, Ma. I'll be fine."

The job I thought would be a piece of cake was starting to look more like a shit show waiting to happen. Nerdy-looking Charles Fraser wasn't who he seemed. Wasn't the mild-mannered nerd in the picture after all. Maybe Kiko *was* just another duped bride.

"I gotta go." I got up and walked toward the door, wondering what one wears to a fetish club. I did have a black leather dress that barely covered my ass hanging in the back of my closet. It was from an old case I'd worked at the bureau. *Nah.*

4

Human blood sport must have been pretty popular, because Sanguine was hopping. I'd argued with Thor about coming with me, but he seemed to think walking into a vampire owned establishment was no big deal. But it was a big deal when the most powerful vampire in the Southeast had a bounty on your head. I agreed to let him tag along if he kept his head low and limited himself to one drink. A drunk wolf could be a real dick and would stick out like a sore thumb.

Instead of trying to fit in with the vampire-groupie crowd, I decided to wear my usual, which was jeans and a T-shirt under my leather jacket. Thor, on the other hand, fit right in, wearing black leather pants and a silk shirt. It gave me the willies every time I looked at him.

We made our way to the bar and ordered some drinks. "Don't disappear on me," I said when I saw him scanning the room. His eyes landed on a blonde, and I could feel trouble on the horizon. "I'm serious, Thor. You'll be walking home."

He leaned back against the bar and grinned at me. "Why did you bring me along again?"

"Because you insisted. Jesus, Thor, you can be a real asshole sometimes."

"And yet you keep me around. A therapist would have a field day with you."

I kept him around because he was useful and we were business partners. "Just make an effort not to fuck this up."

The place was packed, hence the reason we were standing at the bar and not sitting. The dance floor was filled with gyrating bodies, most of which were half-naked. At first, I couldn't tell the vampires from the humans, but then I noticed something odd. Some of the people in the club were wearing red pins. I glanced at a bowl on the bar I'd noticed when we first walked up. It was filled with them. I picked one up and realized it was a pair of bright red lips with the word SUB under it. Another pin said DOM. I dropped it and wiped my hand on a napkin.

Thor looked at the bowl curiously. "Hmm. I think I'll be a sub tonight."

I slapped his hand away when he reached for one. "Don't even think about it."

With a sigh, he trained his eyes back on the blonde and grabbed his drink. "I'll be back. I think I need to interrogate that one over there." After nodding to her, he pushed away from the bar and headed in her direction.

Someone rubbed past me, the heat from his arm traveling into mine as he kept it pressed against me. "Hi." His half-mast eyes fixed on mine. "Is that your boyfriend?"

I took a sip of my drink and watched Thor walk down the bar toward the woman. "Not tonight."

A grin crossed his face as he glanced at the bowl and sucked on the tiny red straw in his drink.

"Forget it. Not gonna happen."

His smile turned into a pouty frown that looked well practiced. "Aww, and you haven't even given me a chance."

"Does that usually work for you?" He wasn't a bad-looking guy. Mid to late thirties, which was the perfect age. The sweet spot. Not so young he needed a mommy to do his laundry, and not so old that he was looking at every twentysomething with big boobs that walked past him. But I wasn't here to find a date.

After slurping the last drop of his drink, he set the glass on the bar and started to walk away. "Sorry to bother you."

"Wait." I was wasting a perfectly good opportunity here. "Do you come here often?" Jesus, it sounded like a pickup line.

"Sure."

I pulled Charles Fraser's picture from my pocket and handed it to him. "Have you ever seen this guy in here?"

He looked at the picture for a moment before shaking his head and handing it back to me. "I don't think so."

"You sure about that?"

He got an uneasy look in his eyes and walked toward the entrance without answering. I considered following him outside and interrogating him properly, the bureau way, but Thor caught my eye from across the bar. He was standing next to the woman, but his attention was on something to my left.

I glanced at a guy wearing dark sunglasses, which was a little strange in a club. But then I recognized him. "Son of a bitch," I muttered, downing my drink before making my way toward the exit. After stepping outside, I walked around to the side of the building and waited patiently.

He came around the corner a minute later, and Uncle Ames took over. My right leg shot out from under me as my boot landed in his side, sending him crashing against the building so hard his glasses flew off his face.

He winced, bending over to catch his breath before looking at me. "Fucking bitch!"

"What did you call me?" My elbow wedged into his windpipe

as I punched him in the kidney, making him stumble sideways. "Do you talk to all women with that trash mouth?"

Without warning, he slugged me in the gut. I fell backward as the wind was knocked out of me. I took a couple of steady breaths, backpedaling as he came toward me. When he reached down and grabbed the collar of my jacket and yanked me to my feet, I sucker punched him in the nuts, disabling him the old-fashioned way.

As he lay on the ground crying like a baby, I kicked him in the stomach for good measure. "Tell your boss I don't appreciate being followed. I'll have her money back to her by morning, minus compensation for my trouble." How I was going to come up with it without taking the rent money back from Ma I didn't know. I'd find something worth selling.

Thor came out of the bar as I was walking away from Kiko's driver. "What happened?"

"What the hell do you think happened? Our *ex*-client has been having me followed all day."

He looked at the guy cradling his scrotum. "Uncle Ames?"

"Well, it sure as hell wasn't you coming to my rescue."

The ancestors invading my head had a tendency to lend me their talents when I found myself backed into a corner. And Uncle Ames's talents came in real handy. He was a Marine with fierce martial arts skills. Don't get me wrong, I was perfectly capable of taking down a guy the size of a truck, like Kiko's driver back there, but he was also capable of breaking me like a twig if he managed to get the upper hand. Uncle Ames just made sure he didn't.

"Hold it!" the driver said as I was walking toward my bike. "I was just supposed to deliver a message."

Intrigued, I reined in my temper. "You've been following me all day. Why?"

He finally managed to climb to his feet and stand semi-erect.

"Mrs. Fraser wants to make sure she can trust you to get the job done. I was just supposed to intimidate you. Send you a message that she has eyes on you."

Damn, that pissed me off. Kiko thought she could intimidate me? Babysit me while I did my job? I walked back over to him and stuck my finger in his face. "Tell your boss I don't need a babysitter. If I ever catch you following me again, I'll castrate you. Got it?"

He backed up but didn't say a word. He didn't have to. I'd made my point.

Relief washed over me as I walked back inside. I couldn't afford to lose that money, and Mr. Wonderful out there was the perfect vehicle to deliver a message back to Kiko. Otherwise, I would have walked.

Thor headed back to the bar, but the blonde had already moved on and was pressed against some other guy on the dance floor.

"Sorry." I snickered and ordered another drink.

He sighed and leaned against the bar, running his eyes down the front of my shirt. "That's all right. I have something better to go home with."

I downed my drink the second the bartender handed it to me. "Fuck off."

His cocky grin suddenly vanished, and his skin lost some of its color as he straightened up and looked across the room. Then he quickly turned around. "Shit!"

"What's wrong?" I glanced over my shoulder as a large figure walked toward us and stopped a few feet down to lean over the bar.

The man ordered a shot of tequila, and Thor turned and stared at me nervously. The guy gazed at me over Thor's shoulder, his eyes lowering as a telltale smile spread across his face.

Thor discretely shook his head when I smiled back. Hey, the

guy was hot. But something urgent in Thor's eyes set off some alarm bells.

The guy raised the shot glass to his lips, revealing a tattoo of an ornate capital *R* on his hand. He was a vampire. A Roman.

Thinking fast, I pushed away from the bar and headed toward the restrooms, fixing my eyes on his as I walked past him. As I'd hoped, he followed me, giving Thor the opportunity to disappear.

Halfway down the hallway to the ladies' room, an arm reached out and cut me off. The vampire planted his hand on the wall and leaned in, his face dangerously close to mine.

"You're blocking me." I tried not to look too closely at his spectacular eyes, but it was difficult.

His lips turned up as he cocked his head and trailed his index finger down my neck with a featherlight touch. "How about a suck?"

"Depends on who's doing the sucking." Normally I would have ended it swiftly, but I had my partner to think about. "And it's not gonna be me." When he ran his finger lower, I almost said to hell with Thor and taught the vampire a lesson on boundaries.

That damn wolf owed me.

"That's what I like about older women. You know exactly what you want. You're not afraid to ask for it, are you?" His eyes bored deeper into mine while his wandering hand wisely stopped an inch away from getting my palm rammed into his chin. Then he planted his other hand on the wall, caging me against it. "Want to find a room?"

I wasn't interested in a set of fangs sucking on the artery of my inner thigh, and I'd wasted enough time taking one for the team. "Tempting, but not tonight." I ducked under his arm and headed back down the hallway. If Thor wasn't out of the club by now, he deserved to get his ass dragged back to Lucius.

Apparently not one to take no for an answer, he followed me

back to the bar. Thankfully, Thor was nowhere in sight, and the spot where we'd been standing was now occupied.

"Look," I said, turning around. I was about to give him the brush-off so he wouldn't follow me outside, but something clawed at my ankle. It was Thor. My heart started to pound as I scooped him off the floor and stuffed him inside my jacket. "There you are, you little shit."

The vampire looked at the tiny dog, and his lustful eyes turned questioning. "What the hell is that?"

"Haven't you ever seen a poodle before?"

He stepped back when Thor bared his teeth. It was enough to cool his engines and send him on his way, which I was thankful for. No need to cause a scene.

After he left, Thor hopped out of my jacket and trotted off toward the men's room.

It was getting late, and we were getting nowhere, so I squeezed up to the bar and beckoned the bartender over. "Have you ever seen this guy in here?" I handed him the picture of Charles.

He glanced at it for barely a second and handed it back to me. "Charlie? Yeah." He shrugged and gave me a funny little grin like it was a stupid question.

"So that's a yes?"

"Are you kidding me? He comes in here two or three times a week. Well, he used to. I haven't seen him for a while."

I looked at the nerdy face in the picture. It was hard enough to image him coming in this place on a dare, let alone as a frequent flyer. A regular in a bloodsucker's club? I showed him the picture again. "You sure it's this guy?"

"Yeah. Good tipper too."

I glanced around the bar. "Are any of his…" What was the term? "…vampire friends here tonight?" Guys were pretty loose with their tongues while getting laid, so maybe he'd mentioned something to one of his companions while getting bitten.

The bartender seemed to be getting impatient. "Vampire friends?"

"Yeah. Is there anyone in particular he likes to service?"

The guy kept looking at me like I was naive or something. Then he lost his friendly demeanor. "The club has a policy about discretion. This conversation is over."

As he was walking away, I reluctantly reached into my pocket. God, I hated to part with money, especially when I was short on it. This was coming out of business expenses.

He walked back over when I slid my hand across the bar with a Benjamin folded under it. After discreetly taking it from me and stuffing it in his pocket, he glanced around and then leaned in to set the record straight. "Charlie doesn't service anyone. He's the one doing the biting."

Motherfucker!

I straightened up and looked around for Thor, spotting him a few stools down with a brunette. She was gazing into his eyes like a viper. As if that was going to work. Shifters didn't fall for compulsion easily.

I grabbed his arm on the way to the door. "Come on."

Kiko's black SUV was still parked on the side of the building with her driver leaning against it.

He took a step back and threw his hand up when he saw me walking toward him. "I wasn't waiting for you. I'm just having a smoke before I leave."

I grabbed his hand and twisted his thumb before shoving him against the SUV. "Tell Kiko we need to have a talk." Before he started to cry, I let go and reached into my jacket for a business card. If she had my address, I was sure she also had my number, but just in case. "The job's off until my phone rings."

On the way to my bike, Thor grabbed my arm and turned me

around. "Are you planning to tell me what's going on, or shall I go back inside and finish what I started with that brunette?"

I didn't care what he did, but I was leaving. "Our new client is playing games with us. Apparently she forgot to mention that her missing husband is a vampire. If she has the guts to call me, we're going to have a little chat about disclosure. Then I think it's time for that trip to New Orleans."

5

WHEN WE GOT HOME, THOR WENT INSIDE WHILE I WALKED across the street to have a word with Ma.

For a late Sunday night, Speaks was fairly crowded. But at least I didn't have to dodge any sharp objects flying across the room. Ma had a rule about Sundays. No axes or darts. Sunday was all about paying respect to her nerves.

She came out of the kitchen juggling several plates and set them down in front of a couple at the far end of the bar. The smell of pot roast hit my nose, reminding my stomach that it hadn't seen food in a while. Then she made her way down to me.

"Are you hungry?" she asked, wiping the bar down in front of me.

"Yeah, but I don't have time." I needed to hunt down my client and read her the riot act.

"Then I'll pack it up so you can take it with you."

What a saint. That list of IOUs was getting longer by the minute. "Thanks, Ma. I appreciate it."

"How'd it go at that club? Did you find what you were looking for?"

Maybe it wasn't exactly the information I was looking for, but it had shed new light on my case. "I found out my client has been lying to me."

She chuckled. "I'm sure it isn't the first time. Is the place as deviant as they say it is?"

I shrugged. "Depends on your definition of deviant. I've been to worse." I'd lived in New Orleans, home to some pretty depraved establishments. "I did get propositioned by a ridiculously hot vampire, though."

"Oh yeah? Did you take him up on it? Or was it a her?"

I gave her a look but didn't answer.

"What?" She stood back and put her hands on her hips. "Don't tell me you passed up a good fuck on account of that *partner* of yours."

"Jesus, Ma! Don't even utter the thought. We're business partners. That's all." With benefits, but that had run its course. The whole don't-shit-where-you-eat philosophy was starting to make a lot of sense.

"Mm-hmm." She continued to wipe the surface of the bar while staring at me. "Where is Thor anyway? Don't tell me you went to that place alone."

"I sent him home so I could have a private word with you."

Something furry grazed my ankle. I glanced down at the tortoiseshell feline on the floor next to my stool. "Oh, it's you."

"You can come out, Pauline. Thor isn't with her." Ma slung the rag over her shoulder and headed for the kitchen. "I'll have Tommy pack up that roast for you."

When I looked back down, the cat had turned into a ten-year-old girl.

She climbed on the stool next to mine and grinned. "Too bad you didn't bring him with you. I was up for a game of chase."

Yeah, and she'd be the one doing the chasing. Thor couldn't stand the cat, but Pauline had definitely taken a liking to *his* alter ego.

Ma came back out of the kitchen. "Tommy will bring it out in a few minutes."

I reached into my pocket and pulled out some cash. "How much do I owe you?"

"Oh, for Christ's sake. Put your money away."

I don't think she'd ever allowed me to pay for a meal or a drink at Speaks, but I always offered. "You don't make a living by giving stuff away, Ma." I slid a bill across the bar. "At least give this to Tommy for packing it up."

She ignored the money and looked at Pauline. "What are you having?"

"The usual." Pauline reached for the bill on the bar. "I'll take it if no one else wants it."

Ma grabbed the rag from her shoulder and snapped it at Pauline's hand. "Touch that money and it'll be a meat cleaver next time." Still glaring at Pauline, she reached for a bottle of gin from behind the bar and poured some into a glass.

I got the willies when she slid the drink in front of Pauline.

"That'll be four dollars," Ma said.

"Put it on my tab." Pauline downed the gin, shuddering as she held the glass out. "Pour me another, but not that cheap stuff in your hand."

Ma gave her a firm look. "Fine, but I don't want to hear you moaning when it's time to settle up."

She slapped her little hand on the bar and leaned in. "Just pour."

Pauline was a good reminder of the old adage—never judge a book by its cover. The first time we met, I nearly choked when she pulled out a cigarette, lit it, and blew a thick plume of smoke in my face. Before I could slap it out of her skinny little hand and give her a lecture about the stupidity of taking up bad habits at her tender age, Ma explained that Pauline was actually a grown woman who could make her own foolish decisions.

Born into a shifter family, Pauline was afflicted with the family legacy at the age of ten, but something had gone wrong. The clock had simply stopped, and poor little Pauline had never seen a sag or a wrinkle since. But despite her youthful appearance, she had the mouth and the sexual appetite of a sailor. A thirty-eight-year-old sailor to be exact. Ma had given her a job helping in the kitchen because no one else would hire her, even with a driver's license to prove her age. I wouldn't have believed that license either had I not known what she was.

She finished her second drink and glanced at me. "Give Thor my regards." Then she slipped off the stool and disappeared around the bar.

I gave Ma a funny look as Pauline walked into the kitchen. "You let her drink like that while she's on the clock?"

"She's done for the night. She's just getting her things."

Tommy came out with my food and set it on the bar. "Here you go, Jesse. There's enough in there for you and Thor."

"Thanks, Tommy." I slipped him the bill while Ma tended a customer at the end of the bar.

When she returned, I got down to the real reason I'd dropped by. "I'm driving to New Orleans in the morning, and I'd appreciate it if you'd keep an eye on the house while I'm gone."

"You mean Thor."

"Gee, how'd you guess?"

"Well, he'd be short a few screws in his noggin to set foot in Louisiana with a bounty on his head." Then she got all serious. "Is there something going on that you're particularly concerned about? Something I should look out for?"

I chuckled. "Yeah. A party. Just keep him in line."

Thor was a grown man, but he came from a different world. Came from privilege until he fell out of his family's good graces and was disowned. Hence his foray into bounty hunting shortly before we met, which he'd failed at miserably. If it wasn't for me, he'd be broke and homeless. Lucky for him he had a good nose for tracking and I needed a partner. But it was a nose that also got into a lot of trouble. The man didn't have a clue about responsibility, and I had to admit it made me very nervous to leave him alone while I took care of business five hundred miles away.

"Unless something real interesting happens in New Orleans" —I almost laughed nervously at the thought—"I'll be back late tomorrow night." At least that was the plan. Get there early to sniff around town and find Charles Fraser's sister and then get out. If I could do that without the Romans detecting me, everything would go just fine. It was the alternative scenario I was worried about. The one where those vampires got wind of me before I even dropped the kickstand on my bike.

I grabbed the bag and left. As I was rounding the corner of the building, I spotted that shiny black SUV parked in front of my place. Kiko had decided to have a face-to face instead of picking up the phone. I guess that was good so I could look her in the eye if she tried to lie to me again. But it was late, and I wanted to eat my dinner before it got cold.

Groaning, I jogged across the street to my house and reached for the door. As I pushed it open, someone grabbed me and slammed me into the wall. My skull cracked against it as Kiko's driver brought his face within inches of mine, the smell of his bad breath hitting my nose. His swollen finger appeared in my line of sight as my vision cleared. "That's for my thumb."

"Go easy on our new business associate, Tok." Kiko walked across the room and made herself at home on my couch. "Ms. Ames will do us no good with a concussion."

"Tok?" I sucked up the throbbing pain, refusing to wince in front of the asshole. "What kind of name is Tok?"

He tensed up and leaned into me like he intended to make sure my head left an impression in the drywall, so I rammed my knee into his groin. He howled and stumbled back, giving me a direct view of Thor standing on the other side of the living room with a gun equipped with a silencer aimed at his head. It was in the hand of a very large man I hadn't seen before. Another one of Kiko's thugs.

"We didn't come here to harm your partner, Ms. Ames, but we need your cooperation." Kiko got up and walked over to where Thor was being detained and replaced her employee's hand with her own so that she was now in control of the trigger. "You ask too many questions." She pressed the muzzle against his temple. "I'd suggest you take the money and do what you were paid to do without being so inquisitive."

"Go ahead. Do it." I locked eyes with her and shrugged.

Thor's nervous grin turned into a frown. "Jesse? What are you doing?"

I reached into my pocket for a cigarette and stuck it between my lips, then muttered around it. "Go on. I was getting ready to dump him anyway, so you'll be saving me the hassle."

Tok struck a match, offering me a light like a real gentleman.

"I don't smoke, asshole." I flicked the cigarette at him and dove to the floor, rolling behind the couch as Thor ducked and knocked the gun out of Kiko's hand. Her henchman scrambled to get ahold of it, but he stopped when he saw the wolf materialize in front of him, standing on top of a pile of clothes. With his amber eyes trained on the guy, Thor pulled his lips back to reveal a set of glistening teeth.

As the guy lost his footing and started to fall backward, Kiko slipped past his scrambling feet and managed to grab the gun. She fired, discharging a bullet that barely made a sound as it shot from the barrel and struck Thor between the eyes. Shaking his head, the bullet fell from his thick fur and dropped to the floor. A moment later, he was on top of her, staring down at her petrified face as he licked his lips and let a drop of saliva fall and land on her cheek.

As Tok pulled out his gun and headed for Thor, I climbed to my feet and pressed my revolver to the back of his head. "Don't waste your time."

Tok halted but didn't turn around. The other guy was damn near climbing the wall trying to find an exit. So much for loyalty.

"Call off your partner," Kiko said, not daring to move more than her lips as Thor hovered over her.

After I disarmed Tok, Thor picked up the gun Kiko had dropped and continued to stand over her with a deep growl coming from his throat. I took it from his mouth but let him taunt her for a few more seconds before putting an end to it.

My food was getting cold.

I looked at the two men and motioned to the couch. "Sit down." Then Thor backed off and allowed Kiko to get up. "You too," I said to her. "You're going to satisfy my curiosity about what the hell's really going on before I kick you out of my house."

Thor grabbed his clothes and trotted off to the bedroom. He came back out a minute later wearing nothing but jeans and a pair of slippers. "You're lucky I bothered," he said when Kiko looked him over.

I gave Kiko a pointed glare, resisting the urge to boot her out of my living room—literally. "Well, now that we're all settled in, why don't we start with you telling me who the hell you really are."

"I've already told you who I am. You know my name and why I hired you, but there are certain aspects about my life that are none of your business. Find my thieving husband and we'll all go on our merry way."

The smugness on her face made me want to slap some sense into her. "I hope you don't take this personally, Kiko, but you're a liar."

I caught a glimpse of her chest heave, but she quickly got her breathing under control and smoothed over it like I hadn't just insulted her. But wait—can the truth be called an insult? I think not. "Your husband is a vampire. A little detail you left out."

For very personal reasons, vampires were on my list of deal breakers. I didn't like the way they looked, acted, smelled, or even the sound of the word. It took a pretty big incentive—or IOU— to get me to hunt one down. And this woman I'd never laid an eye on before yesterday morning thought she could trick me into finding one? No way.

To hell with the truth. Deciding I'd had enough of her, I walked over to the door and opened it. "Get out. I'll deduct the fees for our trouble and expenses from the money you paid me. Text me an address where you want me to send the balance."

Kiko stood up with a look of surprise, or maybe it was anger. It was hard to tell with her. "I'll pay you twice what we agreed upon."

"You can make it a million and I'd still tell you to get your ass out of my house." I hated liars. It was principle.

"Now wait a minute." Thor walked halfway across the room and tried to play mediator, which he was embarrassingly unquali- fied to do. By the way he was licking his lips, he probably already had plans on how he was going to spend his half of the money. Women and overpriced clothes came to mind. "We got off on a bad foot, but I think we can start over."

I wasn't too proud to admit we were desperate for money, but I'd be damned if I let *her* know it. "For starters, tell me the truth about your husband. Then I'll decide if we can work together."

She took a deep breath and sat back down. "I didn't lie about that. I just didn't tell you the truth about who he really is." She looked down at her lap at her shaking hands as a tremble seized her shoulders. "Then I would have had to tell you what a fool I am."

I could barely hear her voice.

Tok pulled a tissue from his pocket and handed it to her.

"Thank you." She took it and dabbed at her nose before looking back up at me, her eyes slightly red, on the verge of a full-fledged meltdown. I hated crying women. Not because it made them look weak but because it made me want to sniffle too. It was the ancestors. Ever since they started showing up on my skin, my hard shell had gotten a little tender in the emotions department.

"Look. I'm not here to judge you. You pay me to do a job and I do it. Your personal life is irrelevant. But I need to know who I'm dealing with. Full disclosure is nonnegotiable. You understand?"

Her eyes went from looking humiliated to hopeful. "Does that mean you'll still work for me?"

I huffed, revisiting the urge to knock some sense into her entitled little head. "Let's get something straight right now—I don't work for you; I work *with* you. And if you ever have me followed or pull a gun on me or my partner again, I'll put you in the ground."

"Watch your mouth!" Thug Number Two said.

"It's all right, Max. Ms. Ames is merely setting the ground rules."

Thor walked over to the man who'd held a gun to his head a few minutes earlier and stopped a few inches away from his face. "That's right, Max. Ground rules." He bared his teeth, and for a second we all got a glimpse of the beast inside. A single brow arched. "Next time I'll take a bite out of your ass."

As the tension in the room started to rise, I reined the conversation back in. My food was on its last leg. "Start talking, Kiko. Who am I hunting?"

"We," Thor said, backing away from Max. "Who are *we* hunting."

She finally came clean. "Charles is a vampire. But he's not a typical one," she quickly added. "He's a half-breed. I didn't know what he was when I met him."

I snorted. "You met him at a Tinder bar for vampires and humans. What did you think he was? At the very least he was looking to get his rocks off by getting bitten." That brought up another question. "Are you a—?"

"No!" She looked at me like I'd just accused her of being a porn star. "I was there with a friend. She convinced me it was a mix of all kinds of people. Trendy and full of A-listers. We'd been out drinking and…"

"And the alcohol gave you some extra courage?" I'd gone to some pretty seedy places while under the influence, but that was back in my college days. College students are allowed to do stupid things. Kiko was a grown woman who ran her own company, which brought up even more questions. "This probably isn't relevant to the job you hired me for, but I'm making it my business. What exactly is Dragon Enterprises?"

She hesitated, which sent up a red flag. But she decided to answer after I gave her a look saying the deal was off if she didn't share. "My company sells fantasies. For a price, we can give you anything you desire."

Thor narrowed his eyes. "You mean sex."

"We provide an experience for our clients."

I shook my head because it was all starting to sound shady. "I don't work with criminals. I did enough of that at the bureau."

"I can assure you, Ms. Ames, this is all legal. Everything is consensual, and all parties involved in the transaction are compensated handsomely."

"Sex for money isn't legal."

"You're right, but Dragon Enterprises doesn't provide that kind of service." I could see her wheels turning as she tried to convince me. "Let's say you have a fantasy about hunting, only you wish to be the hunted. We match you with someone who wants to be the hunter. We provide the introduction and the setting. Two willing adults can figure out the rest. It's all very transparent and consensual."

"People pay for that?" Thor asked.

"There are wealthy people in the world who prefer to have their needs met with discretion. It's better than having them fulfill their fantasies in some back alley, don't you think?"

"Are drugs a part of your business model?" I asked, remembering how Thor tasted cocaine on her.

She got a serious look. "No. Although I admit I partake occasionally, but that's my personal business."

I glanced at Thor and had a silent chat with him. As long as she wasn't trafficking humans or drugs, who were we to judge what consenting adults did to get their kicks? "All right. We'll find your husband. But if I get the slightest whiff of abuse as part of your business, you'll be begging me to hand you over to the police. Got it?"

Kiko smiled and stood up to leave. "Absolutely."

After they left, I grabbed the bag of cold food off the floor where I'd dropped it and handed it to Thor. "Compliments of Ma."

Then I headed for the bedroom to pack a duffel bag. I was about to dive back into the world of vampires. I just prayed I made it out of New Orleans alive.

6

Stopping only once to visit the little girls' room, I made it to Louisiana by noon. The second I crossed over the bridge, I got a wary feeling in my gut I was being watched. But that was just my nerves. I'd be dead by now or at the mercy of a set of fangs if the Romans had caught a whiff of me crossing into the parish. I just needed to lie low and get in and out by nightfall.

I decided to avoid the tourist district for several reasons. Primarily because the vamps were always out. They patrolled the French Quarter like they owned it, which I suppose they did. I was on the Roman's shit list for harboring Thor, and any of the vampires from the lower houses would be stupid not to report me to Lucius if I was spotted in town. The creepy feeling crawling all over me was starting to make me regret I'd dared to come back here. Regret ever laying eyes on Kiko Fraser.

After parking my bike in front of a run-down row house, I looked at the address again. The place looked empty, so either Kiko had gotten her hands on some bad information or her husband came from poorer-than-poor stock. I couldn't imagine anyone living in the place.

"Excuse me," I said to a guy walking toward me on the sidewalk. He looked half out of it, so I doubted I'd get any useful information out of him, but it was worth a shot. "You know if anyone lives here?" I nodded to the house.

He eyed me suspiciously for a few seconds before getting a strange grin on his face. "You lookin' for Silver?"

"Who?" The paper had said her name was Sylvia.

Without another word, he pointed to a worn path between the row houses that looked like it hadn't been used in a while. "Follow that around back. It's on the left."

As he continued down the sidewalk, I debated whether to leave my bike unattended in this part of town. "Hey!" He turned to look at me. "I'll give you a twenty to watch my bike for thirty minutes."

After considering it, he walked back over. "Fifty."

"Fine." I was about to hand him the money when I started to feel like a sucker. "If there's a scratch on it when I come back, I'll find you and fuck you up in ways that you can't even fathom. Understand?"

The shithead had the nerve to straddle my bike and grin at me, patting the tank like a horse's neck. "Ain't got no worries. I'll treat her like she's mine."

I handed him a twenty. "You get the rest when I come back out." Ignoring his protests, I continued toward the path, trying to get the image of my baby being razed out of my head. Or worse —stolen. The things I did to pay the rent.

When I reached the back of the house, I spotted a door. It was open, so I walked inside. "Hello?" I didn't get an answer, but clearly someone was there. I could smell patchouli and franken something in the air. The right wall was covered with shelves holding books, bundles of herbs, and bottles of liquid, and there was a long glass counter spanning the other side of the room. On top of it was a statue of some guy with leaves all over his head.

Herne or the Green Man if I remembered my Paganism correctly.

"Jesus. I'm in Harry Potter land."

A veil of beads hanging from a doorway rustled as a woman walked through it. "We're not open yet."

I could tell she was a lot younger than her silver hair let on. I guess this was who the guy was talking about, but I knew her real name. "Are you Sylvia Fraser?"

Her warm smile vanished as she took a step back. I think it was involuntary. "There's nobody here by that name, so you can leave."

I nodded a few times and took a step closer. "I think I found who I'm looking for." Working at the bureau had made me a bit of an expert on reading people's body language. I was definitely looking at Charles Fraser's sister.

She suddenly dropped her guard and walked over to the counter to reach underneath it. I went for my gun at the same time, but it was only a deck of cards she was grabbing. Tarot cards. "Would you like a reading?"

As she placed the deck on top of the counter, I was overwhelmed by a sea of voices in my head. The ancestors were jabbering so fast I couldn't make out a single sentence. "Shut up!"

She shot her eyes to mine. "Perhaps a palm reading?"

Palm reading, my ass! The woman is a charlatan!

That voice sounded like Samantha's. The mystery relative who'd left the crescent moon on my biceps.

"You're a fake." I didn't intend to blurt it out like that, but Sam took the wheel. "Sorry, but we both know you're full of shit, and I'm short on time. I need to talk to you about your brother, Charles."

That made her change her tune. She tried to smooth it over and act like the name hadn't struck a nerve, but the small tremor in her hand gave her away. "Charles? What do you want with my brother?"

"He's taking a little break from his marriage, and he helped himself to something his wife wants back."

She laughed quietly. "I could see that breakup coming from a mile away. Kiko isn't his type."

"She was enough his type to marry her. Or was it just for her money?"

After perusing the items inside the glass case for a moment, her eyes flicked back to mine. "My brother is a lot of things, but he isn't a thief."

"Tell that to his wife."

"Well, you won't find him here. I haven't seen Charles since he married that woman." Her faint smile vanished as she caught a glimpse of something to her left. "I have a business to run, so if you'll excuse me."

I followed her eyes and spotted two cups on the table against the wall. "I thought you said you weren't open yet?" They could have been sitting there since yesterday, but she didn't look like the messy type, and I had a hunch.

"You need to leave." She nodded to the door.

"If your brother is in the back room, you might as well call him out here." I grabbed one of the chairs next to the table and sat down. "I just drove six hours to have a talk with him, and gas isn't cheap. I'm not leaving until I'm convinced he isn't here."

"Suit yourself." She walked back toward the veil of beads. "Would you like some tea while you stake the place out?"

"I'm not much of a tea drinker."

"Then let's go have a look around so I can convince you to leave."

I got up to follow her, but before I made it halfway through the veil, something hit me in the back of the head. Through blurred vision, I saw a second figure standing next to her. Then I was out.

———————

WHEN I CAME TO, Sylvia Fraser was sitting in a chair with her legs crossed. She had a slender brown cigarette between her lips. The room was filled with a sweet smell as she took a long pull and released a steady stream of smoke. She stood when I struggled to push myself up from the floor.

"Jesus!" I rubbed my head, but it wasn't tender. The way I felt, I expected to feel a crater on the back of my skull. "What the hell did you do to me?"

"A little mental punch." After snuffing out her cigarette—or cigar—she grabbed a glass and handed it to me. "Drink this. It'll help."

I stared at the brown liquid and held back my urge to hurl. "I'm not drinking that."

She shrugged and took the glass back. "If I wanted to kill you, you wouldn't be talking to me right now. But it's your misery." She set it on the table and glanced at the man I'd caught a glimpse of before blacking out. "Get her up."

"Hey!" I shrugged him off when he reached down and tried to lift me. "Get your hands off me!" After climbing to my feet and steadying myself against the wall, I closed my eyes as a wave of nausea rolled through me. I finally reopened one eye and then the other. The guy definitely wasn't Charles. "Who are you?"

"You need to leave New Orleans, Ms. Ames," Sylvia said before he could answer.

Funny. I hadn't told her my name. Then I noticed my wallet lying on the table.

She tossed it to me with a sly grin. "You're a long way from home. If you leave now, you might make it back to Atlanta before nightfall."

I suddenly remembered my bike parked out front in the hands of some drunk or crackhead. "How long have I been out?"

"Long enough to find out who you are. So that bitch has hired a private investigator to find my brother. If you're smart, you'll go back to Atlanta and return the money. Charles is no longer in New Orleans."

"So he was here?"

"It doesn't matter. He won't be back. I made sure of that."

"Why?"

Mr. Silent suddenly stepped forward. "Because it isn't safe here!"

Sylvia shot him a glare to shut him up. "Because this is the first place they'll look!" She gave me a disdainful once-over. "Obviously."

I gave her the attitude right back. "Are you a vampire like your brother? A half-breed?" By the shock on her face, either I'd nailed it or I'd just outed him to his family.

She reined in the anger that suddenly seemed to be oozing from the pores of her porcelain skin and ordered through gritted teeth, "Get out!"

I needed to check on my bike anyway.

"Look. All Kiko wants is her property back." Well, technically I was hired to retrieve the ring and her missing husband, but I'd take what I could get. "You know anything about the ring he stole from her?"

She gave me another contemptuous look and let out a bitter laugh. Before I could ask what was so funny, I felt that brutal pain on the back of my head again. This time when I woke up, I was on the sidewalk next to my bike. The guy I'd left it with was long gone, and so was the house I'd parked it in front of. The number on the mailbox was the same, but the house I was looking at was a different color, and it was occupied. The path leading around back was replaced by a driveway.

I scratched my head and climbed to my feet, deciding to take Sylvia's advice and leave town. I believed her when she said her brother was long gone. I also knew Charles Fraser wasn't what he seemed. More than just a half-breed, as Kiko had said.

After getting my bearings, I drove off. On my way back toward town, I remembered that bag of beignets I'd promised Thor. I wasn't really in the mood to stop, especially in the heart of vampire city, but I'd never hear the end of it if I walked into the house without them. A ten-minute stop would spare me from two days of bitching. A quick in and out with my head down, and I'd be back on the road.

I pulled up to the first café I spotted and went inside. Seeing a line ten people deep, I almost walked back out the door, but the smell stopped me. The last thing I'd eaten was Ma's pot roast the night before, so I was starving.

After checking the menu on the wall to confirm they had them, I got in line. As I waited, I couldn't shake the feeling I was being watched again. What were the chances I'd stumbled into an establishment the Romans had eyes on? But it was just some random hole-in-the-wall, for Christ's sake.

"Give me half a dozen beignets," I said to the guy when I finally made it up to the counter. "Hell, make it a dozen." I'd probably eat half of them before I crossed the bridge driving out of town.

I stepped aside to wait for a fresh batch to finish frying, catching a glimpse of a guy standing near the back. He kept glancing in my direction and then scanning the room. My foot nervously tapped the floor as my heart started to beat faster.

Get out of there, Jesse.

When Uncle Ames gave me a warning, it was best not to

second-guess it. I glanced at a woman behind the counter dumping the beignets onto a surface of powdered sugar, and then I looked at the back of the room again. The guy was gone, but my heart was still in overdrive.

"Miss? Your order."

I took the bag from the cashier's hand and backed up toward the door when another man sitting at a table stared me down without an ounce of discretion. Not wanting to take my eyes off him, I pushed the door open with my back but slammed into someone walking in from the street. He grabbed my arm, and I dropped the bag to reach for my revolver.

"Jesse?"

My adrenaline careened through my veins, and I was ready to blow the vampire's fangs right out the back of his head. The gun was halfway out of my jacket when I turned. "Miller?"

He spotted my hand wrapped around the handle of my gun and instinctively snatched my wrist, losing his smile. "What are you doing?"

I yanked my arm away and stuffed my gun back in my pocket, taking a moment to let my adrenaline subside. "Jesus, Miller! You got a death wish or something?" The easiest way to get your brains blown out—or to crap your pants—was to sneak up behind law enforcement or ex-law enforcement and grab them.

He threw his hands up and took a step away. "Hey, you backed into me."

I glanced around the room again, but both men were gone. "Yeah, sorry about that."

After reaching down to grab my bag off the floor, he handed it to me and cocked his head. "You look a little spooked. Everything all right?"

"Yeah. Rough ride in from—"

"From…?"

He waited for me to finish my sentence, but since I'd left town without telling anyone where I was going for good reason, I responded with another question. "How've you been? Still with the bureau?" Special Agent Jim Miller was an ex-colleague. Kind of an asshole but not the worst I'd worked with. I think he just resented working with a woman.

"Yeah. Got promoted and moved to the Cyber Crime Division about six months ago."

Of course he had.

My skin was starting to crawl again with the feeling that the walls had eyes, so I ended our little reunion. "Good to see you, but I need to get going."

"Come on. Cup of coffee?"

I was about to politely blow him off when I caught movement at the back of the room. I turned toward the front door when I saw the vampire coming toward us, but there was another one walking in behind Miller, and he was looking directly at me. There was only one way out, and it was straight through the kitchen.

"Get out of here, Miller."

His brow twisted. "What? Still pissed at me about what happened in Shreveport?"

Shreveport was ancient history.

"Vamps!" I barked before disappearing into the mob that had squeezed in from the street and lined up in front of the counter. He just stood there looking shocked as I hopped over the counter and ran toward the kitchen, hurling a bowl of powdered sugar at the vampire right behind me. The cloud filled his eyes, stopping him long enough for me to get away. But as I reached the back door, he caught up and grabbed ahold of my jacket and swung me against the wall. I slammed into it hard and slid to the floor.

"Lucius wants to have a talk." He stalked toward me with white powder clinging to his face and hair.

I let out a nervous laugh as I glanced around for options. Something that could take down a six-foot-something vampire big enough to rip my head off. But I was basically fucked. For once, I found myself actually missing Thor. "Is it optional? Because I really need to get on the road."

A grin spread across his face as he licked the sugar from his lips and extended his hand to help me up.

"Aww, what a gentleman." I was about to pull myself up when I felt the familiar rush of someone else taking over inside me.

You're not going anywhere with that vamp, Jesse. If you walk into Lucius's house, you're not coming back out.

"Yeah, you're not the one staring at a bloodsucking linebacker."

The vampire straightened up and cocked his head. "Who are you talking to?"

"My uncle."

As he darted his head from left to right, Uncle Ames introduced himself. I kicked out and swept the vampire's legs, sending him toppling forward. As he came down on top of me, I grabbed his head and smashed my forehead into his.

"Fuck!" That hurt.

He fell sideways and shook his head, growling as he turned to face me. Either Uncles Ames had more moves up his sleeve, or the vampire was about to slam my head into the wall and drag me back to Lucius.

I jumped to my feet and grabbed a cast-iron skillet, swinging it as hard as I could when he started to climb to his feet. This time he went down and remained still. For insurance, I smashed it over his head a second time to buy me a few more minutes.

As I ran for the back door, I heard a ruckus behind me. I turned as the other vampire I'd seen in the restaurant made like a bull and tore through the kitchen after me. Uncle Ames took control again and headed directly toward him.

"Uh… wrong way." He ignored my protest and kept moving my legs toward the vampire. I thought I was about to meet my maker when I jumped into the air and grabbed ahold of a hanging pot rack, swiping a chef's knife from the counter on the way. I swung forward and kicked the vamp in the head, sending him stumbling back against a metal shelf loaded with pots and pans.

He got his footing and clenched his fists. "You're dead!"

"Hmm… I don't think so." All I wanted to do was knock him out like his buddy on the floor, but Uncle Ames did something stupid that I was going to pay for. "No!" I yelled as I hit the floor and slid toward him with the knife gripped tightly. My arm twisted as I found myself back on my feet behind him. Before I could stop it, the blade was slicing through the back of his neck, severing his spinal cord just before his head tilted forward.

Suddenly back in control, I dropped the knife and looked around the empty kitchen. At least there were no witnesses. They'd all wisely taken off.

The other vampire began to stir.

It's time to leave, Jesse!

I ran through the back door into the alley with my heart thumping wildly. By the time I made it around front and jumped on my bike, the vampire was rounding the corner. I floored it, but I barely made it three blocks before I spotted a row of black cars blocking the road.

Romans! Turn around!

"No shit!" I headed north, but the roads were blocked on that end too. There was only one way to go—back toward the café and that very angry vampire. Backtracking, I spotted an alleyway and took a sharp turn. Then I ditched my bike behind a dumpster and took off on foot, ducking into the side entrance of a building.

Taking the stairwell a few floors up, I grabbed my phone and called the one person who could pull off a miracle. "I need help!" I said to Gabriel when he answered on the first ring. "You need to get me out of New Orleans!"

7

Not everyone has a demigod on speed dial, but luckily I did. And he was good at getting me out of tight situations.

The first words out of his mouth seemed appropriate. "Have you been drinking?"

"No, but I will be if I make it out of New Orleans alive."

There was a pause on the other end, and I could visualize him shaking his head.

"What the hell are you doing in New Orleans, Jesse?"

Gabriel and I went way back. He was the reason I was still breathing. But he was also the reason Thor and I were on the Roman's shit list. Lucius had attempted a coup to take control of New Orleans, and Gabriel was the one thing standing in his way of conquering the reigning house of vampires because he had loyalty to its master. A loyalty thick as blood. So Lucius hired Thor to kill Gabriel, but it never happened. The Romans eventually won, but Lucius has never forgiven Thor for failing to deliver Gabriel's head and then absconding with the bounty money. My sin was harboring Thor. But hey, he had a nose for detective work, and he was good at other things too.

"I'm working a case. The guy I'm looking for has family here. I was on my way out of town when I got spotted."

Again, that wolf owed me.

"And?"

"And I just killed one of Lucius's vampires."

He went quiet again followed by a groan. "He'll make you pay dearly for that."

I shrugged. "Well, technically it was Uncles Ames who killed him."

"Jesse…"

"All right! Just get here."

"Where are you?"

I glanced around the stairwell. "I don't know. I ducked into some old building just outside the French Quarter. Can't you just do that thing you usually do?" Gabriel traveled in an unconventional way. The man was a demigod. Paris, Rome, New Orleans —he could be anywhere in the blink of an eye. The only problem was he had to know where he was going. Without a physical address, he couldn't just blindly materialize in a strange place he'd never been to or seen before without some kind of roadmap or a connection to it, and I doubted he'd spent any time in that stairwell.

"You'll have to guide me to you. Stay put and think of dead violets."

"Dead violets?" Was he serious?

"You know. Like the ones you always kill. And think hard."

He hung up, leaving me wondering if it was a bad joke or if he actually had a plan to find me. When I heard the door slowly squeal open a few floors down, I had to make a decision about calling out to see if Gabriel had broken a record getting here or if it was wiser to continue up the steps to take my chances on the roof. The singsong voice I heard calling my name answered the question.

"Jesse. I can smell you."

Taking the steps two at a time—which wasn't easy with my knees—I reached for the door at the top and prayed it was open. It was, but I felt a rush of acrophobia hit me when I ran out on the rooftop. Normally heights wouldn't have bothered me, but the fear of a vicious vampire forcing me to jump certainly did. I estimated I had about thirty seconds to find another way off, but when I ran toward the edge to see if there was an adjoining rooftop, all I saw was the street below.

The door swung open, and three vampires walked onto the roof, including the one I'd knocked out. "It's over, Jesse. Let's go." His sadistic grin told me I was about to pay for that lump on his forehead. And *then* he'd kill me if Lucius didn't do it himself. That street below was looking better by the second.

Glancing over the side, I spotted a fire escape ten or twelve feet down, but it was my only option. I steadied my trembling hands and reached for the edge. The Romans seemed to realize what I was about to do and rushed toward me. I slipped over the side and hung on to the ledge of the wall, praying I'd stick the landing and not tumble over the railing of the narrow platform. Or miss it completely, which was more my luck.

I shut my eyes and whispered, "Dead violets," visualizing a row of potted flowers shriveled up on my windowsill.

One of the vampires grabbed my arm, and I let go. I slipped out of his grasp and felt a painful jar to my right ankle when I hit the rusted metal grate of the fire escape. As I fought to keep my balance, pain shot up my leg, sending me stumbling back against the railing. I saw the faces of three vampires leering down at me as I tipped backward and fell over the edge, catching a view of New Orleans while I flipped awkwardly through the air.

I was dead.

It's hard to imagine your body smashing against asphalt from a five-story fall. It's even harder to describe what it feels like. But at that point, I didn't care. It was over and I was numb. I could feel myself slipping away from my body, but then I caught a fading glimpse of a pair of eyes. Beautiful green eyes staring down at mine.

Gabriel.

I was looking down at him from above. Watching him slice his wrist open and drip his fiery blood into my mouth.

Gasping from the rainbow of colors exploding in my mind, I sat straight up as the rocket fuel—as his blood had been described—raced through my veins and repaired every destroyed cell in my body. "Damn!" My heart was pounding as my adrenaline flowed. "What the hell just happened?" I'd just been blessed with the nectar of the gods, that's what happened.

He stood up and pushed his golden hair over the top of his head. "*Fuck*, Jesse! You almost got yourself killed!"

I felt invincible as I climbed to my feet with a cocky grin on my face. "But thanks to you, I didn't, did I?" Still a little shaky, I was pretty sure I could run a marathon.

He wagged his finger at me. "Five more seconds and even my blood wouldn't have saved you! You would have been worm food!" Pacing the alleyway, he grumbled under his breath.

I quietly sobered up. "We need to get out of here."

He beckoned me toward him for one of his fancy demigod exits, the kind of embrace that would have us both back in Atlanta in a matter of seconds. But pulling me along for the ride would exhaust him, and I wasn't leaving my bike. "I'm riding out of here."

"You can build another bike."

"Jesus, Gabriel, I'm not twenty-four anymore." I cringed just thinking about scouring junkyards and Craigslist for parts. "I'm not leaving it."

"You'll have to go through a gauntlet of vampires to get it out of New Orleans."

"No, *we'll* have to go through a gauntlet, so let's figure it out. I need to get home before Thor turns the place into a frat house." I didn't stand a chance without Gabriel's help, and if push came to shove, he could disappear and leave me to fend for myself.

Gabriel shook his head. "It's a shame you didn't bring that wolf. He could have been your ticket out of here."

Ignoring him, I headed down the alley to the dumpster I'd stashed my bike behind. The second I started it up, the side door of the building flew open. Time was up.

Careening past the vamps, I stopped at the end of the alley long enough for Gabriel to climb on.

"Remind me why I shouldn't just leave you here?" he yelled over the roar of the engine.

"Because then you'll never get to collect on all the favors I owe you."

Full throttle, we headed toward the roadblock I ran into earlier. There were other ways out of town, but I knew the Romans would have every exit blocked, and it wasn't worth wasting our time to find out.

We made it to the spot where the Romans had cut me off, but there was no sign of them. It had to be a trap, but I gunned it anyway and headed for Atlanta. We were almost to the bridge over Lake Pontchartrain when I spotted something in my rearview mirror coming up on us fast. A big black sedan. One of the same cars that had barricaded the road earlier.

Motioning to Gabriel to hold on tight, I put my bike to the test and accelerated. I don't know what kind of engine that car had, but it was keeping up. They probably let us out of town, hoping we'd lead them straight back to Thor.

We had less than a quarter mile to go over the lake when Gabriel leaned forward and motioned for me to go faster, but I was already pushing it. If the engine blew, we were going into the water. He eased back into the seat behind me, and suddenly his hands slipped away from my waist. When I reached behind me, he was gone.

I kept going. When I looked in the mirror, I spotted a wave building over the bridge that was coming from both sides of the lake. It curled inward, making the cars entering the causeway from the opposite direction hit their brakes to avoid driving into the storm. The only car behind me was the one full of vampires.

When I reached the end and drove over land, all I could see in my rearview mirror was a tsunami of water rolling over the entrance of the bridge. I pulled to the side of the road and looked back. The black sedan was history.

When Gabriel's arms appeared around my waist again, I looked over my shoulder at him. "What was that?"

"An obstacle. Drive!"

"Yes, sir." I pulled back onto the road and took off toward home with a list of questions on my mind, like how he'd pulled off that stunt. Then I needed to come up with a new game plan for finding my target. Charles Fraser was a slippery one.

WE MADE one stop in Atlanta before going home, and that was only to keep Thor from bitching all night. I didn't hear any noise or see any strange cars out front, so at least he wasn't wrecking the place with a wild party.

He was shirtless and lounging on the couch, watching TV, when we walked inside. I tossed him a box of Krispy Kreme donuts, straight out of the oven and still warm. "Sorry, New Orleans was fresh out of beignets."

He caught the box and looked at it with a furrowed brow. "Fresh out of—" Then he saw Gabriel walk in behind me. "What is he doing here?"

"Nice to see you too, Thor. Don't worry, I won't be staying long."

I wasn't much of a drinker, but after the day I'd just had, a stiff shot of something was in order. "Do we have any alcohol in this place?"

Thor looked back and forth between me and Gabriel as I kicked my boots off and threw my jacket over the chair. "Wait. Were the two of you together in New Orleans?"

"Why? Jealous?" He looked downright horrified. If it was anyone but Gabriel, he probably wouldn't have given a shit.

"I suppose he's staying here for the night?"

I groaned and headed for the kitchen to check the cabinets for a bottle of booze. "What is it with you two?"

Gabriel followed me. "Well, he did try to kill me once." He opened the refrigerator and inspected the empty shelves. "Did sunshine over there drink all the beer?"

"I was *hired* to kill you," Thor yelled across the room around a mouthful of donut. "But you're still breathing, aren't you?"

"I've had better men try," Gabriel said, shutting the refrigerator door. "Don't worry, I'll be leaving soon. I have my own woman to get back to, so I'll leave you to yours."

I shot him a glare. I wasn't Thor's woman. Never had been. It was strictly business between the two of us from now on.

"Does he know that?" Gabriel muttered to me.

"Get the hell out of my head." I hated when he did that. But since the man had just saved my life, I decided to go easy on him and change the subject instead. "How's Emmaline?" His girlfriend was the nicest witch I'd ever met. The woman didn't have a mean bone in her body, but she was capable of conjuring a hurricane in her sleep if need be.

"Never better. Things are peaceful for a change in Savannah, but I need to get back there just in case it doesn't stay that way." He looked at me sideways. "If you're foolish enough to go back to

New Orleans in the future, I suggest you bargain with your lapdog over there instead of calling me."

Thor stood up and narrowed his eyes at Gabriel. "What was that?"

I decided to put an end to the pissing contest before it really got going. "Both of you, shut up."

"On that note," Gabriel said, "I'll be on my way."

Thor smirked. "What a shame. And I was going to offer you the couch."

It was time to call in a favor, although I was pretty sure he'd just repaid me handsomely. "Can I convince you to stay until morning?"

He glanced at Thor. "No."

"Please."

Exhaling a deep sigh, he closed his eyes and rubbed the bridge of his nose, contemplating our friendship, no doubt. "Why?"

"Because I need you to go somewhere with me tonight. I have a job to do, and as much as I hate to admit it, I'm hitting a wall here." One thing I was convinced of—Charles Fraser was not in New Orleans. I think he went there to see his sister and then possibly returned to Atlanta. The only way to find out for sure was to look for him here, and the only place I knew to start looking was that cesspool disguised as a legitimate club. "I need to go see some bloodsuckers, and I'd rather not go alone. The guy we're looking for is a regular at a club called Sanguine. I hear it's owned by vampires."

He snickered quietly. "You mean a club for blood sport."

"Sanguine?" Thor looked like he'd just bitten into a lemon. "Why in God's name would you go back there?"

"Because if Charles Fraser is back in Atlanta, he'll need to feed. But he'll need to do it discreetly so no one gets wind of him."

His brow twisted as he looked at me like I'd lost my mind. "Why the hell would he come back here?"

Gabriel took the liberty of answering Thor's question. "For the same reason you turn into a canine the size of a sewer rat—no one will be looking for him here."

He'd read my thoughts exactly. Just as the Romans would never go looking for a teacup poodle, Atlanta was the last place Kiko's goons would waste their time searching for her husband. Or at least they'd already done that and come up empty-handed. Hence the reason they hired us. Of course, I could have been way off, but we didn't have a lot of other options.

Knowing my extreme aversion to vampires, Gabriel shook his head at me. "You really do like to make your life difficult."

"I also like to eat, and I didn't know what he was when we took the job."

"Mind telling me what that is?"

"He's a half-breed. Half vampire."

He cocked his head. "And the other half is…?"

I assumed his other half was human, but now I was beginning to wonder. "I guess we'll find out if we ever track him down."

Thor got up and headed for the bedroom. "This case just keeps getting better and better."

"Where are you going?" I asked.

"Well, I'm pretty sure they won't let me in the door without a shirt and shoes."

Before I could inform him that he was out of his mind if he thought he was walking back into that club, Gabriel brought up a good point. "Let him come. He can keep an eye out from the parking lot."

Thor scoffed. "I'm not a sentinel."

"You are tonight," Gabriel said. "Get dressed if you'd like, but you won't be wearing clothes for long."

8

SANGUINE WAS CROWDED FOR A MONDAY NIGHT, BUT IT
stayed open until two a.m. seven days a week for a reason. But
something told me the place closed down whenever the hell it
wanted. They were the vampire cartel, for God's sake. The cops in
the area were probably some of their best customers.

I drove to the back of the lot so Thor could climb off my bike
without being seen. Since three was a crowd on a Harley, Gabriel
had to get himself to the club, which should have been a piece of
cake considering I'd given him the address, but he was nowhere
in sight.

"I should have stuffed you in my pocket so I could give
Gabriel a ride." But then I would have had to lug around a backpack full of his clothes.

Thor glanced toward the road. "There he is."

Gabriel looked irritated when he crossed the street and found
us at the back of the parking lot.

"What took you so long?" I asked him.

He held up his cell phone so I could see the text message I'd
sent him. "Next time get the address right. You sent me to the gas
station across the street."

"Sorry." I turned around to tell Thor to get going, but he was already on all fours with his clothes in a pile at the edge of the parking lot. He didn't even wait for instructions. He just took off into the woods behind the club and disappeared. The only thing giving him away were his amber eyes glowing from a thicket of shrubs and trees.

"Come on." Gabriel nudged me and set off for the entrance.

I climbed back on my bike and started the engine. "I'll meet you at the door." After driving around to the front, I pulled into a small triangle that wasn't actually a parking space at all. It was now.

A guy grabbed my arm as we were walking inside. "You can't park your bike there."

"What are you?" I asked, unsuccessfully trying to yank my arm away. "The parking lot police?" They hadn't had a bouncer last time.

Gabriel held the man's gaze before glancing down at his hand gripping my arm. A moment later, the guy got a funny look in his eyes and let go of me. Then he stepped out of our way.

I squinted at Gabriel's eyes as we entered the club. "That was a nifty little trick."

"Yeah, well, it's a good thing he isn't a vampire. You'd be moving your bike by now if he were."

"Like hell."

As I surveyed the room, I prayed I didn't come eye to eye with that Roman from last night because I didn't have time to fend him off again. And while Gabriel and Lucius had called a truce, his vampire might not have gotten the memo.

The second we slid onto a couple of stools that were conveniently being vacated, a woman with platinum hair and lips with a little too much filler started to protest. Her friend with the manufactured double Ds looks just as annoyed.

She put her hands on her hips and gave me a catty look. "We've been waiting for those stools."

"Don't worry, we won't be here long." By the look in her eyes and the length of her fake fingernails, I was kinda nervous about turning my back on her. But time was of the essence, and we needed to get friendly with the bartender for information. When he walked over, I flicked my head toward the two women. "Buy them both a drink on me."

The blonde lost some of her attitude when I made the peace offering, but it was Gabriel who defused the impending catfight. When he turned around and looked at her, her face melted into a weak smile as her breasts stood taller. He had that effect on women. Gabriel was the definition of gorgeous. A unicorn. Movie-star handsome.

He quickly turned away when she slid past me like I was invisible and wedged herself between him and the guy sitting on his other side.

"I'm Tammy." She grazed his arm with her tits before extending her hand.

Don't do it, Gabriel.

He smiled at her politely. "It's nice to meet you, Tammy, but this isn't going to happen."

Good boy.

Her man-eating grin flattened as she pushed away from the bar and gave him some room. Then she turned her eyes on me and huffed. "Must have mommy issues."

I wasn't *that* old, but I shrugged. "Yeah, but guess who he's coming home with?"

When the bartender brought their drinks, I grabbed them and set one down in front of Gabriel while I prepared to drink the other. "Buy your own damn drinks." I downed the alcohol as they headed to the other side of the bar, wincing as it slid down my throat. "Jesus, Mary, and Joseph! What the hell was that?"

The bartender snickered. "It's called a Motor Oil. Don't worry, it won't kill you."

Wise enough not to drink his, Gabriel slid the glass away. "I'll have a shot of Wild Turkey, but you might want to bring her some water first."

After downing the entire glass the bartender kindly handed me, I started in with the questions before he could disappear. "You remember me from last night?"

He suddenly lost his friendly grin. "Yeah, and I said all I'm gonna say."

"I just want to know if you've seen Charles tonight?"

He shook his head and glanced up and down the bar, barely raising his eyes. As he started to walk away, he discreetly nodded to a woman sitting at the other end. A redhead with big blue eyes. The way they kept darting around the room, she was definitely looking for someone.

"You see that redhead down there?" I said to Gabriel.

He followed my gaze. "The one who looks like she's been stood up?"

"Yeah. The bartender just pointed her out. How much you want to bet she knows Charles Fraser?" I got up to have a word with her, but Gabriel grabbed my arm.

I glanced down at his hand. "Why is everyone manhandling me tonight?"

"Because you're about to scare her off." He stood up and finished his drink. "Order me another one. I'll be right back."

He headed down the bar and slid in next to her. The guy on her right wasn't too happy about it, but he took one look at Gabriel and probably realized he didn't stand a chance and left. She shot him a glare, but when she got a thorough look into his big green eyes, she lost the attitude. Another one of his nifty little tricks. He could charm the panties off a nun.

After ten minutes of conversation, he ordered her another drink and handed her something before he walked back over. He took his seat and look down at the bar. "Where's my drink?"

I motioned to the bartender for another round of bourbon and noticed the woman was staring at us. "So?"

"She's definitely waiting for your client's husband."

"You didn't come right out and ask her, did you? I don't want to spook her. She's the closest thing we have to a lead."

"You know me better than that. I just asked her if she was here alone or waiting for someone." He let out a muffled laugh as he picked up the shot of bourbon the bartender set down in front of him. "She volunteered his name. Said she was waiting for someone and muttered something about Charlie never being late. I got a good look at the guy inside her head. Do you have a picture of him?"

"You got inside her head?"

"It was impossible not to. The woman's emotions are all over the place. In fact, I think she got inside mine without even realizing it."

I pulled the photo of Charles out of my pocket. "Is this the guy?"

"That's him all right. Who would have thought *that* guy had a set of fangs." The glass went still at his lips. Then he set it back down and slid his eyes sideways without turning around. "A bullet won't do you any good."

I gave him a funny look. "What the hell are you talking about?" Then I noticed a guy looming over us. He pressed something hard against my back. The barrel of a gun if I wasn't mistaken. Then he nudged Gabriel again with the one gripped in his other hand.

"Maybe not," the guy said, "but I bet a bullet will do some damage to your lady friend here."

73

I craned my head to look up at him. A vampire no doubt. I could tell by his cold and lifeless eyes. And then there were the fangs sticking out of his mouth when he grinned at me.

He leaned down and came dangerously close to my face. "Wouldn't that be a shame?"

"Yeah, wouldn't it." I locked eyes with Gabriel, trying to read him. We—*I*—was in a bit of a quandary. He had the ability to leave anytime he wanted.

"What do you want?" Gabriel asked.

"Mr. Bastian would like to have a word with you."

Without turning around, Gabriel took a deep breath. "Tell your boss I'm not interested in talking."

Now I was curious. "Who's he taking about?"

Gabriel downed his drink and stood up. "We've been summoned."

The guy jammed the gun harder into my back. "You too, princess."

I shrugged him off, which was probably a stupid thing to do with that gun pointed at my spine. "Lower the gun, asshole." Another stupid move, but I had a feeling he didn't have the authority to shoot me.

He motioned for me to hand over the gun tucked inside my jacket. I don't know why. A bullet wouldn't do any more damage to a vampire than it would to a demigod. Seemed I was the only one imperiled at the moment, and I wasn't planning to shoot myself with it.

After reluctantly parting with my revolver, I got up and glanced at the bartender, wondering if he'd sold us out to his boss or if we'd been under surveillance since walking into the place. Probably the latter. And obviously Gabriel had a connection to the Bastian cartel he hadn't mentioned. If we made it out of here alive—and by *we,* I meant *me*—I planned to ream his ass for holding back that little bit of pertinent information.

We walked toward the back of the club and headed down a hallway. When we reached a door at the end, I held my breath as the vampire opened it, not knowing if we were about to walk into an ambush of fangs or a closet. It turned out to be an office filled with guys who looked more like good old boys than vampires. There wasn't a dark suit or a cape in sight. Just a bunch of men wearing jeans and cowboy boots. Expensive-looking cowboy boots, but still boots. The big cheese was sitting behind a desk in a chair facing the wall, his sandy-blond hair reaching down to the middle of his neck.

I glanced around the room. "What is this?"

Gabriel reached into his pocket for a cigarette, which wasn't a good sign. He rarely smoked and usually stuck an unlit cigarette between his lips when he was agitated or something bad was brewing. I'd gotten my habit of doing the same thing from him.

"Puffery," he said as he rolled the smoke between his fingers.

The chair swiveled around slowly, and the boss looked at us from behind a pair of dark sunglasses. His legs were planted wide, and a black button-down shirt hugged his abs. A smile slid up his face as he laced his fingers together with his elbows planted on the armrests. There was a large ring on his index finger with a symbol on it. "Gabriel."

I hated to admit it, but his deep voice sent a shot of warmth down my torso. The bastard.

The cigarette continued to roll between Gabriel's fingers. "Blain."

The vampire's smile flattened. "It's Blade."

Blade? Typical.

I kept my eyes on the guy with the gun, although I was pretty sure they were all armed.

Gabriel finally shoved the cigarette back into his pocket. "You called, *Blade*?"

The vampire stood up and walked around the desk to lean

back against the front edge. "I was just wondering what you're doing in my club. In Atlanta." He had a refined Southern accent, but the rest of him said born-and-bred country boy, which totally contradicted the whole vampire thing.

"I'm visiting a friend."

Even with him having sunglasses on, I could feel his eyes shifting in my direction. I had a feeling I was about to be questioned next, which posed a problem because vampires are good at smelling bullshit. If I lied, he'd probably know it. On the other hand, if I told him we were looking for one of his customers, he might make me an example to anyone else who dared to walk into his establishment and pull a similar stunt.

What to do? What to do?

"We're looking for someone," Gabriel said, clearly sensing my nerves. "He's one of your regulars. A guy named Charles Fraser."

So much for holding back.

Blade's smile vanished, and he finally removed his sunglasses. I hadn't expected to see light blue eyes, but they quickly went dark with that familiar vampire glow. He pushed away from the desk and snapped his fingers at one of his men, who walked over to a table on the other side of the room. The top was covered with liquor bottles. "Would anyone like a drink?"

Gabriel declined the offer, but I just stared at him, trying to anticipate what he was up to. He kept glancing at me. Sizing me up.

The vampire handed his boss a hefty glass of whiskey. After taking a swig, Blade sat down in his chair and swung his boots up on the desk. "What's your name, darlin'?"

"You mean me?"

He sipped his drink and waited.

"Jesse. Jesse Ames."

"Why are you looking for Charlie, Jesse Ames?"

Charlie? That cleared up any doubt he knew the man. "His

wife hired me to find him. He stole something from her and disappeared. A ring. It's a family heirloom and she wants it back." I got a little brave. "You wouldn't happen to know where I can find him?"

His glass went still at his lips, and the room went eerily quiet. I think I heard my own heart beating. But then he smiled, and his dark eyes began to lighten up again. "Well, if I did know where he was, I'm not sure I'd tell you."

"Why not?"

Gabriel muttered something under his breath. I'm pretty sure it was something about me shutting up. But after eleven years at the bureau, I'd learned a little something about psychology. About mutual respect. If you acted like a doormat, you got treated like one. Nothing wrong with asserting a little confidence in a respectful manner.

I started to regret opening my mouth when the vampire got up and walked around the desk again, hopping up on it as his eyes fixed on mine and then traveled south.

After an uncomfortable moment, I said, "What do you think you're looking at?"

He brought his eyes back up to mine. "Why you, darlin'."

"You can keep them right here." I pointed my forked fingers at my eyes, not giving a damn who or what he was. The ladies were off-limits.

His brows cocked. "Is that what you think I was looking at?" Then he nodded toward the door. "I've got plenty of that right out there."

The awkward conversation ended abruptly when the door flew open. Thor came stumbling into the room with a couple of large vampires behind him. I took one look at their shredded arms and Thor's busted lip and figured he'd put up a fight. The skin on his arms kept shifting to fur and then back again like he couldn't quite get the wolf under control.

Blade hopped off the desk and walked over to him, shaking his head slowly. "Well, would you look at that." Then he glanced back at me like he was putting the pieces together, his grin growing wider as he patted Thor on the shoulder. "I believe you have a bounty on your head."

9

SOMEONE THREW A TOWEL AT THOR. "COVER THAT shit up."

Before wrapping it around his waist, he turned to face the vampire. "If you had let me grab my clothes before dragging me out of the woods, I wouldn't be standing here swinging my jewels at you."

Gabriel gave Thor a firm nod. "Good for you, Thor. Stick it to the man who holds your very future in his hands."

"Go find his damn clothes," Blade ordered.

Glancing around the room, Thor finally had mercy on us and covered himself up. "If you want this towel to stay put, you'll get me a chair." He spotted the one behind the desk and strolled toward it.

Blade stepped in his path. "I'll castrate you like a bull if your ass touches my chair. It doesn't matter to the Romans how I deliver you as long as you're alive."

Thor stepped back and pointed to me and Gabriel. "I'll just stand over by those two."

With Thor safely tucked between us, I decide to address the

LUANNE BENNETT

elephant in the room. I glanced back and forth between Blade and Gabriel. "How do you two know each other?"

"Mr. Bastian and I have something in common." Gabriel had a brief, silent conversation with the vampire before continuing. "Lucius has tried unsuccessfully to kill us both."

Blade sat back down and crossed his booted foot over his knee. "For a master vampire as old as he is, he's not very good at killing. But then again, I'm not very good at being killed."

I snickered. "He did a pretty good job of killing things when I lived in New Orleans."

Blade was staring at me with that look again. "So you're the one."

"The one what?"

"The woman who outsmarted him and snuck that shifter over there out of New Orleans. I bet he *really* hates you."

If Blade only knew I'd done it again this afternoon. If Thor and I didn't find a way out of this room, he'd hand us over to Lucius and both of our heads would be on a spike by morning. I assumed he intended to collect on that bounty. Why wouldn't he? He was a drug dealer. Integrity didn't fit into his business model.

"Can we get back to Charles Fraser?" Gabriel said. "Why are you so interested in why we're looking for him?"

Blade finally lost interest in me and focused on Gabriel. "A demigod starts sniffing around my club and asking questions about my clients, I'm gonna be curious. I have a reputation for discretion, you know."

"You could have just thrown us out, but something tells me there's more to it. Why don't you just cut the bullshit and tell us why you're guarding your bone with this particular client?"

In the blink of an eye, Blade had Gabriel pressed to the wall. His fangs were an inch away from Gabriel's face a second later. "Because he's mine!"

Gabriel vanished, sending Blade tumbling face-first into the wall. A moment later, he reappeared behind the vampire. "You're embarrassing yourself in front of your men. Don't make it any worse."

Blade collected himself and smoothed his disheveled hair before looking at me. "Sorry you had to see that, Jesse. Gabriel and I were just having a little discussion."

I locked eyes with him as I tried to ignore all the voices jabbering in my head. Uncles Ames was trying to convince me to let him take over, which was unusual because he rarely bothered to ask. The others were just arguing with each other about the best way to approach the predicament.

"Shut up," I growled under my breath.

Blade cocked his head. "What was that, darlin'?"

"Nothing." I shook it off. "Why are you protecting Charles Fraser?"

"I'm not protecting him—I'm hunting his sorry ass. The man stole from me, and I plan to get my money back and then make an example out of him." He shot Gabriel a wicked glare before looking back at me. "Charlie is mine."

This case was getting more convoluted by the minute. I was tempted to give Kiko her money back and call it a day, but first I had to get out of the room. "How did he steal from you?"

"I loaned him money and he disappeared on me. A lot of money. No one does that to the Bastians. No one's ever been stupid enough to try, and I'm putting myself at the top of the debtors list when I find him."

Kiko's husband was on a roll. I wondered how many more disgruntled debtors were about to come crawling out of the woodwork. "All these big bad vampires of yours and you can't find a half-breed like Charles Fraser?"

"Charlie isn't your average fox. If he can hide from me, either someone's helping him or he's smarter than any of us thought. I know one thing for sure. He hasn't left town."

"What makes you think that?"

He glanced around at his men. "Because all these big bad vampires have had the exits sealed. He'd have to go through us to get out."

Okay. That made my job a little easier if I managed to get out of the room in one piece. "Why don't we work together? One of us will eventually find him." It would also take care of the bounty problem looming over our heads.

The vampire who had been dispatched to find Thor's clothes walked back in the room and tossed them on the floor. Thor picked up his pants and shirt and quickly put them on before slipping into his shoes.

Blade leaned back on the desk and gave Thor a thorough look. "I have a better idea. A little insurance."

Gabriel shook his head and let out a laugh. "You'll regret that decision after about five minutes with him."

I looked back and forth between them. "What are you two talking about?"

Blade snapped his fingers at one of the vampires. "Set him up with a nice cell downstairs. He'll be staying for a while."

Two of them grabbed Thor and started to manhandle him toward a door at the back of the room. His eyes went wide. "Jesse? What's happening here?"

"I believe you've just been confiscated as collateral," Gabriel said, looking at Blade. "Correct?"

The vampire nodded. "That's right. Bring me Charlie, and your wolf is free to go. I'll even forget about that bounty."

It wasn't a bad offer, although it meant I'd definitely have to give Kiko her money back. I doubted there'd be anything left of her husband when the Bastians were through with him. Although there was still the ring.

"Deal," I said.

Thor looked horrified. "What?"

"But I want Thor back in one piece. There better not be a hair out of place. Got it?"

Blade walked across the room and came close to me. So close I could feel his breath on my face as he spoke. "You bring me Charlie and I'll even protect you from the Romans."

"Seems reasonable." I was dancing inside. Not only was I walking out of the room intact, I had protection against those lowlife vamps in New Orleans. Now I just needed to find Charles so they didn't kill Thor. Piece of cake.

I gave Thor a pointed look. "Do what they say, and don't fuck up." I couldn't save him from himself if he mouthed off one time too many. I cringed as he pleaded while I walked out the door, but my hands were tied. I intended to get him out of here if it killed me, and it just might.

After Gabriel and I walked outside, I stopped to let my adrenaline settle. "We got lucky. Charles Fraser just saved our asses from being shipped back to New Orleans."

Gabriel laughed. "Blade despises Lucius. No amount of bounty money could convince him to hand either of you over. He wouldn't give Lucius the satisfaction."

"So that's how you two know each other. From New Orleans. You could have mentioned that when I told you we were coming here tonight."

"You didn't tell me the place was owned by the Bastian cartel. Christ, Jesse, only you could get yourself into this mess."

He had me there. The things I did to put food on the table. "You know what they say—no risk, no gain."

"Yes, but it's only meaningful if you're alive to enjoy the gains." He walked ahead of me toward the bike. "We need to talk to that redhead and find out what she knows."

Now I was questioning his bad decisions. "You're out of your mind if you think we're coming back here to interrogate the customers. Blade will kill Thor for sure."

"No, he won't. I could see the gleam in his eye when he realized he has what the Romans want. He'd rather dangle Thor in Lucius's face. A very *live* Thor." He reached the bike and waited for me to catch up, climbing on behind me. "Besides, Blade has taken an interest in you, so I doubt he'll harm your partner."

"Yeah, no kidding. I can't believe I'm in bed with the cartel."

"That's not what I mean, Jesse. He's taken a *liking* to you."

I looked over my shoulder at him. "Why the hell would you say something like that to me?" Especially when he knew how much I despised vampires.

"Because he wasn't looking at your breasts tonight when you called him out on it. He was looking at your left hand. For a wedding ring."

"What?" I blew it off. "You're crazy."

He had a chuckle at my expense. "You're about to find out how persistent he can be when he wants something."

I started the bike and took off. Now I had to worry about offending Blade when I gave him the brush-off. The list of vampires out for my ass was about to get even longer.

GABRIEL GAVE me a funny look when I pulled around the house and headed back toward the street. "Where are you going?"

I glanced over my shoulder at him. "Come on. I'm hungry."

He followed me across the street but stopped when I passed the restaurant front and headed around the corner toward the back of the building. "I'm hungry myself, but I draw the line at dumpster diving."

"Suit yourself."

I waited for him to catch up before going inside. The place was kind of empty, so there were plenty of stools at the bar.

"What is this place?"

Before I could tell him, a dart sailed past his head, barely missing his ear as the sharp tip embedded itself in the door behind him. Randy walked up and yanked it out of the wood. "Who's your friend?" He kept his eyes locked on Gabriel's.

Gabriel snatched the dart out of his hand. "I'm the man who's going to shove this pointed tip up your ass if you don't apologize and convince me that you mean it."

Randy took a step back but continued to glare at Gabriel.

"Hey! Take it down a notch!" I grabbed Gabriel's arm and gently eased him back. "It was an accident. Right, Randy?"

"Well, I don't know." He got a stupid look on his face and leaned closer. "Was it?"

Gabriel finally handed the dart back to him. "The proprietor should be a little more careful about allowing challenged individuals to handle sharp objects."

Randy got a blank look on his face as he processed the comment, but before he could figure out that he'd just been insulted, I steered Gabriel toward the bar. "You're in my backyard now, Gabriel. Don't start anything in here."

"Me?"

I took a seat and glanced back at Randy. Luckily, he was already heading back over to the dartboard. Ma didn't tolerate fighting in her place, and she didn't give a shit who started it. They'd both be out.

Gabriel sat down next to me and looked up and down the bar. "Nice place if you like a side of douchebag with your dinner."

"We don't all live in fancy houses, Gabriel." He and Emmaline lived in a cottage on one of Savannah's finer estates. Before that, he'd spent his days in a grand house in New Orleans. The house currently occupied by Lucius and the Romans.

"It's not the place, it's the clientele." He glanced around

the room before bringing his eyes back to mine. "I hope the food's better. I can't imagine what else would bring you in here."

Before I could tell him about Ma and her connection to Uncle Ames, Pauline came out from the kitchen. She walked around the bar and got an eyeful of Gabriel, then made a beeline for the stool next to his. After climbing on it, she turned toward him and crossed her legs, gazing at him like she was good and hungry.

"Here we go," I muttered. I was about to warn him, but he'd already gotten himself snared.

He looked at her when she wouldn't let up on the staring. "What?"

"I was just admiring your eyes. They're so green." She leaned closer and extended her hand. "I'm Pauline."

Her ten-year-old face had hunger written all over it, and I could see the disturbed look in Gabriel's eyes when he glanced at me. He was definitely on the menu.

"That's enough, Pauline," I finally said.

With her eyes still fixed on Gabriel's, she slipped her hand under the bar.

Gabriel practically knocked his stool over when he stood up abruptly and gawked at her. "Jesus! Someone needs to teach you a lesson, little lady!"

Her smile turned into a pout as she gave him a submissive look.

"Isn't it a little late for you to be in here? Where are your parents?"

I was about to let him in on Pauline's little secret when Ma came out of the kitchen and made her way over. She glanced at Gabriel before pouring a glass of gin and sliding it to Pauline. After downing her drink, Pauline hopped off the stool and headed back into the kitchen.

"Christ!" Gabriel's brow twisted. "What kind of depraved place is this?"

"You hungry?" Ma asked me. Then she turned her eyes to Gabriel. "Who are you?"

"A friend of Jesse's. Who are *you?*"

Randy strolled over and leaned against the bar next to me. "A friend of Jesse's, huh?" He snickered and almost dared to rub up against me but wised up when he saw the look I was giving him. "A round of drinks for Jesse and her... friend. Put it on my tab."

Ma kept her eyes on Gabriel as she grabbed a glass from under the bar. "You don't have a tab, Randy. Now you can leave on your own or I can have Tommy put you out."

He straightened up and huffed. "What the hell did I do?"

"Tommy!"

Finally getting the message, he walked toward the door, grumbling on his way out.

When he was gone, I made proper introductions. "Ma, this is Gabriel. He's an old friend of mine from New Orleans."

She was laser focused on him. "Friend, eh?" Finally easing up on the suspicious glaring, she asked me what I was drinking.

"Club soda is fine."

Her eyes turned back to Gabriel. "And you?"

"Bourbon. Neat."

After pouring him a glass from the bottom shelf—what was all the hostility about?—she slid the cheap booze in front of him. "And what might you be?"

Gabriel chuckled quietly. "Me? Just a man with an appetite."

She seemed unconvinced. The way she was eyeing him, you'd think he was on the FBI's most-wanted list. I assumed she'd picked up on his powerful blood. Any self-respecting witch would have sensed it.

"Let it go, Ma. He's just an old friend."

"Mm-hmm. Where's Thor?"

"He's a little tied up tonight." Well, I hoped he wasn't actually tied up.

She nodded a few times but continued to glare at Gabriel. Then she finally backed off.

"Is there a menu?" Gabriel asked.

I cringed a little, hoping Ma didn't get riled up again. Speaks usually didn't offer choices, and the regulars knew it. Whatever Tommy decided to cook that night was the menu, and it usually consisted of one item.

Ma smiled at him. "Tommy made a batch of chili tonight. It's either that or a burger."

I guess Tommy was feeling his inner Julia Child tonight. I was hungry enough to eat two burgers, but we both ordered the chili.

Ten minutes later, Ma came through the swinging doors with a bowl in one hand and plate in the other. She set the chili in front of me and slid the plate over to Gabriel. After reaching under the bar to grab me a few packs of saltines, she folded her arms and waited for us to dig in.

Gabriel looked at the burger. "I ordered the chili."

"Did you now?"

"Just eat it," I muttered. Something was up her ass, and I wanted to leave before it climbed all the way out.

Gabriel picked it up and took a bite. As he chewed, his expression began to change. Either the cow was way past its prime, or it was laced with too much pepper. He dropped the burger and stood up, spitting a mouthful of food on the plate. "What the hell!" He spit a few more times, grimacing as he wiped him mouth.

Ma gave him a firm look and grunted. "Well, I guess we cleared that up."

I looked back and forth between them. "Cleared what up? What's going on?"

"Your friend here just tried to poison me!" Gabriel tossed the napkin on the bar. "Belladonna?"

"So you're a witch," Ma said. "A good one or a bad one?"

"Neither!" I shot her an astonished look. "Jesus, Ma! Are you out of your mind?"

She cocked her head. "Did you hear what I just said? The man's a witch. Or a warlock, which is even worse. From where I'm standing, I think you owe me a debt of gratitude for flushing him out."

Funny, considering *she* was a witch.

"What is it with this place tonight?" I gawked at her like she had three heads. "First Randy tried to skewer him with a dart, and now you try to poison him?"

She waved me off. "Nonsense! I knew he was a witch the second I laid eyes on him, and no sane witch is gonna swallow a mouthful of belladonna. It's a foolproof way to ferret one out. I mixed it in with the lettuce on the burger."

I was starting to lose patience. "He's not a witch. He's a demigod. Are you happy now?"

She took a step back and gazed at him. "Holy…" After letting it sink in, she pulled herself together. "Why didn't you just say so?"

"I didn't know I had to."

She stepped closer and looked into his ethereal green eyes. "I ain't never met a demigod before. And to think I could have killed you!"

Gabriel spat one more time. "No sane demigod would eat belladonna either. It wouldn't have killed me, by the way, but it tastes like ass."

"Gabriel's girlfriend is a witch though," I said to Ma. I seriously doubted it could kill her either.

Her eyes lit up. "Really? What kind?"

Gabriel gave her a look. "The kind that doesn't try to poison me."

"Ma is a hedge witch." I pointed toward the kitchen. "Hence the separation between the front and back restaurants. The space back here is by invitation only, although the occasional uninvited walks in and lives to regret it."

Ma scooped the burger onto the plate and walked back toward the kitchen. "I'll get you that chili now. It's on the house."

After she left, Gabriel looked at me sideways. "That kid from earlier. Is she…?"

"Don't worry. You didn't just get felt up by a child. She's a shifter, and she's old enough to get arrested."

The look of relief on his face was palpable.

Ma returned with the chili and set it down in front of Gabriel. "Are you helping Jesse on her new case?"

He thought about it for a second. "I guess I am."

"Good. I think she needs some help with this one."

I looked at her sideways. "Thanks for the vote of confidence, Ma."

"So sue me for caring."

She got busy wiping down the bar while I mulled over what we knew about Charles Fraser. "I don't understand this guy. If he married Kiko for her money, why not stick around for a while and enjoy a life of leisure? Let his sugar mama take care of him? Why steal the ring and then rip off the Bastians?"

He took a bite of chili, chewing it slowly for a moment to test the water. When it passed the nonlethal test, he gave me his opinion. "That's a good question. But one thing's for sure, he's still in Atlanta."

At first I wasn't as convinced as Gabriel—or Blade. But it was starting to make sense. "Hiding in plain sight?"

Gabriel nodded. "You heard what Blade said. The city is

sealed off. Mr. Fraser may be able to hide within its walls, but he'll never get past those vampires."

"Now all we have to do is tear the entire city apart to find him." It was like looking for a ghost. The only lead we had was that redhead back at Sanguine, but getting in there to have a chat with her could get dicey if I wanted to keep Thor safe and sound. Under the circumstances, maybe Blade would make an exception about questioning a client, but not likely. Discretion was everything to a club like Sanguine. A breach of privacy would spread like wildfire and jeopardize his business. And then there was the other thing Gabriel had mentioned. The thing about Blade taking a shine to me. I needed to stay far away from that place.

Gabriel took a final bite of chili and pushed his bowl away. "Then I guess we better start tearing."

"You're a demigod. Can't you just look into your crystal ball and find the man?"

He laughed. "It'll take a bloodhound or a psychic, and I'm neither of those things."

"What I need is someone who knows Atlanta inside and out. Someone who knows the underbelly of the city. Where a vampire might hide."

Ma stopped pretending she wasn't listening to the conversation. "Well, I think you know just the right person."

10

Zᴇʙ ᴡᴀs ᴀ ɴɪɢʜᴛ ᴏᴡʟ, ʙᴜᴛ I ʜᴀᴅ ᴀ ꜰᴇᴇʟɪɴɢ ʜᴇ ᴡᴀsɴ'ᴛ going to appreciate me knocking on his door this late on a Monday night. Ma wrapped up some cookies to bribe him with so he didn't take my head off when we showed up.

"Where are you taking me now?" Gabriel asked when we walked back across the street. "To another loony bin for someone to try to kill me again?"

I threw him a sideways glance. "Where am I taking you? Shouldn't you be getting home to your future wifey?" Emmaline might be a nice witch, but women were territorial when it came to their men, and I didn't want to rub her the wrong way. "I know you told Ma you'd help me with the case, but I won't hold you to it. You've done enough, so vamoose. Go home."

"And leave you to get your ass killed?" With a laugh, he headed for the bike. "I don't think so."

I cocked my head. "Aww. You care about me."

"And don't you forget it."

He climbed on the bike behind me, and I started her up, taking off toward Zeb's studio with a knot in my stomach. Either the chili had done a number on me or my confidence was starting to wane. Or it was just my nerves. I really hated the thought of giving that money back to Kiko, but I also couldn't stomach the thought of having Thor returned to me in a box if I didn't cooperate with Blade.

We were almost there when I noticed a flashy little sports car in my rearview mirror. Nothing unusual about that, but it had been behind us for a while. It took a right turn just as I was about to try to lose it.

Zeb's lights were on when we pulled up to the studio, so at least there was no fear of waking him up. Just before I cut the engine, I saw that sports car coming slowly down the street that crossed over Zeb's. It stopped in the middle of the road for a few seconds and then continued.

Gabriel nudged me from behind when I backed the bike out of the parking space. "Where are we going?"

"I think we have company."

I pulled back onto the road. When I saw the car behind me again, I headed up the street and pulled into a convenience store. "I doubt it, but let's see if I'm being paranoid."

Without looking over at the car, Gabriel and I walked into the store to see if the driver would get out or if I could get a look at him through the tinted windows. Strolling down the middle aisle, I grabbed a bag of potato chips.

Gabriel looked at it. "Cholesterol, Jesse."

"You should talk." He had a candy bar in his hand. "Oh, I forgot." He could eat dog shit and be healthy as a horse.

He glanced at the car through the window. "Recognize anyone?"

I shook my head. The windows were tinted so dark I was surprised a cop hadn't pulled them over yet. I couldn't even make out how many were inside. After dumping the bag back on the shelf, I headed for the door. "Let's go."

He tossed the candy bar and followed me out. "What are you doing, Jesse?"

I walked toward the car, but when I was halfway to the driver's side door, the car kicked into reverse and did a backward U-turn around the side of the building and took off.

"Christ, woman, you're gonna get yourself killed one of these days!"

I laughed. "If they wanted me dead, they would have done it about five miles back." I climbed on my bike. "Get on."

As I was about to pull out of the parking lot, I spotted the car at the corner. "Son of a bitch. Hold on." I made a right turn and took off down the road, testing my bike as I pushed the engine. I maneuvered tightly around cars, but that fancy little sports car kept up with me.

I spotted an alleyway up ahead and took a sharp right, nearly skidding into the side of the building when a dumpster appeared in front of me. Successfully avoiding it, I almost careened into a couple conducting business against a wall. I hit the brakes, giving them the scare of their lives before backing up and continuing past them. I came out the other end, right into the path of the car.

"Fuck!" Gabriel growled as I slammed on the brakes. "I'll take care of this." He tried to climb off the bike, but I turned around and took off back down the alley before he could lift his ass off the seat. This time I beat them to the other end and kept going, weaving in and out of side streets until I lost them. Gabriel kept yelling over the engine for me to stop, but I ignored him.

I pulled into Sanguine and parked, preparing myself for a tongue-lashing.

"Don't ever ignore me again!" he barked as he climbed off the bike and ran his hand over the top of his head. "Fuck, Jesse!"

"Are you finished?"

He finally calmed down and glanced at the club. "The Bastians? Really?"

"Well, who else would it be?"

"Oh, I don't know." He followed me across the parking lot toward the entrance. "Maybe Kiko?"

"She tried that already and I put an end to it. My bets are on the vampires."

On the way to the hallway that led to the office, I nodded toward the bar. "Go find that redhead while I have a word with Blade." I was pissed off, but my legs were also shaking. I was about to storm into the office of the vampire cartel and try to bluff my way back out in one piece. But Blade needed to understand something. Either we had some mutual respect for one another, or the deal was off. I just hoped he saw my boldness as a sign of strength and Thor didn't suffer for it.

Before I could bang on the door, it opened. One of Blade's men motioned me in. Of course he'd seen me coming. The entire club was monitored by cameras.

The vampires parted as I walked into the office and headed straight for their boss. "What the hell's going on, Blade?"

"Jesse Ames." He smiled and sat deeper in his chair, his legs spread wide. "Twice in one night. I'm beginning to think you like me."

"You're having me followed?"

His grin vanished as he stood up, towering over me. "What are you talking about?"

"That little red sports car tailing me tonight. Are you going to lie to me and tell me it wasn't one of yours?"

His forehead tightened as he seemed to give it some thought. "Well now. If I was going to have you followed, I'd do it myself. But I wouldn't be caught dead in a red sports car. I prefer black."

If it wasn't the Bastians, then who the hell was it?

"Well, someone's been following me, and I can't think of

anyone with a reason to do that but you. Maybe you wanted to make sure I was doing your dirty work fast enough."

For the first time since I'd met him, he looked dead serious. "It wasn't us."

"And I'm supposed to take your word for it? A drug dealer holding my partner hostage?"

He had me against the wall before I could blink, and his fangs were showing. "If it was me following you, darlin', you'd know it."

The door flew open and Gabriel stepped inside. "Get off her." It was his scary voice. The quiet one. The vampires stepped in his path, but if I was really in danger, those thugs wouldn't have been able to stop him.

Blade waved them off and gave me some breathing room. As he composed himself, his fangs disappeared. He smoothed his hair back. "Like I said, it wasn't us."

"He's telling the truth," Gabriel said.

"Great!" Maybe Kiko didn't get the message after all.

Blade gave me that grin again. "I can make it happen if that's what you're into."

Jeez. Enough with the horny innuendo.

I glanced around the office. "Where's Thor?"

"Tucked away in the basement."

"Well, go get him."

"Now why would I do that?"

"Proof of life. I want to know he's still breathing."

After mulling it over, he walked to the door at the back of his office. When I didn't follow him, he looked over his shoulder at me. "Well?"

I wasn't keen on the idea of following a drug-dealing vampire down a flight of dark stairs, but I decided to trust him because he clearly wasn't planning to bring Thor up to me. Besides, Gabriel nodded for me to go with him.

We took the stairs down to the basement where I spotted a cell at the end of a corridor. *A cell!* "Keep many prisoners down here?"

Blade glanced back at me. "Only those who rub me the wrong way."

I guess it was better than the alternative. Halfway down the corridor, I heard a familiar voice.

"It's all about the butter," Thor said to the vampire keeping him company on the other side of the bars. "You have to get it good and hot before pouring the eggs into the pan. Then you slide the pan back and forth."

The vampire looked at us as we approached, and I could see a glazed look in his eyes. The look I'd seen in the mirror many times while listening to Thor prattle on about whatever he was an expert on at that moment. Apparently tonight he was an expert at making omelets.

He swallowed a mouthful of the eggs on his plate and brightened up when he saw me. "Jesse! Come to fetch me? It's about time."

"Not yet. I'm just here to make sure they're keeping up their end of the bargain."

The vampire guarding him looked at Blade and groaned. "You got to get someone else down here for a while. I can't take it much longer."

Thor took another bite. "What's the matter? A French omelet is too overwhelming for you?"

"Is it really necessary to keep him in a cage?" I said to Blade. "A handcuff on a chair will do."

Blade snickered under his breath. "In case you haven't noticed, he's a shifty little shit. Literally. Can't be trusted on this side of the bars."

"You hear that?" I said to Thor. "I can't save you from yourself, so sit tight and behave. I'll find Charles Fraser, but it might take a day or two."

A low growl came from Thor's throat as he turned back to the guard. "Get me a beer! Please," he added with a smile.

Way to go, Thor. Piss off the vampire holding the key to your cell.

I walked up to the bars and leaned closer. "Please don't give them a reason to kill you."

"Aww, Jesse. You miss me, don't you?"

I stepped back and gave him a firm look. "You're my partner. Rebranding my business would be a royal pain in the ass. Now sit down and make nice."

"Satisfied?" Blade asked.

"Yeah." I headed back up the stairs and walked out of his office with Gabriel right behind me.

"Jesse!"

I turned around. "What?"

"I like you, but the clock is ticking."

"Did you find her?" I asked Gabriel when we walked outside.

He shook his head. "She wasn't here. Besides, those cameras were watching." He got a grin on his face. "But I did run into our bartender friend on his way out of the men's room. He gave me a name."

"The redhead's name?"

"Not exactly." He handed me a piece of paper with the word Six written on it.

"What's this?"

"It's a name."

I looked at it again and what was written underneath it. "What kind of name is Six?"

"I guess we'll find out in the morning when we pay her a visit."

11

WE DROVE BACK TO ZEB'S STUDIO, ONLY THIS TIME WE weren't followed. I made sure of that by keeping an eye on the rearview mirror the entire way.

Gabriel climbed off the bike and gazed at the orange dinosaur. "Very interesting."

"He's a real character. Just don't rub him the wrong way like you did with Ma."

"I'll keep that in mind."

The door was unlocked, but Zeb was nowhere in sight when we walked inside. "I need to get on him about that door." It was late, and this part of town wasn't exactly Saintsville after dark. Then we heard banging and clanking coming from the other room along with the sound of singing. Bad singing.

"Zeb?"

The singing abruptly stopped, and Zeb stuck his head around the corner. "Jesse?" He took one look at Gabriel and narrowed his eyes. "What's wrong?"

"Do I reek of trouble?" Gabriel muttered.

"Sorry to come by so late, but we need to talk to you."

He glared at Gabriel again. "Who's we?"

Some other sounds coming from around the corner reminded me of why Zeb was so comfortable leaving his door unlocked at night. Lula and Raven came tearing into the room like a herd of elephants and made a beeline for Gabriel. Before I could tell him they were nothing but big pussycats, he was engulfed by the Great Danes. Lula decided to throw her paws up on his shoulders and give him a proper greeting, backing him against the wall with her considerable weight.

"Off!" Zeb ordered.

She dropped down on all fours and Raven took a seat next to her.

"They like you," he said to Gabriel, "so I guess you passed the sniff test."

"This is my friend Gabriel," I said. "He's been getting tested a lot lately."

"A friend? Where's Thor? Did you dump him for this one?"

I needed to set the record straight about my relationship with Thor before the whole damn town got the wrong idea. Before *he* got the wrong idea.

"He's busy, so Gabriel's in town helping me on a case."

Zeb stepped closer to size him up. "Gabriel, huh? Like the archangel?"

I snorted a laugh. "He's an angel all right."

His eyes narrowed. "No, he ain't. Something in there ain't right."

We didn't have time to beat around the bush. "He's a demigod." Now that we'd gotten that out of the way, we could avoid Zeb spending the next twenty minutes trying to figure out what Gabriel was. Or worse, putting him to the test like Ma did.

"A demigod? Is that right? I never met one before."

Gabriel extended his hand. "I've never met a wizard, so we're even."

After they shook, Zeb snapped his fingers and gave the dogs a hand signal. They trotted over to their beds and lay down while we went into the other room to have a talk about the less savory side of Atlanta.

"So," Zeb said, pointing to his latest creation, "what do you think?"

I looked at the giant abstract heap of metal. I had to be careful with my words because Zeb was temperamental about his work. I also had no idea what it was, so I opened my mouth to make a neutral comment that wouldn't be construed as offensive.

"Never mind," he said, cutting me off. "It'll just influence my artistic vision."

I handed him the cookies Ma wrapped up for him. "I brought you something."

"A bribe, huh?" He took them from me and bit into one. "Get on with it so I can get back to work."

"It's about the case I'm working on. The guy who stole that ring I showed you the other day. Turns out he's a little slipperier than I expected."

He put his glasses on and eyed the sculpture while he talked. "You mean he skipped town on you."

"See, that's just it. We think he's still in Atlanta, but he's found himself a nice little hidey-hole."

"And?"

"And he's also a half-breed. Half vampire."

Zeb stopped inspecting his work and gave me his undivided attention. "What's the other half?"

"Uh... asshole?"

"We have no idea," Gabriel said. "Jesse tells me you're familiar with every inch of the city, including the less savory parts. If he's still in town, more than likely he's hiding in one of those places. Somewhere he can feed freely without being detected. A place where even the local vampire cartel can't find him."

"The cartel?" Zeb's face had disappointment written all over it. "Who've you gotten yourself mixed up with, Jesse?"

"It's a long story, and we don't have time to explain. Do you have any idea where someone like that could be hiding?"

He gave it some thought and nodded a few times. "Yeah, I think I know a place where you can start."

"So?" I waited for him to elaborate.

His brow furrowed. "Hold your horses. Let me think on it for a second."

As we watched Zeb scratch his head and try to recall this mystery place, we heard the front door squeak open.

I glanced toward the other room. "Are you expecting someone?" The dogs hadn't made a sound, which worried me on a couple of levels.

Zeb shook his head. I automatically pulled a gun from my jacket and pointed to the door leading to the back rooms. "Go," I whispered to him.

Reluctantly, he complied, and I walked toward the second entrance of the studio to circle around to the front room. "Keep an eye on Zeb," I said to Gabriel when he started to follow me.

"He's a wizard. He can take care of himself. It's you I'm worried about."

Gabriel suddenly vanished, and I stepped silently around the corner and saw the backside of two men wearing dark suits. They weren't from the IRS, that was for sure.

"Are you the guys who've been following me?" My gun was pointed at their backs.

They barely moved when I spoke, and I could see Lula and Raven sitting in front of them like obedient dogs, panting with their tongues hanging out as they looked up at the strangers in anticipation.

One of them slowly turned, his perfectly coiffed head of hair resembling shiny black plastic as the light hit it at an angle. When he looked at me, I couldn't hold back my gasp.

"Who the fuck are you?" I demanded, wondering where Gabriel was as the man with the snake eyes stared back at me. "You better start talking because my hand is getting a little shaky." It wasn't an idle threat. There was a slight trembling in my trigger finger.

The second guy with the salt-and-pepper hair looked down at the dogs, causing them to retreat backward, a low whine coming from their mouths as they disappeared into the studio I'd just come from.

"Lower your gun," the one with the dark hair said, his voice deep and raspy.

"I don't think so." When his buddy turned around and gazed at me with the same strange eyes, I took an involuntary step back. He came at me, and I fired. He stepped aside with freakish speed, and the bullet flew right past him and hit the wall.

The guy with the black hair didn't even flinch. "Come with us. Mrs. Orochi would like to speak with you."

"Who the hell is Mrs. Orochi?"

He gave me a venomous sneer. "Your boss."

"I don't have a boss, so fuck off!"

When he came at me, I felt the Marine Corps tattoo crawl around my wrist. My body surrendered, and I closed my eyes and went into a reverse spin, pulling my arms toward my center as I came around and snapped the heel of my foot into his chin. He flew backward into his buddy, sending him slamming into the wall.

I waited for him to get up, but he didn't move. I must have snapped his neck. His friend looked pissed though. He steadied himself against the wall while I looked for the gun that had flown out of my hand. I spotted it halfway across the room and figured running was a better option.

I'd almost made it to the front door when I saw my reflection in the window. The guy was about to be on top of me. I lost my footing and fell, twisting around on my back when I hit the floor. He loomed, looking down at me with his strange eyes.

Gabriel appeared behind him with a knife in his hand. I rolled out from under the guy a moment before the blade reached around and sliced through his throat, escaping the spray of blood coming from the wound.

I jumped to my feet and stared down at the nearly decapitated body while I caught my breath. "Where the hell were you?"

Gabriel dropped the knife. "Taking care of the guy waiting outside in the car."

"There were three of them?"

"He got away. It was the same car that was following us earlier."

I thought about what the guy had said just before coming at me. "I think they work for Kiko. They said my boss wanted to have a talk with me, but they called her Mrs. Orochi." I kicked the body in the side. "Boss, my ass."

"Then she's lying to you."

"No kidding. Not only about what her husband is but what *she* is. Her men in black here aren't human, so I'm guessing neither is she." I grabbed a folding chair and sat down, dropping my head in my hands. "Is Zeb okay?"

"I don't know. I haven't seen him since he ran out."

"We better go find him." I was getting up when I saw someone appear behind Gabriel. The one I'd kicked in the chin raised a gun and aimed it at Gabriel's head, but then he shifted the muzzle to the right until it was aimed at me.

I heard something that sounded like a war cry, and a shiny object sliced through the air. It swept across the guy's shoulders, taking his head clean off, barely missing Gabriel as it swung around and continued across the room.

Zeb was standing in the doorway, looking at the body on the floor. "I tried to hex him, but it didn't do a damn thing. The guy must have an aura fit for an elephant." He took a step closer. "Did I kill him?"

I glanced at the severed head. "Yeah, I believe you did."

There was a long piece of metal with a sharp edge lying on the floor. It must have been material from his latest project, and it was covered with blood. At least I think it was blood. Had to be.

Zeb nodded firmly. "Good! He did something to my dogs." He whistled, but they didn't come running as fast as they should have. "Come here, girls!"

Lula eventually came in with her head down and her tail between her legs. That same whimper I heard earlier was coming from her mouth. Raven followed a minute later, looking just as spooked.

Gabriel got down on his haunches to examine them. After having a silent conversation with the dogs, he patted them on the head and stood up. "They took a mental browbeating from whatever those things were, but they should be fine by morning."

Zeb shook his head. "I've seen a lot of strange things in my sixty-four years, but I've never seen something with eyes like that. Did you recognize them?"

"No, but I know who they work for. They're my new client's henchmen."

"The lady with the missing husband? The one looking for that ring?"

"That's the one."

He scratched his head and looked down at all the blood on the floor. "Well, ain't that interesting."

I followed his gaze. "What?"

He shrugged. "I've been thinking about the stone in that ring. Kinda looks like that blood on the floor."

I pulled the picture out of my pocket where I kept it next to the one of Charles. "You're right. That is interesting." The colors matched perfectly. But we were comparing the stone in a valuable ring to a pool of blood on the floor. I'd say it had to be a coincidence, but this case was getting weirder by the second, and we had the severed head of something that clearly wasn't human.

A hissing sound got our attention, and the three of us looked at the head on the floor a few feet away. It was still as a stone. So was the body. We followed the sound and realized it was coming from the other one. The one Gabriel had nearly decapitated near the front door. And the body was quivering.

When I looked closer, I saw the skin on the half-severed neck start to undulate like something was trying to work its way out. "What's happening to it?"

A second later, a forked tongue slipped out of the wound that ran from ear to ear.

"It's a snake!" Gabriel grabbed my arm and yanked me back as the serpent slithered out of the man's body and started to race across the floor. It suddenly stopped and turned around, moving its head back and forth as it eyed the three of us. When it slithered in our direction, we moved back toward the wall.

Gabriel and I both glanced at the knife he'd dropped on the floor.

"Be my guest," I said. Snakes give me the creeps.

He grabbed the knife, but before he could use it, Raven came charging into the room with a growl. Her giant paws dug into the wood floor as she slid and collided with the serpent, wrapping her large jaws around its body a few inches from the head. She crunched down and shook it violently, sending the tail end flying across the room.

"Drop it, girl!" Zeb ordered before she could swallow it.

The dog obeyed.

While Zeb checked her for bites, I inspected the head to

make sure it wasn't about to sprout a new body like a lizard regrowing a tail or something. When I bent down to look at it, it started to move. It was shriveling. A few seconds later it was nothing but a dried-up piece of leather the size of a quarter.

I straightened back up and watched it go still. "What are the chances that thing could reconstitute? Like one of those sea monkeys or a sponge?"

Zeb pulled a handkerchief from his pocket and picked it up. Then he walked over to a jar of turpentine and dropped it in and screwed the lid on tight. "Good luck to it."

It was getting imperative that we find Charles Fraser and get this mess over with, so I got back to the original reason we were here. "You were about to tell us where we might find a half-breed lying low."

"The place doesn't exactly have an address. At least not one you want to be giving out. Sharing that kind of information could get you killed."

"Thanks, Zeb. That's real helpful."

He got that irritated look again. "Keep your pants on. I know someone who might be able to help, so I'll see what I can do. Call me tomorrow afternoon."

We didn't have time to wait, but we didn't have much of a choice either.

Gabriel started for the door. "We have to go, Jesse."

I felt uneasy leaving Zeb and the dogs alone, but those things had come here looking for me. And Zeb was a wizard, although not much of one.

"Lock up tight, Zeb. While you're at it, throw up some creep deterrent, just in case."

12

THE FRONT DOOR WAS AJAR WHEN WE GOT BACK TO MY place. Gabriel tried to go in first, but I beat him to it, slipping inside with the hair on the back of my neck bristling. The furniture was all intact, which was a good sign. I didn't see so much as a piece of paper on the counter out of place. But then I noticed the light from the refrigerator. The door was open.

Gabriel shook his head when I walked toward the kitchen. With the image of a severed head or something equally gruesome perched on the shelf, I let him take the lead. He slowly opened the refrigerator door and stumbled back.

I stopped in my tracks when something came out of it and slithered to the floor. Through the darkness, all I could make out was a tail. A tail that swished back and forth under the door and seemed to be growing at an alarming rate.

"Stay back!" Gabriel pulled a knife from his boot and stepped closer to it. "It's a dragon."

"A what?" I thought he'd lost his mind, but when I flipped the lights on, I saw it with my own two eyes. There was a Komodo dragon in my kitchen. A venomous monitor lizard the size of one of Zeb's dogs.

He glanced at his knife and let out a nervous laugh. "Lot of good this will do against that armor. Where's your gun?"

The lizard swung its heavy legs forward and crossed the kitchen floor in the blink of an eye. Gabriel disappeared as it lashed out at him. It turned its head and zeroed in on me, moving so swiftly it knocked me to the ground before I could aim my weapon. The gun slid from my hand from the force of the impact, and I came face-to-face with the creature as it lowered its head and opened its mouth, the stench triggering my gag reflex. It stared down at me but didn't strike, crushing me against the floor with its enormous weight.

Get ready, Jesse!

About time he showed up.

I wiggled my right arm out from under the heavy beast and wrapped it around its neck. With my left arm and leg, I shoved hard, harnessing the strength of Uncle Ames as I gave the dragon's neck a firm yank, throwing the lizard off-balance and onto its back. Then I quickly turned the tables and straddled it, knowing I'd be right back underneath it in a few seconds if someone didn't intervene.

Gabriel materialized near the front door and grabbed my gun off the floor. He shot, piercing the lizard's tough armor when it righted itself and climbed on top of me again. The beast let out a loud hiss and slithered off me. Gabriel stabbed it when it came at him with its jaws wide open. He managed to shove the blade clear through the back of its neck but let go when the creature bit down hard.

"The poison!" I yelled, recalling the venom Komodo dragons carry in their glands. I doubted it could kill him, but we weren't dealing with your average lizard.

Its jaws opened as it thrashed, and Gabriel pulled his arm free. When it backed up and shook its head, he reached inside and grabbed ahold of the knife still lodged in the back of its throat. He twisted it sideways until it sliced the reptile's neck from shoulder to shoulder, nearly toppling its head.

The dragon stumbled back toward the refrigerator and dropped to the floor, its body shriveling like that snake back at Zeb's studio. A moment later, it vanished, leaving no trace that it had ever been there.

I examined the deep wounds on his forearm. "Jesus, Gabriel! You're hurt!"

He flexed his hand as the cuts and gashes started to heal before my eyes. I don't know why I doubted they would.

Relieved, I sidestepped the spot where the lizard had been a moment earlier and looked inside the refrigerator. "How the hell did that thing get in there? How did it *fit* in there?"

"It didn't. There was a snake on the shelf. It shifted after slithering out."

I shuddered. "I'm gonna need a new refrigerator."

Gabriel grabbed the gun off the floor and handed it to me. Then he glanced around the kitchen.

"What are you looking for?" I asked.

"A message. That thing was sent here to intimidate you, so there might be something he left behind."

I laughed. "Well, it worked. I was a second away from meeting my maker."

"You wouldn't be breathing right now if your client wanted you dead. That lizard would have finished the job before I got to it."

There was no doubt now that Kiko wasn't human. Deserted newlywed, my ass. Her husband probably had a damn good reason for disappearing. But tonight's little incident did solve one problem—I no longer had to worry about a conflict of interest. As much as it pained me, I intended to tell Kiko she could shove her money where the sun doesn't shine. I was on the Bastians' dime now, with Thor's spared life as payment for services rendered.

I brushed past him and headed for the bedroom.

"Where are you going?" he asked.

"To prepare."

I walked into the living room a minute later with a shotgun in one hand and my revolver in the other. "Which do you think I should wave in Kiko's face to get her to talk?"

He looked wary when he saw the shotgun. "Do you even know how to use that thing?"

"Eleven years with the bureau?" I raised it and pointed it at the wall to check the sight. "You bet your ass I know how to use it. Kiko's gonna shit her pants by the time I'm through with her."

He walked up and grabbed the end of the barrel to lower it. "Don't you think this is a little much?"

A little much? Kiko's men in black had crossed a line tonight. Breaking into my house was one thing, but coming after me at Zeb's studio was a whole other story. You didn't go after my friends without paying a price. And now that I was working on behalf of the Bastians, I planned to get some useful information out of her after I returned her dirty money.

I laid the shotgun on the couch and opted for the revolver instead. "Yeah, you're right."

Gabriel groaned and rubbed his eyes. "I'm probably going to regret this, but where do we find this woman?"

Good question. I pulled out her business card and handed it to him. "This is all I have."

He read the business name on the front. "Dragon Enterprises. How appropriate."

I took the card back and dialed the number, doubtful anyone would pick up. To my surprise, someone did, but there was no greeting. Just breathing on the other end.

"You've got my attention," I said into the phone, "so why

don't you save us both a lot of time and tell me what this is all about."

She finally spoke up. "This is about you doing your job. You work for me, Ms. Ames, not those lowlife vampires."

"We need to talk. Face-to-face."

A quiet laugh came across the line. "I'm having a party at my apartment tomorrow night. I'll text you the address. And bring your friend."

I hung up and glanced at the shotgun on the couch. "I guess I won't be bringing that. We just got invited to a party."

KIKO WAS LOADED. Anyone who lived in the Walden was rich. Since her unit was listed as the penthouse, I figured she was *rich* rich. The kind of rich that made people off their relatives.

I glanced down at the marble floor in the lobby. "The business of fulfilling fantasies must be lucrative."

The doorman stepped in our path when we walked toward the elevators. "May I help you?"

Pardon me.

"We're here to see Kiko Fraser. She's expecting us."

He got a puzzled look on his face. "We don't have a resident by that name."

I double-checked the address on my phone. "Says right here the Walden on Peachtree." He didn't budge. "She's in the penthouse."

That seemed to jog his memory. "You mean Mrs. Orochi."

"Yeah." That was the name her thugs mentioned at Zeb's studio. Must have been her maiden name.

"Jesse Ames and my plus-one. Check your list."

He walked back to the desk and took his time running his finger down the page of a book. "You can go up."

Gabriel and I stepped into the elevator and hit the top button with a *P on it*. In jeans and leather, we weren't exactly dressed for a fancy party, but we also weren't here to socialize. As the elevator approached the floor, I got a little uneasy. "I hope we're not walking into a den of freaks when that door opens."

Gabriel took a deep breath. "Like I said, if she wanted you dead, you'd already *be* dead. Just keep your cool."

"Easy for you to say, Houdini."

When the door opened, I was hit with the smell of something awfully tantalizing. There were people milling around everywhere. After walking past the foyer, I made it about five feet into the main room before some guy with a pencil-thin mustache and slicked-back hair accosted me.

"Giovanni Russo. And you are?" He smiled with a mouth full of veneers so white they were blinding.

"Not interested."

I grabbed a glass of champagne from a tray carried by a passing waiter and kept moving, looking over the crowded room for a familiar face. Short of finding Kiko, I'd settle for Tok.

A woman wearing a bright magenta dress that actually hurt my eyes a little tried to hand me her empty glass. "I'll have another martini. Vodka. Three olives."

"Yeah, so will I," I replied, walking past her.

When I turned around to see where Gabriel had wandered off to, I nearly collided with mustache man. "Are you following me?"

He gave me that toothy grin again. "I was just wondering if we've met. Perhaps at Kiko's annual fantasy ball?"

It suddenly occurred to me that I was about to piss away an opportunity if I blew him off again. "Fantasy ball? I must have missed my invitation. I'm one of Dragon Enterprises' newer clients."

His face lit up. "Well, you're in for a treat. Kiko likes to spoil her recipients." He squinted at me while he sipped his drink. "Let me guess. The eyes."

"The eyes what?"

A hand wrapped around my arm and steered me away from the man. "Hands off, asshole!" I yanked out of Max's death grip and shot him a fuck-off glare. "That's a good way to get your fingers bitten off."

He grinned. "Got a foul mouth on you. Gives me a hard-on."

"Does that shit really work for you?"

"Every time." He shoved me toward a hallway.

"I guess there's no accounting for brains." I grinned back at him and looked at the door at the end. "Am I going to find Kiko in there, or are you planning to show me more of your bad moves?"

His cocky smile faded. "Why are older chicks so jaded? A little rusty down there?"

"I bet you'd like to find out." I took a step closer to him and leaned in. "Us older chicks have something guys like you will never have." I tapped my temple. "Confidence. I don't need someone half my age to stroke my ego."

"Move!" He shoved me forward.

Gabriel caught up to us and gave him a warning look. "Touch her again, and I'll slit your throat."

Max met him eye to eye but wisely kept his mouth shut.

"Where've you been?" I asked. "Max here was just about to escort me to Kiko's office."

The double doors opened as we approached, and two men with those same snakelike eyes motioned us in. It was a large room with ultramodern furniture and a panoramic view of the city through a wall of windows. Kiko was sitting in a chair behind a sleek desk with nothing on it but a laptop and a vase holding a single tulip, facing the view. I guess she was a real minimalist.

She swiveled around in the chair and crossed her legs. "Ms. Ames, you disappoint me."

"Then I guess we're even. I don't appreciate you having me followed and barging into a colleague's home."

"Colleague? Is that what that old wizard is?" She motioned to the chairs on the other side of the desk. "Please have a seat." Her eyes were on Gabriel as he refused her offer and didn't budge. "Who's your friend?"

"Ask him yourself."

Gabriel was easy on the eyes to just about every breathing woman on the planet, and she stood zero chance of seducing him if that's what she had in mind. Although I would have taken enormous pleasure in seeing the fair Emmaline put Kiko in her place.

"Gabriel," he said. "I'm an old friend of Jesse's. I'm helping her out while her partner is tied up with other cases."

Finally pulling her eyes away from his, she waited for me to take a seat.

I plunked myself down in the dainty chair that looked like it could barely support the weight of a child and threw my feet up. A second before the heels of my boots landed on the desktop, I swung them back down to the floor, dusting off the sleek surface with the edge of my hand. "Sorry. Force of habit."

She looked like she was about to have a conniption.

After regaining her composure, she got down to business. "I hired you to find my husband, so where is he?"

"That's a very good question." I stood up and reached into my jacket for the envelope of money she'd given me. "I don't think we can work together, Kiko. There are too many secrets between us." I tossed in on the desk. "It's all there, minus expenses I've incurred to date. And a little restitution for my friend for upsetting his dogs and trashing his studio." Aka Ma's rent money. She stared at me in disbelief, so I said, "You can count it if you'd like."

She glanced at Gabriel, maybe thinking he could knock some sense into me. When he shrugged, she looked back at me. Her neutral stare might have fooled some, but I was really good at reading people. Picking up on controlled fury and hidden agendas behind their eyes. There was real anger there, and I was beginning to regret defying her in front of her men.

She finally spoke. "I think there's been a misunderstanding between us."

"I'll say. You lied to me repeatedly, and I don't work with liars."

Her chilling grin returned. "The misunderstanding is that you think we're equals. You work for me now, and I expect results."

I hopped up from my chair and nearly came across the desk, stopping a foot away from her to slam my fist on the surface. "No more lies, Kiko Fraser. Or is it Orochi? What the hell are you?"

She stood up and brought her face within inches of mine. "I'm your new master!" Her eyes flashed green for a second and then returned to their normal dark brown.

I straightened up and laughed. "You're delusional." After glancing at the envelope on the desk, I reiterated my stance on our working relationship. "Like I said, I quit."

I felt the floor rumble slightly under my feet and motioned for Gabriel to follow me out, hoping her lizard men didn't do something stupid like try to block the door. Instead, they stepped aside and allowed us to leave.

"That was easy," Gabriel muttered when we were outside her office.

"Yeah, a little too easy. Watch your back."

He chuckled, but there was nothing funny about it. "It's not *my* back I'm worried about."

We walked into the room full of party guests, but it seemed twice as crowded as before. A shindig of massive proportions. I bumped into Giovanni Russo again, but it was his skin that got my attention this time. It had a rosy glow like a baby's bottom.

"Ah, we meet again." He flashed me his pearly whites. "How nice."

"Not really." His lecherous stare was revolting.

I turned right and ditched him, pushing my way through the crowd toward the elevator. Gabriel was right behind me, but when I looked at him, I saw a couple of Kiko's men following us. When I turned back to the elevator, a woman stepped in my path. Her eyes were glowing, illuminating her long platinum-blond hair. It was unworldly.

"We need to speed it up," Gabriel said.

"No shit. Tell me I'm not seeing things."

He glanced around at the guests as we worked our way across the room. "You mean the eyes?"

"Yeah, and look at that guy." I motioned to a man standing a few feet away. His skin had a strange golden aura emitting from it. He was laughing at something the woman next to him had said, and when he suddenly turned to look at me, his eyes lit up in a blaze of purplish blue.

"Your eyes are fine. Theirs are not. Let's get out of here while we still can."

It felt like an eternity before we reached the elevator. After pushing the call button, I turned around and saw the entire party come to a standstill. All eyes were on us. It was like I'd dropped a tray of glassware and gotten everyone's attention. But it was the freaky look in their eyes that had me pressing the button about ten more times.

The elevator finally arrived. We got in, and the door shut just as the crowd was starting to head toward us. A wave of relief washed over me when the car started to descend. "Talk about creepy."

Gabriel let out a pent-up breath. "No, Jesse. That was foreplay."

"For what?"

"You don't think your client intends to let you just walk away, do you?"

I snorted as the elevator reached the lobby. "What's she going to do? Force me to work for her? Let her duke it out with the Bastians when she finds out I'm working with them now."

Working with *vampires*. God, I hated to admit that.

As we entered the underground garage, I looked left and right to make sure none of Kiko's men in black were waiting to pounce. There wasn't a thug in sight.

"Where to now?" Gabriel asked.

I shrugged. "Waffle House?"

"Tempting, but we still have to find Mr. Fraser before the vampires show up. Let's head back to your place to regroup. I could use a drink."

As we walked toward my bike, I felt a set of eyes on us. It was going to be a long ride home… if we made it there.

13

W<small>E WERE ON THE ROAD FOR LESS THAN FIVE MINUTES WHEN</small> I spotted that same sports car that had tailed us to Zeb's studio the night before.

After motioning to Gabriel to hold on tight, I took a sharp right, accelerating as we turned down a one-way street. It was late, but there was plenty of traffic competing for the road, so I decided to stick with the side streets. The car followed, and when we came out on the other end, there was a second identical car waiting. I guess those fancy sports cars were part of the uniform.

I hung a U-turn as the car behind us approached, driving right past it, heading in the wrong direction. After driving three blocks, I stopped.

"I'm going to lose these guys and head north." There were plenty of places outside the perimeter of the city where Kiko wouldn't find us. At least until we had a chance to figure out what to do next.

Gabriel agreed, and we took off down the road and got on the interstate. After driving a mile, I veered onto the north ramp, but one of the cars I thought I'd lost cut us off, sending us careening back into traffic. A second car paced me in the next lane, repeatedly trying to run me off the road.

Kiko's drivers were either immortal or they didn't give a damn if they died. They weaved in and out of traffic, keeping us closed in from the side and front. When another car showed up and boxed us in from the rear, I knew we were fucked.

With nowhere to go but straight ahead unless I wanted to risk climbing a retaining wall, which I didn't, I slowed down and cooperated. I wasn't wrecking my bike over Kiko. They were herding us somewhere. Probably straight back to that penthouse now that she'd made her point and had her fun.

Gabriel nudged me and pointed up ahead. It was a group of bikers driving in a neat formation that spanned five lanes of the highway. When we approached, they slowed down, keeping us at a low speed for the next mile.

The car boxing us in from behind suddenly swerved out of its lane and drove up to the bike at the end of the line. The driver's side window lowered, and an arm holding a gun appeared. But before it could fire, the bike swerved closer to the car, nearly colliding with it. The biker jumped, clinging to the window while he wrestled for the gun. His feet were dragging along the highway.

"What the fuck," I muttered, not fully believing what I was seeing.

The car flipped, sending the biker airborne. It kept flipping until it smashed into the concrete wall separating the highway.

The other bikes suddenly sped up and disappeared down the road at breakneck speed. Within seconds, they were gone from sight.

No longer boxed in from the rear, I was about to fall back and dip out when I saw something coming straight at us. The bikes had turned around and were barreling back down the road toward us.

I hit the brakes and swerved onto the shoulder as the bikers came within seconds of smashing into the two oncoming sports cars. At the last moment, the bikes veered out of the way and turned around, ending up behind Kiko's thugs.

One of them pulled up to where we'd stopped. It was a woman. "Follow me."

Not one to look a gift horse in the mouth and with Gabriel urging me on, I took the ramp behind her and followed her through the back streets of Atlanta. We finally pulled into the parking lot of a club that looked like it had gone out of business.

Gabriel and I climbed off my bike and walked over as she was getting off hers.

The first words out of my mouth were "I think your friend is dead."

She swung her head toward me, a set of fangs disappearing before she spoke. "Digger? He's fine."

"What the hell?"

Gabriel extended his hand. "Thank you."

She looked at it suspiciously for a second and then took it, giving it a firm shake. "Hilli."

"I'm Jesse, and this is—"

"I know who you are." Cocking her head, she ran her eyes up and down my body. "I expected you to look more like my mother, but you're definitely nothing like her." She let out a chuckle. "I get it now."

My brow pulled tight. "Get what?"

"You work for Blade," Gabriel said.

She let out another laugh. "That's debatable."

The other three bikes pulled into the lot before she could elaborate. One of them had an extra passenger, and the leather around his feet was shredded. He walked straight up to me with an irritated glare. "You owe me a new pair of boots."

"I owe a lot of people, so get in line."

He walked around my Harley and nodded. "Nice. What is it? A '67?"

"'65. Sorry about your bike back there." I hoped he didn't expect me to buy him a new one of those too.

He continued to inspect my bike. "It was brand new. I can get another one."

There were five of them. All Bastians, I gathered. "So Blade is having me followed after all. I appreciate the help back there, but I don't like being tailed."

Gabriel gave me a warning look. "Jesse…"

"What? Should I be giving him status reports every night like some stiff wearing a suit behind a desk? I left that shit behind when I walked away from the bureau."

The vampire with the ruined boots leaned against a short wall bordering the lot and pulled out a cigarette. "Now I see what my brother meant."

"Brother?"

He lit the cigarette and took a drag, exhaling as he spoke. "He said you'd be difficult."

Gabriel squinted to him. "You must be Digger. Used to run the northern territory of Louisiana until the Romans took over."

The vampire got a bitter look in his eyes and dropped his cigarette, snuffing it out with his shredded boot as he pushed away from the wall. "Yeah, that's me. I'll be taking that territory back someday."

"Digger, huh? That's an interesting name. You like to garden or something?" I couldn't help myself.

Hilli filled me in. "He got it because he's dug his own grave so many times we stopped counting. But he just keeps digging himself right back out."

I knew the type, and based on that little stunt he just pulled on the highway, I could see what she was talking about.

"Like I said, I appreciate the help back there, but tell Blade he needs to get off my ass. When I find Charles, he'll be the first to know." I walked back toward my bike, hoping that was the end of it.

It wasn't.

Digger stopped me. "My brother has another job for you."

Shit. This was why it's never a good idea to get tangled up with the cartel. You know what they say—once you're in, you never get out. Working at the bureau taught me all about family ties, but anyone who's ever seen a half-ass mafia movie could tell you that.

I turned around, catching Gabriel's wary look before giving the vampire my undivided attention. "What's this job?"

"A simple drop." He held out a small package that was tightly wrapped, so I couldn't easily peek inside even if I wanted to.

I stared at it for a moment but didn't take it. "I don't use drugs, and I sure as hell don't deliver them. Tell Blade he can go fuck himself." Christ! Did I really just say that to a cartel leader's brother? With four more Bastians within striking distance?

Gabriel stepped up and took the package. "What's inside?"

Digger held his gaze. "You don't need to know."

"Oh, I think we do," I said, digging my own hole deeper.

One of the vampires who hadn't introduced himself yet had me against the retaining wall before I could react, and his fangs were fully extended. Gabriel was on top of him a second later.

It was a real lovefest.

Hilli came to my defense. I liked her. "Get off her, Evan!"

Gabriel backed off so this *Evan* guy could take his hands off me.

I straightened my jacket and gave the vampire a nasty look, trying to keep my hands from shaking so he wouldn't feed off my fear like a predator. "You ever touch me again, *Evan*, I'll disappear and let you find Charles Fraser yourself. To hell with Thor." I was banking on the bluff.

Evan smoothed his black hair back and pierced me with his hazel eyes. "Sure. No problem. Wouldn't be a fair fight, would it?"

"Not with those fangs in your mouth." I'd kicked the asses of men half my age. And if I didn't, Uncle Ames sure as hell would.

Gabriel and Hilli both stepped between us as the vampire raised his left brow and came closer.

"You'll have to go through me to touch her again," Gabriel said. "You really don't want to do that." He gazed at Evan, and I thought I saw a brief twinge of pain in the vampire's eyes. Gabriel had a way of convincing you to do things. No gun or knife necessary.

"Don't worry," Hilli said. "He won't put his hands on her again." Now she was leering at Evan. When she was done sending him a message, she nodded to the package in Gabriel's hand. "You need to deliver it to your client."

"I don't have a client anymore. I gave her my walking papers earlier tonight, hence the little exit interview on the interstate."

She took a deep breath and smiled at me. "Then I guess you'll have to face her one more time. My brother doesn't like to hear the word no, and neither do I."

I glanced back and forth between her and Digger. "Let me get this straight. You two are sister and brother?"

"Yeah, but I'm the one with the normal genes." She glared at Digger, who was standing aside with his arms crossed while he watched the show. "I know how to reason with people."

"So that makes you Blade's sister." I looked over at the other two whose identities were still a mystery. "How about those two?"

"That's James and Destiny. No relation other than our Bastian blood."

She took the package from Gabriel and held it out to me. "Take the package, Jesse."

It was killing me to think about what was inside, but it was killing me even more to think about delivering it. "You do realize what will happen if I face Kiko again."

"You worry too much. It'll give you ulcers. Kiko needs you alive just like we do."

"You know what she is, don't you?"

She gave me a sly smile. "We didn't at first. Blade usually never parts with money before doing a little due diligence on his debtors—and their significant others. Apparently he didn't do enough this time, but that won't happen again."

"Why don't you deliver the package yourself?"

"What fun would that be? Besides, coming from you will solidify who's in charge when you tell her who your new client is."

I didn't have much of a choice, so I took the package. "I'll do it, but I want to know what's inside."

"You'll find out when she opens it. Trust me, she'll let you live once she sees it and accepts the fact that you're working with us now."

"And what if she refuses the package when she finds out it's from you?"

Hilli walked back over to her bike and climbed on. "Tell her it's from her husband. She'll open it."

"Tell me what Kiko is!" I yelled as she turned her bike toward the street.

Without another word, the vampires took off, leaving me and Gabriel standing there with the box. It was wrapped so tightly there was no way I was getting it open with my bare hands. The damn thing was hermetically sealed with all that tape.

I mulled over my options for a few seconds. "Give me your knife."

He laughed at me. "Like hell. You're not opening it, Jesse."

"You want to know what's in it as bad as I do, and I'm not ripping my fingernails off trying to get through all that tape."

"Don't be foolish. For all we know, it's booby-trapped. You might blow yourself to smithereens."

I bounced the package in my hand, gauging its weight. Couldn't have weighed more than half a pound, and that was from all the tape. "You have an active imagination."

He snickered. "You don't know Blade. Now let's go. We have a delivery to make."

"You don't have to do this, Gabriel. You did what I called you here for, so you can go home to Emmaline if you want."

He shook his head. "Right."

Reluctantly, I stuffed the package in my inside pocket and found myself walking slowly toward my bike. Slow enough not to detonate whatever was in that box. "I'm gonna regret this."

WE LEFT the parking lot with every intention of driving straight back to the Walden, but I couldn't bring myself to walk into that place again, not with all those bizarre partygoers mulling around like human flashlights. It was wiser to wait until tomorrow when the freak show was over. And since I was now on her shit list, we needed a plan to get out of there if she didn't like what was in that package. I was also hungry, and Speaks was still open.

It was Taco Tuesday. Actually, it was Fajita Tuesday, but that just didn't sound right. Speaks's fajitas were right up at the top of my list with my father's pot roast. You wouldn't think a Scottish cook like Tommy would have such a knack for them, but they were finger-licking good.

"Damn, Ma. You got to get that recipe from Tommy."

She picked up our empty plates and walked toward the kitchen. "Since when do you cook?"

"Since… never. But I might if I knew how to cook these."

"I'll see what I can do."

After she walked through the swinging doors, I pulled the small package from my jacket and set it on the bar. "Looks harmless enough."

A hand reached over my shoulder and grabbed it. "Aww… you brought me a present." Randy held it to his ear and shook it.

"Jesus! Don't do that!" My heart went into overdrive when he tossed it up in the air and caught it like a baseball. "I'm not playing, Randy. It's fragile!"

He held it out to me with a puppy dog expression but yanked it back when I reached for it. That went on a couple more times until he pushed his luck a little too far.

Gabriel stood up and wrapped his hand around Randy's throat. "I've had about enough of you." He let go, shoving Randy toward the door. "Now leave."

I think it shocked the hell out of the guy, but it worked.

"Hold on," Gabriel said as Randy started to walk toward the exit. "The package."

It was still in his hand. He passed it to Gabriel and then landed his remorseful eyes on me. "Sorry, Jesse."

I closed my eyes and shook my head. "Just go."

Ma walked out of the kitchen and fisted her hand in her side. "What do you have there?"

"Nothing. Just a package that could possibly blow the place up." I cringed the moment I said it. I'd learned the hard way that even a simple joke about such things could have repercussions, and most of those repercussions usually happened before you had the opportunity to clarify.

"A bomb?" A guy sitting a few stools down from me got up and grabbed his jacket on his way to the door. Then the couple at the table behind us did the same, but not before yelling a warning to the rest of the place. Not one of them took the time to pay their check either.

Ma let out an ear-piercing whistle as the entire place went into a panic. "Settle down! There's no bomb!" Then she leaned closer and muttered, "Is there?"

I stood up and went into damage-control mode. "Just a misunderstanding, folks. Take your seats."

A few people put money on the bar on their way out, but most went back to drinking and throwing darts. When I sat back down, Ma gave me a look. "What's in the package?"

Scratching my head, I tried to come up with a suitable reply. "That's a good question. Einstein over here"—I pointed my thumb at Gabriel—"has me thinking it's something dangerous."

"And you thought it was a good idea to bring it in here? Get it out! Now!"

Like usual, Gabriel calmed the situation. "My apologies. I put the idea in Jesse's head to save her from herself. To keep her from opening it."

I shook my head at him. "Do I look like a kid?"

"No, but you have the curiosity of one."

Ma nodded to the package. "So what's in it then? And where's Thor? I've been seeing a lot of you lately but not him. Is he all right?"

Gabriel shrugged and gave me the floor.

"Long story," I said. "You were right about Sanguine. We should have stayed clear of the place. The Bastians are babysitting him for a while."

Her look was incredulous. "Thor's being held by vampires?"

"That's right. My client's husband has been burning a lot of bridges. He owes the Bastians money, and they want me to turn him over to them instead of his wife. By the way, she's my ex-client now. I gave the money back tonight. Well, most of it. Now those vampires are blackmailing me to deliver this package to her or they'll kill Thor." It sounded absurd coming out of my mouth. "I have no idea what's in it, and Gabriel here won't let me take a peek."

Ma leaned over the bar to get a closer look at it. "You don't think it's drugs, do you?"

I shook my head. "Not likely. They could deliver drugs themselves. They're playing some kind of game with her, and I'm stuck in the middle."

She straightened up and walked back into the kitchen. When she came back out, she handed me an envelope. "You'll be needing this."

"What is it?"

"The money you gave me for the rent."

"No, Ma. Keep it."

"Like hell. Give it back to that snake."

If she only knew how accurate that statement was.

"I already told her I was keeping some for expenses. And as far as I'm concerned, the predicament she got me and Thor into falls under that category." I slid it across the bar. "Keep it."

Reluctantly, she picked it up. "How can I help?"

"I have to make that delivery. Got a miracle to get me out of her fancy penthouse in one piece?"

She let out a shuddering breath and muttered something under her breath. "I think I just might."

14

I ENTERED THE LOBBY OF THE WALDEN, PUMPING MY clammy fists to dispel some of my nerves. Kiko would smell my fear like a horse with a rookie rider on its back. I almost turned around the second I set foot on the marble floor, but the doorman was already staring at me.

"I'm here to see Kiko Orochi."

"Yes, Mrs. Orochi is expecting you."

I'd called her that morning to let her know I wanted to talk. I figured I'd surprise her with the package when I got up there. Gabriel stayed behind at the house. He was my backup plan, ready to sound the alarm with the Bastians if I didn't make it out of there in a reasonable amount of time. But the vampires had seemed pretty confident she'd let me go after taking a look at what was inside that box. If they were wrong, I'd sic Uncle Ames on her and fight like hell.

I reached inside my jacket to feel my gun, the steel reassuring against my hand. In my other pocket, next to the package, was a small carved totem Ma had given me the night before. Something called a Cù-sìth. As a hereditary witch, she had a few tricks up her sleeve. But she rarely used her gifts. The family tradition had all but faded away with her. She gave it to me with a warning to only use it as a last resort, to use my weapons first. I only took the thing to be polite. Hell, she didn't even tell me how to use it. Said I'd know if it came to that.

As I stepped into the elevator, I could feel eyes on me. There was a shiny little lens near the ceiling. A security camera. I'd bet my bike Kiko and her horde of vipers were the ones monitoring it. She probably owned the entire building.

I stepped into the foyer and glanced around. The place was immaculate. No sign that a crowded party had taken place in the penthouse the night before. There wasn't a dirty glass or a rug stain in sight. No Kiko or anyone else either.

"Hello."

Not a peep.

The second I walked into the living room, I was being escorted down the hallway toward Kiko's office. "What's with you guys yanking women around?" I pulled my arms free from the two thugs manhandling me. "Ask me nicely and I'll walk."

Neither of them so much as broke a grin. They just ushered me through the double doors and closed them on their way out, leaving me alone with their boss. Evidently I'd interrupted Kiko's lunch. Without even doing me the courtesy of looking up, she kept tearing at the bloody steak on her plate. The thing was practically raw, and she was mopping up the blood with a piece of bread and stuffing it into her mouth.

"Late lunch or early dinner?" It was just after four o'clock. "You know, if you scar that steak for another minute, it might actually be edible."

She stopped eating and finally looked up. Normally her skin had a perfect porcelain glow, but it was paler than usual today. And her eyes were dull. She speared a piece of meat with her knife and held it up. "Would you like a bite?"

"I'll pass." I took a seat without waiting for an invitation and watched her have at it. "Don't mind me."

After inhaling her food, she washed it down with a glass of red wine and snapped her fingers. One of her men came through the door immediately and cleared away her empty plate.

"Wow! Help like that is hard to find. He must have dog ears."

She wiped her mouth with a napkin and leaned back in her chair. "Among other things, you owe me a Porsche."

"You mean that car your men tried to run me off the road with last night? It wasn't me who taught them a lesson." I pulled a cigarette out of my pocket and placed it between my lips.

"Don't even think about lighting that in my office."

I pulled it from my mouth and rolled it between my fingers. "I don't smoke."

Her brow furrowed as she glared at me, but then she got a curious grin on her face. "Where's your handsome friend?"

"You mean my insurance?"

"Don't play with me, Ms. Ames. You're in no position."

"Wouldn't dream of it. Gabriel isn't here because he's waiting to notify the Bastians if I don't walk out of this building in"—I glanced at the time on my phone—"about twenty minutes."

"The Bastians?" She let out a curt laugh. "What do those bloodsuckers have to do with this?"

She should talk after what she just stuffed in her mouth. It was time to get this over with.

I reached into my pocket, pulled out the package, and slid it across the desk. "The Bastians send their regards."

As if a cold chill had rolled through the room, she shivered. "Max!"

He came rushing into the room when she barked. "Yes, Mrs. Orochi?"

She nodded to the package. "Take it in the other room and open it."

Nice. Blow up your employee.

I'd be damned if I wouldn't see what was in that package with my own two eyes. "They said it's from your husband."

She threw her hand up when Max went to reach for it. "Charles?"

"That's what they said."

Cautiously, she picked it up and examined it. With her index finger, she poked her long nail into the tape and slowly slid it along the edge, bringing it all the way around until the wrapping started to fall away.

Talk about deadly claws.

She pulled the rest of the packaging off and set the small wooden box on the desk. As she stared at it, I started to get nervous because her breathing was getting more erratic by the second. It was like she could feel the object inside.

If Charles Fraser's finger was in there, I was in trouble.

She eventually reached for the lid and slowly lifted it. When she looked inside, she gasped. Not a normal gasp; a gasp like her airway had completely closed up.

Her breathing came back with a vengeance when she barked, "Check the tomb!"

As Max ran for the door, I leaned forward and saw what looked like a gemstone nestled in a bed of velvet. An emerald or tourmaline. "What is it?"

There was pure hatred in her eyes when she pulled them away from the box to look at me. She didn't say a word for what felt like an eternity. Just pinned me with a heavy gaze that dared me to ask another question.

Eventually her phone rang. And not a second too soon, because I thought she was about to come across the desk at me. She showed no emotion as she listened, and then she set the phone down. "They're gone."

It seemed like a smart idea to stand up. "What are gone?"

"You bitch!"

"Me? What did I do?"

Her eyes lit up for a moment but then dulled as she grabbed the edge of the desk to catch her breath again. "Where's the other one?"

I shook my head. "I don't know what you're talking about. The other what?"

"The other eye!" It was no longer Kiko's voice coming out of her mouth.

Looking back at the package, I noticed a piece of paper wedged under the velvet. "There's a note."

She read it and then tossed it on the desk as the floor began to rumble.

I grabbed the note and read it myself.

YOU GET THE OTHER ONE WHEN I GET MY HANDS ON CHARLIE.

"UM… did I mention I'm working with the Bastians now?" Hilli seemed to think it would help my situation.

Max came bursting through the door as the entire room started to shake. "The tomb has been breached."

"I know that, you idiot!" Her strange voice was getting deeper with each word. *"How?"*

With Max preoccupied, I tried to run for it. But the tornado of wayward energy in the room hurled me backward into the wall. I slid to the floor, shaking my head to clear it. When I looked up, Kiko's sleek desk was moving toward me. I ducked as it slid over my head and slammed into the wall. The entire contents of her office came flying across the room next.

I crawled out of the way. When the dust cleared, the far side of the room was one big pileup of furniture.

Furious, Kiko turned to me. "An eye for an eye! Cut them out!"

Self-preservation had me running for the door again.

On your left, Jesse!

I pulled my gun out as I ran through the double doors, taking aim at the guy lunging for me on the other side. The bullet hit him right between his eyes, but he stirred the second he hit the floor, shaking it off as if I'd hit him with a paint gun. I grabbed the knife I'd stuck in my boot and slashed it across his neck. His head started to fall backward, but he kept coming, so I lashed out again. This time his head fell, landing on the floor between my feet.

Two more of Kiko's men came down the hallway, cornering me. "What now?" I asked myself. Or Uncle Ames. Or anyone else who was listening.

The totem.

It was a gentle voice in my head, and the crescent moon on my biceps started to crawl.

I reached inside my pocket and felt for the carving. *What do I do with it?*

Call it forth! Cù-sìth!

Hey, whatever worked. I closed my eyes and said the name aloud, feeling a sickening sensation in my stomach as the two syllables came out of my mouth. Whatever it was slammed me into the wall. It was like something had crashed into my body and exited through my chest. When I slid to the floor and opened one eye, I saw an apparition of an animal. A dog or a wolf.

A hound from hell to be exact.

The ghostly animal turned to look at me. Then it lowered its massive head and bared its razor-sharp teeth as a growl reverberated off the walls. It crashed into Kiko's men. They stabbed at the beast, but their knives just thrashed at the air. Its teeth looked real to me, and the blood spraying the narrow hallway confirmed it. The gray walls looked like pink abstract art.

The hound grabbed ahold of one of the guards by his neck and shook its head violently. The man's eyes started to change, narrowing into slits as a hiss filled my ears. Within seconds, I was watching a battle between serpent and canine. The snake wrapped around the hound's body and started to squeeze. The creature dropped and rolled, crashing into the wall as it sank its teeth deeper into the serpent's flesh. A spray of that strange pink blood came from the snake's neck when its body detached and flew across the hallway, slamming into the opposite wall. It was still moving when it hit the floor.

While the Cù-sìth focused on its next victim, I climbed to my feet and slipped through a doorway that led to the kitchen. It was a clear shot to the living room from there and then to the elevator. As I ran for it, I felt a painful stab to the back of my right thigh. When I turned around, I saw a serpent a few feet away, recoiling for a second strike.

The room started to spin, and suddenly Max was standing where the snake had been. He had a wicked grin on his face. "You should have taken the money and done your job. Now we'll have to make you cooperate the hard way."

Stumbling, I turned back toward the living room. My legs were going numb, refusing to move in the direction I was telling them to go. The room was a blur as someone grabbed me from behind. I turned around and slammed my fist into his throat over and over again, my hearing quickly fading as my strength slipped away. The last thing I remembered was seeing Gabriel's face as I fell to the floor and closed my eyes for what I thought was the last time.

"Wʜᴀᴛ?" I sat straight up, shivering from the sweat covering my body. Everything was out of focus, but I could see the couch I was lying on, and it wasn't mine.

"Ah, there she is." Ma bent down and set a tray on the coffee table next to me. "You had us worried there for a while."

"Where am I?"

"You're in my living room." She handed me a cup of steaming-hot tea. "This will help with the headache."

I glanced around the room. "Where's Gabriel? He got me out of there. I saw him."

"And it took the wind right out of him. He's resting in the spare bedroom."

Gabriel could pop in and out with ease, but it took all his energy to drag someone along for the ride. Emmaline was the exception. She had enough energy for both of them.

"Hold your horses," Ma said when I tried to get up. "You've been through the mill. Drink up before you try to stand."

I took her advice when the room started to spin. "What time is it? Jesus, what *day* is it?"

"Still Wednesday. You've been asleep for about four hours. If it wasn't for Gabriel's blood, I doubt you'd be breathing at all."

He'd saved my ass again. What was I going to do when he left and I was cut off from that healing gold running through his veins? Although vampire blood froze nicely.

The memory of Max biting me quickly came back. "I don't think they were trying to kill me. I think they planned to make me one of their puppets."

Gabriel emerged from the hallway, looking a little scruffy. "What was in the box?"

"Well, look what the cat dragged in. You look like shit,

buddy." And it took a lot to make Gabriel look bad. I was just relieved to see him standing there. "Thanks for the ride."

He sat down next to me, squinting as he examined my eyes. "That was some powerful venom. Took an extra dose of my blood to reverse it. What happened back there?"

"It was a stone. It looked like an emerald or some other green gem. Kiko blew a gasket when she saw it. Then she mentioned something about a tomb and went ballistic." I scratched my head while I tried to remember all the details. "I think it was an eye."

Gabriel looked at Ma and then back at me. "Maybe you should drink a little of that tea."

"I'm not loopy, for Christ's sake. There was a note in the box saying she'd get the other one when the Bastians got Charles. I think that stone is one of a pair of eyes from something inside the tomb she mentioned." I shrugged. "I don't know. Maybe some kind of statue or something? People sink all kinds of money into memorializing the dead. Wasn't King Tut's tomb made of gold?"

Gabriel wasn't buying it. "Or maybe they're just valuable stones."

"It's possible. Hilli said it was a gift from her husband, so maybe that ring isn't the only thing Charles stole before disappearing. He probably used them as collateral for that loan Blade made to him." I set the cup down and dropped my head in my hands. "This case is getting weirder by the second." I shuddered when I remembered Kiko mentioning an eye for an eye. There was something more to those stones, and I planned to find Charles Fraser so he could enlighten me.

Ma stuck her hand out. "The totem."

"Oh yeah. The other strange-as-fuck detail about today." I reached for my jacket, which was thrown over the back of the couch, and pulled the carving out of the pocket. "Cù-sìth is all yours."

138

"Hush! The summons is still fresh. Wouldn't want to call it forth in the middle of my living room."

"What exactly was that thing?"

She took the totem and walked over to a desk. "A faery dog. The hound of the highlands. But there aren't many of them left. My people are caretakers for one of the last remaining. Consider yourself honored to witness it." After retrieving a wooden box from the top drawer, she placed it inside.

"I consider myself lucky it didn't focus its fangs on me."

She laughed. "It serves its summoner. You were never in danger."

As my head continued to clear, I started to get pissed off. I stood up to see if my legs were stable. Satisfied they were in good working order, I threw on my jacket and headed for the door. "Where's my bike?"

Gabriel got up and walked after me. "Where do you think you're going?"

"To knock out a few fangs."

15

THE BOUNCER GRABBED HIS PHONE WHEN I WALKED PAST him. So did the bartender. I guess the cameras weren't enough and Blade had given all the staff strict orders to report it if I entered the place.

Not bothering to knock, I pushed the door open, but one of his men stepped in my path.

"Let her through." Blade swiveled around in his chair with a wide smile on his face. "Jesse."

"You said I'd be safe. What the hell happened today?"

His smile turned into a frown. "You'll have to be more specific."

"Specific?" I wanted to pull my pants down and show him the bite mark from that snake, but I didn't want to encourage him. "Kiko ordered her men to gouge my eyes out. I believe she referred to it as an eye for an eye."

"What a shame that would have been." He eased back in his seat and found his grin again. "I like those eyes."

"Cut the crap! What are those gems? And while you're at it, you're going to tell me exactly what Kiko is."

"Haven't you figured that out yet?"

Gabriel finally caught up and came into the office. "Ah… I see the fun has started without me."

I took a deep breath to rein it in before I said some things I'd regret. "Tell me about those stones." I grinned back at him. "Please."

"They're emeralds. You didn't think I would hand Charlie a bunch of cash without collateral?"

I wasn't buying it. "Emeralds are pretty, but they're not that valuable."

He got up and hopped on the desk. "They're not just any emeralds." He reached over and opened the top drawer and pulled out a box. "This is what Kiko meant by an eye for an eye, but I didn't think she'd have the guts to risk never seeing the other one again."

He removed the lid, and I got a gander at the matching one. It looked bigger right under my nose. Or maybe it was the bed of black velvet it was sitting on that made the emerald pop. "What was she talking about when she mentioned a tomb?"

"It's where Charlie got them from. They're the eyes from some corpse, but that's all he said, and I didn't ask questions."

I looked at Gabriel but refrained from an I-told-you-so moment. "You're a demigod. Ever seen anything like this before?"

He shook his head. "No, but I don't like it. If they were found in a tomb, they were put there for a reason. Possibly to appease the dead."

"Perfect. Just what we need." I turned back to Blade. "What the hell is she?"

He let out a soft groan as his fangs descended. "Kiko Orochi, aka the Red Widow."

"You'll have to explain that." Gabriel seemed just as mystified when I glanced at him.

"There's not a lot I can tell you about her, but I do know how she got the title."

"Let me guess. She's been married a few times."

Blade nodded. "That's right. And they all end up dead."

It was all starting to make sense. "I guess Charles wasn't interested in becoming her next victim."

He closed the box and shoved it back in the drawer. "There's no proof that she offs her husbands. Who knows why she bothers. She's the one with the money, so it isn't for that. I guess we'll find out when you get your hands on Charlie."

I stared at him, wondering if he was playing with a full deck. Delivering that package had almost gotten me killed, so I'd say we were even. "You almost got me killed tonight. I'm done."

He grabbed my arm when I started to walk away. "We're just getting started. Now she knows you're working for me. You find Charlie, Kiko gets her emerald eyeball back, and I get my pound of flesh."

"And the ring? Who gets that?" It was the reason Kiko hired me in the first place, although her husband was part of the original deal. I guess she'd have to choose between her precious emeralds and Charles because Blade was only giving up one of them. The two of them could hash that out.

He finally let go of my arm. "I don't give a damn about the ring. All I'm interested in is that deadbeat husband of hers."

Gabriel asked the next question that was about to come out of my mouth. "You still haven't told us what she is. Is she a shifter like her guards?"

"You mean the serpents? Probably, but I have no idea. Other than her reputation, she's a bit of a mystery."

I let out a short laugh. "Well, she's something. You should have seen her unleash her wrath on me today. I saw the woman's eyes practically glow."

"Then I guess you need to watch your back, darlin'. I can give you a room downstairs next to your partner if it'll make you feel safer."

"I'll pass. But speaking of Thor, I think it's time for a check-in."

His brow tightened. "Don't you trust me?"

"Take me downstairs or the deal is off."

Releasing a dramatic sigh, he hopped off the desk. When I started to follow him to the door, he threw his hand up to stop me. "Stand right there." He opened to door and yelled down the stairs, "Speak, wolf!"

"Are you kidding me?"

Thor yelled back, "I'm hungry!"

"Thor?"

"Is that you, Jesse? Get me out of here! There's a vampire down here who looks like she wants to eat me!"

I glared at Blade. "I swear, if anyone touches him—"

"Do your job and there won't be a scratch on the lad's head when I hand him over to you." He slammed the door shut before I could say another word. "I don't know what you see in that wolf. He's annoying as hell."

Damn right he was annoying. But we were partners, and I was loyal. "Don't worry. I'll find Charles."

"Fantastic." His eyes lingered on mine for a moment. "Do you like steak? I know a hole-in-the-wall that serves the best T-bone in town."

All I could do was shake my head. "You blackmail me and almost get me killed, and now you're offering to buy me dinner? You don't date very much, do you?"

When he actually opened his mouth to reply, I headed for the door. "Come on, Gabriel. Let's get the hell out of this loony bin."

As we made our way out, I scanned the room for that redhead. She wasn't at the bar, but I remembered the name the bartender had given Gabriel the last time we were here. It was time to pay the woman named Six a visit, but first we had to find a new place to stay. No way was I going anywhere near the house so Kiko could sic her snakes on me again.

The night air washed over me like a calming breeze the second we walked outside. "Jesus, I feel like I'm suffocating every time I walk into that place."

"It's the energy from all the life force flowing in the back rooms. The blood. The place reeks of it."

As I headed for my bike, I looked over my shoulder at him. "You know of a good Airbnb around here?"

———

WE DROVE north for twenty minutes. When we finally arrived at the house we'd be staying at, I climbed off my bike and eyed the bungalow before surveying the area. It was cute, but the neighborhood didn't feel right. "Where the hell are we?"

"It's called the suburbs. You've heard of them, haven't you?"

I glanced up and down the quiet street, wondering what I'd done to deserve this. "The burbs, huh? I never thought I'd end up in one again."

"It's either this or a hotel."

The place belonged to a friend of his. After a quick call, we'd been invited to stay for a few days. If it took longer than that to find Charles Fraser, I was skipping town and leaving Thor to the mercy of the vampires.

I followed Gabriel around back to where he located a key tucked under a pile of rocks. When we walked in through the kitchen door, I headed for the refrigerator to see if there was anything edible inside. It was empty except for a few cans of soda and a Tupperware container with more mold than a petri dish. "I guess we'll be eating out."

"You seem disappointed. Were you planning to cook?"

I closed the refrigerator door. "You're a funny guy, Gabriel."

The place had its charm. Based on the decor, I figure it was a female friend. "Does Emmaline know about your little love shack up here?"

"Love shack?" His irritated look morphed into a grin. "How do you always know how to push my buttons?"

I shrugged. "Years of practice. Seriously, Gabriel. Thank you."

"For what?"

"For being a friend." God, I was getting soft. "You're the only person I can count on to drop everything and show up. That kind of friend. I owe you."

"Seems like we're always owing each other. We might as well get used to it and call it even."

I nodded and decided to take a stroll through the house just to make sure we were alone. Another habit I'd acquired at the bureau. Letting my guard down was tantamount to stupidity. The three bedrooms were empty. So were the bathrooms, but I wasn't about to climb the folding ladder in the hallway to check the attic, the one place in any house that gave me a severe case of the creeps.

Satisfied that the house was clear, I met Gabriel in the living room and pulled out the piece of paper with Six's information on it. "What's this written underneath her name? Nervona?"

"The bartender said she works there."

"And?"

"And nothing. The cameras were watching. I was lucky to get a name."

I pulled out my phone to do a search. "There's only one place coming up, but it doesn't say anything about what kind of business it is. No phone number or website either. Just an address in a less than pleasant part of town."

What kind of business didn't have a phone number listed?

"Then let's go. It's still early. Whatever this place is, it might still be open."

After thinking about it, I decided it would be best if I went alone. "You're staying here." Was I wearing a tutu? "Don't look at me like that. She sees the two of us, she might get spooked."

"There's no reason for her to get spooked unless she has something to hide."

"Something to hide? How about Charles Fraser? If she does know where he is, she'll be looking for the nearest exit."

"Point taken, but I'm still not letting you go alone."

I got up and stuffed my phone in my pocket. "I didn't ask your permission. And do I have to remind you what I used to do for a living? Jesus, Gabriel, I used to walk into houses, looking for serial killers. I think I can handle it."

"Then I'll wait outside. If you need backup, you can throw up a signal."

I could live with that. "Fine. You can watch my bike." I'd like to see some asshole try to lift it from a demigod. In fact, I'd *pay* to see that.

"It's your investigation." He got up and walked toward the kitchen door. "It's also your life."

16

THE STREET WAS EVEN SEEDIER THAN I'D THOUGHT IT
would be. If Gabriel hadn't agreed to stay behind, I might have
waited until morning when the lowlifes would have to try to steal
my bike in broad daylight.

The place had a neon sign in the window that lit up the name
NERVONA in red letters. It kind of reminded me of a hole-in-the-
wall bar or a tattoo parlor. The light over the front door was on,
and I could see someone inside.

We parked across the street at the end of the block where
Gabriel could keep an eye on the place and he could easily see a
smoke signal if I sent one up. Just as I suspected, there were
people on several corners, and they didn't look like they were
selling Girl Scout cookies.

"How did that bartender say Charles knows her?" I had my
doubts about a guy like Fraser socializing with someone from this
part of town.

"He said she comes into Sanguine, trolling for clients. He
didn't say what kind of clients though."

"If Blade gets wind of it, she's toast." I patted the gas tank.

"Don't take your eyes off her. If you have to come in after me, just ride straight through the front door."

He smiled but didn't laugh. "I just might do that."

Chuckling nervously, I started across the street. Other than an old pub a block down, Nervona seemed to be the only business open. I glanced at the time. It was almost ten o'clock, and to be honest, I was surprised anything but the bar was still open. I noticed a sign posted on the door with their hours. The place was open until 11:59 p.m. It seemed a little strange to close a minute before midnight, but this was a pretty strange case. Nothing about it surprised me.

I pushed the door open and walked inside but didn't see a soul. The place was illuminated by a dim pink bulb reminiscent of a few unsavory establishments I'd visited in the course of my former career. To my left was a doorway with a veil of floor-length red beads covering it. Probably to warn anyone in the back room that company was coming. There was a sign on the wall with a list of what I assumed were products or services.

I stepped closer to read it. The first item was something called an aura tonic. It cost half as much as my rent. "Pepper rub?" I muttered. "Depends on where you're supposed to rub it."

"Would you like a sample?"

When I turned around, there was a woman with chartreuse hair standing behind me. Her eyes were almost as green, and her skin was shockingly pale. She almost glowed like a black light was shining down on her.

"My aura is just fine." I was a little startled by all the bling. "And I'm not a fan of pepper." That was a lie. The hotter the better.

A grin edged up her face as her eyelids lowered slightly. "I thought I detected a little jumpiness."

I was jumpy all right, but a tonic wasn't going to fix it. "Are you Six?"

Her smile flattened. "No. I'm Nine. Is there something I can help you with?"

Nine? What the hell was this place?

"I really need to talk to Six. Is she here?"

Without answering, she walked behind the front desk and slid a piece of paper toward me. "Six isn't available, but here's a list of our specials tonight. Twenty-five percent off. I'm available, or you can work with Seven if you'd like."

I glanced at the flyer.

AURA TONIC
PEPPER RUB
LIGHT STIMULATION
NERVE MASSAGE

"WHAT EXACTLY IS THIS PLACE?"

She gave me a blank stare for a moment, as if I'd asked the question in a foreign language. "A day spa."

A day spa in this part of town that stayed open until midnight? Right. "Why don't you just tell me where I can find Six and I'll be on my way."

The beads hanging from the doorway rustled, and another woman walked into the room. She had jet-black hair and blue eyes, and her complexion was a little warmer. She gazed at her coworker for a moment before turning back to me. "Can I help you?"

"That depends. Are you Six?"

Her smile widened. "Yes."

Something told me she was full of shit, but they obviously had no intention of producing the mysterious Six, so she was all I had. It was worth a shot to see if I could get some information out of her. I reached into my pocket for the picture of Charles Fraser. "I'm looking for this man. He's a regular at a club called Sanguine. The bartender over there said you know him."

She came closer to get a better look at the photo. As she stepped back, she glanced at Nine. It was a brief glance, but I caught it.

Putting on that fake smile again, she turned and beckoned me to follow her. "Let's talk in the back where it's more private."

My instincts were telling me not to walk through that doorway, but Thor wasn't getting out of that basement until I produced Charles. With a deep breath, I headed for the hippie beads.

"Hold it." Nine pointed to the sign over her head that said No Weapons Allowed. "Your gun please."

Did I look like a cop? I needed to work on that.

My instinct to keep my weapon was even stronger than my instinct to stay away from that back room, so I reached into my other pocket and handed her the small Glock I'd been carrying for backup since walking into the Walden that afternoon. Something told me I'd be needing it. If she called my bluff and demanded my revolver, all bets were off.

For good measure, I put up a little protest, eventually handing it over. Luckily, they didn't try to pat me down, and I was given the green light to follow the impostor down the hallway. There were rooms on both sides, but the doors were shut, so I had no idea if there were legitimate customers in the place.

She closed the door behind her when she followed me into the last one on the right. "Have a seat."

"I prefer to stand." I glanced around and spotted a massage table in the center of the room and a single folding chair in the corner. There was also a built-in cabinet against the wall like you'd find in a doctor's office.

As I was turning back around, I felt a jab in my neck. It was a needle, made clear by the warmth suddenly rushing through my veins. A moment later, I slipped to the floor and watched the room start to spin above me.

A pair of faces came into view, and someone lifted me off the floor and laid me down on the table. When I felt my arms and legs being spread and tied to the corners, I knew I was in real trouble. Shortly after the restraints secured me, my head started to clear rapidly.

The impostor leaned over the table and dangled the revolver in my face. "I guess we missed this one."

Half expecting gibberish to come out of my mouth, I was surprised when I managed to get out coherent words. In fact, I felt downright lucid. They must have reversed the drug. "What did you give me?"

"That's the least of your worries, Ms."—she opened my wallet and looked at my driver's license—"Ames."

I yanked at the restraints, but they had me tied down good and tight. "I'm guessing you're not Six."

"You guessed right." She had a sly look in her eyes.

Nine was in the room with us, and there was a third woman standing near the door. I raised my head to look at her. "Let me guess. Seven?"

"You can go back to work now," the woman said. "Ms. Ames and I have things to discuss."

The other two women left the room, closing the door behind them, and I had a feeling the conversation was about to get unpleasant.

"Why are you looking for Charles?"

If there was any doubt the bartender had steered us in the right direction, it was gone now. She knew him all right. "I was hired to find him. I'm just doing my job."

"By whom?"

That was a little trickier. I thought it best not to mention I was being blackmailed by the vampire cartel. "His wife. He stole something from her, and she wants it back."

The woman let out a brief laugh but quickly turned serious again. "I think you're lying to me."

"Now why would I do that?"

She walked over to the counter and pulled something out of the drawer. It was a rod that looked like a curling iron, only it sizzled when she turned it on. The blue light crackling around it reminded me of a mini electrical storm.

A nervous laugh slipped from my mouth when she walked toward me with it. "What are you planning to do with that thing?"

"It's a powerful tool for restoring balance to the nervous system. It's very popular with our clients. On humans it can also be very dangerous, though. And persuasive."

She lowered the rod just enough for the electrical charge to touch my shirt near my navel. I had to admit it felt kinda good, but then she ramped up the voltage and I felt it all the way up and down my body. It started out almost ticklish but then escalated to an unbearable sensation of being burned from the inside out. She pulled it way when I let out a howl.

"Fuck!" I winced and panted when a muscle spasm took hold of my stomach and tightened to the point I tried to curl into a ball, which was impossible when you're tied to a table spread-eagle.

She fired the rod up again. "We're just getting started. Tell me the truth and this will all end."

"Get Six in here and I'll talk!"

"I don't want to do this, Ms. Ames, but I'll blind you if I have to. Please don't make me."

I reconsidered coming clean about the Bastians, but a commotion outside the room got our attention. The door swung open, and Gabriel rushed inside. She lunged at him, jabbing him with the rod.

He yanked it out of her hand and ran it slowly across his arm. "That feels rather nice. Where does one get one of these?"

She backed away from him, looking unsure of herself. "What are you?"

"A considerable problem for you."

"You're fucked now, lady." I yanked at the restraints. "Will someone untie these damn things?"

Gabriel flicked his head at me. "You heard the woman. Untie her."

The fear on her face eased as her eyes darted over his shoulder. "As you wish."

Nine flew at him from behind with a syringe in her hand, but before I could warn him, he caught her wrist. I doubt the drug would have done more than piss him off anyway.

He shoved her over to her accomplice and took a frustrated breath. "Whoever unties her gets to live."

The one who got off on torture had me untied in less than a minute. The second the last restraint was undone, I jumped off the table and landed my fist in her jaw. She stumbled back against the wall and slid down to the floor.

"We're not even close to being even, but that'll do for now." I pointed my thumb over my shoulder. "See that man over there? Tell us where we can find Charles Fraser and he won't kill you both."

Nine spoke up. "We don't know where he is. That's Six's job."

Job? What the hell was going on?

The woman on the floor glared at her, and Nine clammed up so tight I don't think she was even breathing.

I was getting impatient. "We're not leaving until we get information." When neither of them budged, I grabbed my revolver from the cabinet where it had been carelessly tossed and headed for the door. "I'll make sure the place is empty so we can have a more persuasive chat with the ladies. By the way," I said to Gabriel, "where's my bike?"

"Priorities, Jesse."

The building started to rumble before I reached the door. I grabbed the edge of the counter to steady myself when the floor shifted under my feet. "What's happening?"

The women were both as calm as could be. They didn't even flinch when the room started to shake again and a chunk of the ceiling came down.

Gabriel looked at the floor as a crack appeared and quickly started to spread. "We have to get out of here!" He grabbed my arm on his way out when I didn't move fast enough for him. We managed to stay one step ahead of the collapsing hallway and ran out the front door without a scratch. After crossing the street to where my bike was parked, we turned around, expecting to see the building crumbled to the ground, but it was perfectly intact. Not a brick out of place or a cracked window. Not even a cloud of dust.

I glanced at Gabriel, who seemed just as dumbstruck. "What just happened?"

He just stared at the building without saying a word.

When we walked back over, the neon sign was gone and there were no lights on inside. I peered through the dirty window at an empty room without a stitch of furniture inside. The building might have been in one piece, but Nervona was gone.

"I'm not crazy, am I?" I asked.

"If you're crazy, so am I." He shook his head. "You sure know how to pick a case."

"Yeah. I can't just walk away now, can I?"

He gave me a questioning look. "Can't you? This case has been nothing but a headache for both of us."

"Not unless I want to seal Thor's fate." He was a handful, but he was my partner. "Maybe I should talk Blade into letting Thor go so *he* can track down Charles."

"Good luck with that. Blade may like you, but that doesn't mean he trusts you." He placed his hand on the brick exterior of the building as if he wasn't convinced it was real. "I know one thing for sure. Kiko Orochi isn't the only one who isn't who they seem. It appears her husband has just as many secrets."

"By the way, how'd you know I was in trouble?" He'd rushed in like the cavalry just before I was about to get my eyes worked over. What was it about my baby blues? First Kiko wanted to cut them out and now this.

"Are you serious? The same way I found you in New Orleans. My head nearly exploded from that wail you let out."

"Lucky me."

My phone rang as we were walking back across the street. It was Zeb. After a brief conversation, I hung up and climbed on my bike, which luckily was still in one piece in the spot where Gabriel had left it unattended. "That was Zeb. Looks like he came through for us. We're going to a blood lounge tomorrow night."

17

WE GOT TO THE STUDIO A LITTLE AFTER NINE O'CLOCK.
There was an old Chevy parked out front that I didn't recognize,
so I assumed it belonged to our escort for the evening. I was
kinda worried he wouldn't show because Zeb had sounded a little
on edge when I talked to him the night before. Like he wasn't
sure himself if he should have called me and made the offer.

Lula and Raven went straight for Gabriel when we walked in.
After letting them slobber all over him for a moment, he removed
Lula's paws from his shoulders and sent her into an obedient sit
position.

"You've got a way with my girls," Zeb said, shaking his head.
"But something tells me you've got a way with all the ladies."

I chuckled. "He's a real Casanova."

We followed Zeb into the other room where he was still
working on that monstrous Venus flytrap. Standing on the other
side of it was a short man with a thin ring of hair around a large
bald spot. Raven ran toward him but stopped a few feet away and
let out a low growl.

"Would you get those damn dogs out of here!"

Zeb snorted. "This is their house. But don't worry, they won't touch you unless I give them the okay. Don't tempt me."

The man shifted his eyes to me and Gabriel. "So this is them?"

I was having second thoughts because the guy was twitching like he was on the verge of a seizure. "Is he okay?" I muttered to Zeb.

"He's fine. Just needs a little fix."

Great. Zeb had hooked us up with a junkie who was supposed to be taking us to a blood lounge. But then I noticed the tips of a pair of fangs protruding from his upper lip. "He's a vampire?"

Zeb raised his right brow. "Is that gonna be a problem?"

"Well, look at him. The man looks like he's ready to take a bite out of someone."

"The name's Dizzy, and you ain't my type, lady." His eyes slid to Gabriel as his lips quirked, revealing more of his fangs.

Gabriel groaned and gave him a warning look. "I'll snap your scrawny neck if you try it."

Zeb grabbed a mallet and pounded it on his worktable. "Cut the crap! There ain't gonna be no biting going on." Then he glared at Dizzy, who suddenly revealed how he'd earned his name. The man was teetering back and forth like the noise from the mallet had startled him.

"You might want to get him a chair," I said, not wanting to lose the opportunity to find that blood lounge if he fainted.

Gabriel kept eyeing the man. "I don't think it's a chair he needs. He needs some blood."

"Then let's get going. I'm sure he can find plenty of it there."

Zeb tossed the mallet on the tool bench and grunted. "Mm-hmm, but you'll be paying for it. Dizzy here isn't the charitable type. He agreed to take you there in exchange for a free session with one of the donors and a little extra money to hit up the liquor store after that."

I reached into my pocket for some cash. "How much?"

The man gave me a thorough once-over. Probably to assess my net worth. "Two hundred."

Gabriel countered. "Fifty."

After thinking about it for a few seconds, Dizzy countered back. "A hundred."

"You greedy little shit!" Zeb glared at him. "You owe me!"

We needed to get moving, and the vampire who was supposed to get us there was looking a little peaked. "It's okay, Zeb. I'll put it on the Bastians' tab."

He squinted at me. "So you are mixed up with those vampires. Christ, woman, are you out of your mind!"

I glanced at Dizzy. "We can talk about it later."

Gabriel grabbed my wrist when I reached for the money. "Fifty," he said to the vampire, "or we walk out of here and you get nothing." He pulled a bill from his own pocket and offered it to the man.

Dizzy gazed at it, licking his lips. "Deal. But you're still paying for a donor when we get there."

"Of course." With that settled, Gabriel pointed to the door. "Let's go."

I headed for my bike when we walked outside. "We'll follow you, so don't lose us."

He looked at me like I'd lost my marbles. "Follow me? That wasn't part of the deal." After shooting Zeb a glare, he walked over to the Chevy and reached inside. "I'm driving, and you're wearing these."

"A blindfold?" I huffed at him. "I'm not wearing that."

"Get in the back seat and put it on, or the deal's off."

Gabriel was a little more comfortable about putting his life in the hands of a blood junkie than I was. "We're not going anywhere unless we cooperate with him, Jesse."

"He could get himself killed for even offering to take you there," Zeb said. "Even I don't know the location. I'll pull your bike into the garage until you come back for it."

I grabbed the blindfold from the vampire's hand, and we climbed into the back seat and tied them around our heads.

"Tighter!" Dizzy ordered when he saw the fabric hanging a little too slack for his liking.

When he finally started up his piece-of-shit car, we took off with a jerk and headed down the road. After about ten minutes, I began to feel queasy. "Speed it up. I'm about to puke back here." I get carsick easily, so I'd always gotten the front seat during family trips when I was a kid.

A few minutes later, the car stopped and the engine cut off. I reached for my blindfold, but our chauffeur grabbed me and practically yanked me out of the car. He was strong for a little guy. I could feel concrete under my feet as he gripped my arm and led me straight ahead. Either we were on a very quiet street or in a parking deck.

"You can take them off now," he said.

When we pulled the blindfolds off, we were standing in front of a door. There was no sign on it, and the street around us was empty. The whole neighborhood seemed deserted. I couldn't even see a street sign, but the city skyline was visible over the dark buildings.

Dizzy pushed the door open. "Quit nosing around and get inside."

We'd started to walk down a hallway when a huge bald guy perched on a stool got up and blocked us from following the vampire. I guess it made sense for a blood lounge to have a bouncer.

Dizzy jerked his head toward the guy. "Pay the man."

Mr. Clean held out his hand. "One fifty."

I wasn't sure if I'd heard him right. "You mean a buck and a half?"

He didn't seem amused. "Fifty bucks a head. Anything extra is between you and your partner for the evening." He gave me a wide smile that immediately flattened as his patience wore off.

Extortion wasn't on my list of expectations tonight, so I hadn't brought a wad of cash with me. I reached into my pocket and pulled out two twenties. I could have sworn there was an extra hundred in there. "I don't suppose you take checks?"

Once again, Gabriel stepped up and took care of it. The guy took the cash and shoved it through a slot in the door behind him. Then he gave us the green light to continue.

"I'll pay you back when I give Blade his invoice for expenses."

"Don't worry about it."

I'd never asked Gabriel where he got his money from. He never flaunted it, but he always seemed to have a lot of it.

We followed Dizzy down the hallway toward a room at the end, the music getting louder as we approached. When we walked inside, I was hit by the smell of something rich and coppery in the air. It wasn't exactly what you'd think blood would smell like. It was different than the smell at Sanguine. Powerful but not as overwhelming.

The place was crowded with people lounging on sofas and pressed against the walls in various stages of lewd activity. But I'd seen worse in the brothels I'd encountered in my previous line of work.

I leaned into Gabriel. "I can't tell the vampires from the humans."

"Easy. The humans are the ones with the stupid smiles on their faces. They're all high as hell."

Now that he'd said it, I could tell the difference. "I don't get it. Who wants a pair of fangs biting them?"

"It's quite pleasant actually."

He should know. He'd spent some time imprisoned by a vampire. Six years to be exact. It started as a love affair and ended in a nightmare when she drained him daily to keep him powerless and submissive.

Did I mention that his current girlfriend, Emmaline, is half vampire?

"I never plan to find out." I'd had enough fangs gunning for me over the years. Although I'd be lying if I said I wasn't curious about consensual nipping. I was also curious about skydiving, but I never planned to try that either. "Let's ask some questions without sounding any alarms."

Someone came up behind us. "Are you looking for anything in particular?"

When I turned around, there was a tall woman with auburn hair standing behind us. Her voice was like silk. At first, I thought it was that redhead from Sanguine, but something told me this one wouldn't be caught dead fishing for a companion at a bar. Although we were in a blood lounge, and I was pretty sure she was soliciting us. I couldn't tell if she was a vampire or a woman looking to get bitten.

Dizzy stepped between us before I could open my mouth to reply. "I'm looking for a donor." He flashed her his fangs and ran his tongue over one of the sharp tips. "Are you available?"

After pulling her eyes away from mine, she looked at him disinterestedly. Out of courtesy I imagined. She nodded to a woman at the other end of the room. "Maybe you'll have better luck over there."

The vampire was way out of his league. Finally getting the message, he scowled and headed across the room to try his hand there.

As he walked away, her eyes slid to Gabriel. "I do couples."

Cocking my head, I squinted at her. "Exactly how does that work?"

She smiled, revealing a set of delicate fangs, clarifying what she was looking for. "Any way you'd like. One at a time, or I can join the two of you." She glanced at the staircase. "I have a room upstairs."

I curtailed a laugh. "Wrong tree, honey. We're looking for something else." I reached into my pocket for the picture of Charles but got a little uncomfortable with all the eyes around the room looking at us. "Is there somewhere a little more private where we can talk? It'll only take a minute."

Her hand settled on her hip as she lost her hospitable smile.

"I'll let you suck on my finger," I said.

She let out an inpatient sigh and ran her eyes over me. "Don't bother. Just make it quick. I'm hungry." She beckoned us to follow her back into the hallway and up a flight of stairs on the other side.

After entering an empty room at the top, I pulled out the picture. "We're looking for this man. Have you ever seen him in here?"

She took the photograph from my hand and studied it for a moment. Then she handed it back to me. "No. Who is he?"

"Are you a regular here?" I asked without answering her question.

Shrugging, she walked over to the window and looked out. "Honey, they don't get any more regular than me." She pulled out a cigarette and lit it before turning around. "What did you say his name is?"

I stuffed the picture back in my pocket. "I didn't."

She kept her eyes on me while taking a long drag. Then she walked to the door. "If you'll excuse me, I have business to attend to."

"She's lying," I said to Gabriel as I watched her leave.

"Well, she isn't talking, so we're back to square one." He walked to the door and watched her disappear down the hallway. "I think it's time for a tour of the place. If he's here, we might get to him before she has a chance to warn him."

Halfway to the stairs, a noise coming from one of the rooms got our attention. I made my way quietly to the second room on the left. The door was ajar. When I peeked inside, I got an eyeful of what went on in a blood lounge. There were two men going at it on a bed. One had his arms and legs spread-eagle and tied to the four posts, and the other one had his teeth sunk into the guy's pectoral. The part that had me practically blushing was seeing the vampire working his companion's hard-on like a jackhammer.

My jacket rubbed against the doorframe, creating just enough sound to draw attention to us. With his teeth still embedded in his partner's chest, the vampire's eyes shifted to mine. Having an audience didn't seem to bother him at all. I think he liked it.

We moved on to the room on the right. This one had a three-some going on. A man was sitting in a chair, and there were two women on their knees on either side of him, each sucking at a wrist. I was surprised they had their clothes on.

I pulled my head out of the doorway. "He's not up here. Let's go downstairs and ask around. Maybe we'll get lucky."

As we descended to the first floor, I couldn't shake the feeling we were being watched. "I think we need to get out of here."

Gabriel glanced up and down the hallway. "Yeah. We're close. I can feel it in my bones, and I think whoever's hiding Charles Fraser knows it too."

I spotted Dizzy coming toward us with a satisfied look like he'd gotten his fill. Good thing since he was our ride.

"We need to go." I grabbed the vampire's arm and steered him toward the door.

He yanked it free. "Wait a minute!" After adjusting his shoulders, he smoothed his hair back. What little he had. "What's your hurry?"

"Move!" Gabriel ordered.

Dizzy reached into his pocket and pulled out a small round container. I don't know what came over me, but when he lifted the lip, my instincts told me to knock it out of his hand. Before I could, he tossed the contents, sending a fine powder into the air.

The last thing I remembered was hitting the floor hard. Semi-conscious, I tried to fight as someone grabbed my ankles and dragged me back down the hallway. I looked back and forth for Gabriel, but everything was a blur. Whoever it was finally dropped my legs and stepped over me. When I finally managed to prop myself up, I spotted Gabriel slumped over next to me. At least he was moving.

Barely able to focus my eyes, I spotted someone sitting in a chair on the other side of the room. A woman wearing blue pants and a matching jacket, her skin a shade of coffee, and her hair shaved almost down to her scalp. "Who the hell are you?" I slurred out.

She crossed her long legs and smiled. "The person who holds your fate in her hands, but you can call me Six."

18

I MUST HAVE PASSED OUT, BECAUSE AFTER MY introduction to the woman we'd been looking for, my memory went blank and I woke up on a different floor. This one had a rug on it, providing a little cushioning, and the room smelled like... bacon?

Blinking several times, I tried to clear my eyes. I saw two women standing near a stove. It was hard to make them out clearly with the haze still clouding my vision, but one of them was wearing a long dress that skimmed the floor. The other one was dressed in slacks and a blouse and had long gray hair that reached halfway down her back. I'd seen her before, but the other woman, the one who kept fading in and out like an apparition, was a mystery. When she spoke loud enough for me to catch a few words, her voice rang a bell.

"Gabriel?" I glanced around the room and saw him sitting on the floor with his back propped against the wall.

Other than throwing me a weak wave, he barely moved.

After hearing the mystery woman's voice again, I finally recognized it. The crescent-moon tattoo on my arm was buzzing like a bunch of bees were swarming under my skin. "Sam?"

The two women stopped and looked at me. A moment later, Sam was gone and I was focusing my eyes on Sylvia, Charles's sister.

She stopped stirring whatever was on the stove and walked over to me, her feet inches from my face as she stared down. "You're lucky. Your aunt has convinced me not to kill you."

Aunt?

"You'll have to go through me first." Gabriel struggled to climb to his feet, but he only made it to his knees. "What the hell was in that powder?"

"Something that even a demigod isn't immune to."

Well, that was interesting. Anything that could take down Gabriel didn't come from a regular pharmacy. And she knew what he was, which was even more interesting.

She walked back over to the stove and turned off the burner. "It should wear off completely any minute now. Just in time for breakfast. Although you'll probably have a headache for a few hours."

"Where are we?" I asked.

"You're in my kitchen."

"Yeah, I get that, but why?"

She sighed heavily and turned around. "You're looking for Charles, aren't you? He'll be down in a minute."

I glanced at Gabriel, but he looked just as confused as I was. Finally managing to climb to my feet, I swayed to the left and grabbed the edge of a chair. "*Fuck* me."

"Language, Ms. Ames."

"Call me Jesse." I think getting drugged and dumped in a strange kitchen warranted a first-name basis. "You want to tell me what's going on?"

Six walked into the room and glanced at me and Gabriel. "I see you decided to let them live. I hope we don't regret that." She grabbed some plates from the cabinet and started setting the table.

"Her aunt had a nice chat with me. Convinced me Jesse isn't trying to kill Charles. She's just a pawn."

I couldn't argue with that. I *was* being used as a pawn. "You said Sam is my aunt?" Finally a little information about who put that tattoo on my arm.

Sylvia gave me an odd look. "Yes. Your great-aunt. Who else would she be? We spoke witch to witch. She's a damn powerful one, by the way."

"Good to know." I rubbed the tattoo as the vibrations finally stopped.

Gabriel climbed off the floor and stood next to me, whispering, "I'd get us out of here if I could."

"Save yourself, Gabriel. I won't hold it against you."

"Don't worry," Sylvia said. "You'll have your strength back soon. First we're going to enjoy this nice breakfast while we discuss your predicament."

I heard someone coming down the steps. The man at the center of it all walked into the kitchen and gave me a wary look on his way to the table. "So you're the one Kiko hired to hunt me down."

He looked a little different than his picture. In particular, his violet eyes. Last time I checked, humans don't have eyes in the purple range. I guess a half-breed could, but I couldn't recall ever seeing a vampire with violet eyes either.

Sylvia brought a platter of food to the table and told everyone to sit. I don't think it was a suggestion.

I suddenly realized I was missing something. "Where's my jacket?"

She nodded to a chair on the other side of the room. "Over there. You'll get your gun back after we've come to a mutual understanding. It won't do you much good anyway."

Instead of eating when I sat down at the table, I dove in with questions. "What is she?"

Charles looked up from his plate. "Kiko? Surely you've figured that out by now."

Why did everyone keep saying that to me?

"I'm pretty sure she's a shifter like those slithery goons she has working for her."

He glanced at his sister and then at Six. All three of them got an annoying smirk on their faces. "She's not just a shifter. She's the queen." He swallowed his food and wiped his mouth. "You don't know anything about her, do you? Some investigator you are."

I leaned back in my chair and squinted at him, not liking his attitude one bit. "I'm a damn good one."

"Really? Do you work for heathens on a regular basis? Is it just about the money?"

Heathens? I was starting to get the feeling I knew even less than I thought I did. And I hated to admit that. "Exactly what is Dragon Enterprises?"

Six filled me in. "Procurement of despicable goods."

"You'll have to clarify that. I know they fulfill fantasies for people with a lot of money, but that's not illegal."

She laughed. "How about organs? Is that illegal enough for you?"

"Organs?" Gabriel suddenly got real interested. "You mean black market organs?"

Charles put his fork down and pushed his plate away, seeming to lose his appetite. "Oh, it's worse than that." He ran his eyes down Gabriel's neck and stopped at his chest. "I wonder how much the heart of a demigod is worth?"

A sickening feeling began to crawl up my throat. "Supernatural organs." It wasn't a question because I already knew the answer. I'd heard rumors about an underground network selling them to the highest bidder. Usually humans seeking immortality. But I hadn't known if it was real or just another urban legend.

Charles looked me dead in the eye. "Exactly. I was just a product to her, like all her other dead husbands, only my organs were slated for personal use. Kiko's personal use. In particular, my heart."

It was all starting to make sense. The clients at Kiko's party and their strange eyes. I recalled Mr. Russo's remark as he gazed at me.

Let me guess. The eyes.

He was wondering which body part I'd acquired. "Son of a bitch! Let me guess, the eyes are one of her top sellers."

"Ah, the light bulb has finally gone off." He shook his head as he looked at me with slight contempt. "Now you know the truth. The question is, what will you do now? Choose greed and force us to kill you or help us stop her?"

I gazed at him for a moment. "What are you?"

Sylvia grabbed his plate and walked over to the sink. When she turned around, her irises were violet like her brother's with a golden aura around them. "We're fae, but my brother is a little more complicated. He's half vampire as well. It's incredibly rare. In fact, Charles is the only one as far as we know. The power that a human could harness from harvesting his organs is… Well, I don't know. I can't even imagine." She smiled at Six. "We've been protecting him. Managed to keep his secret for a very long time."

Six scoffed. "Until he opened his mouth."

"I thought she loved me!" he shot back.

I glanced at Six. "Are you a faery too?" She didn't fit the stereotype.

"I prefer fae."

The puzzle was starting to come together. Not only was the Red Widow hunting supernaturals for their organs, she was saving the best ones for herself. A real Frankenstein in the making.

While I was fuming with revelations, Gabriel asked another important question. "What about this ring and the emeralds you stole from her?"

Charles released a steady breath and stared at the table for a moment. I could tell he was still on the fence about whether or not he could trust us.

"Tell them," Six said. "We can always kill them if they betray us."

You mean kill me. With or without that powder, I doubted they could do any serious bodily harm to Gabriel. His blood was the elixir of life. If Kiko only knew.

Charles finally completed the puzzle. "Those stones are her source of power. Kiko is the leader of the Red Dragons."

Sylvia let out a bitter laugh. "More like snakes."

He continued. "If you haven't already figured it out, they're serpent shifters. There isn't an ounce of compassion in their cold veins. It's all about power. They'll kill you the moment you've outlived your usefulness." He looked me in the eye. "You know too much, Ms. Ames. Once you deliver me, Kiko will get rid of you. And if you don't, she'll kill you for failing."

"Why'd you marry the woman in the first place?" I was dying to know. "Don't take this personally, but you two seem like an odd couple."

"I was in love with her."

"Kiko Orochi is a master manipulator," Sylvia said. "She sets her sights on her prey and goes after it. Just like she did with you, Jesse. Charles saw exactly what she wanted him to see. Combined with a spell, it was easy to make him fall for her."

Gabriel was getting impatient. "Let's get back to the ring and emeralds. And what about this tomb she mentioned to Jesse?"

Charles went still and stared straight ahead. "Have you seen it?"

"We haven't seen anything," I said. "The Bastians blackmailed me into delivering a package to Kiko. It contained one of those emeralds. It had a note saying she'd get the other one back if I delivered you to Blade. Kiko went ballistic when she saw it and nearly brought the building down."

He chuckled quietly. "I bet she did. Those emeralds are the eyes of the dragon. The mother of them all. I have no idea how she died, but Kiko keeps her corpse in the basement of the Walden. In a sarcophagus inside the tomb. I stumbled onto it along with a book detailing Kiko's conquests. It was like her spell suddenly wore off when I read my name in that book with the word *heart* written next to it. She was actually keeping an inventory. That's when I knew I had to get out."

"Talk about a coldhearted bitch. Must have been a hell of a spell."

"But it's the ring that holds the real power," he continued.

"It's not a ruby, is it?" I'd had my doubts, and so did Zeb.

He shook his head. "It's the fossilized blood of the serpent. Without it, she'll grow weak and eventually die."

I remembered how peaked she'd looked in her office when I delivered the package. "She's already getting weak."

"Good!" Sylvia spat out. "I hope she starts to rot!"

Charles cocked his head at me. "You said the Bastians black-mailed you? How?"

"It's a long story, but they're holding my partner hostage in the dungeon below Blade's office at Sanguine. He's a little upset about that money you stole from him."

An incredulous look crossed his face. "Stole? That bastard! He *gave* me that money."

"What? He said it was a loan and you skipped out on him. And now he's blackmailing me to hand you over to him instead of Kiko. Said he wants his money back. I'm sure he intends to make an example out of you to anyone else who tries to rip him off."

He shook his head. "You've been played, Ms. Ames. The fae have an alliance with the Bastians. We've been helping them keep the Romans out of Atlanta for years, and now Kiko has shown an interest in expanding Dragon Enterprises into the business of drugs, including vampire blood, which is Blade's territory."

"Blade's territory? I thought the Bastians were running drugs like cocaine or heroin?"

He shook his head. "The Bastians deal strictly in blood. Vampire blood is much more lucrative."

I guess that explained the cocaine Thor tasted on Kiko. She must have been sampling the product. But I was a little surprised to hear about the vampire blood.

"Did you know this?" I asked Gabriel.

"About the vampire blood? Yes. I assumed you knew."

"Blade gave me that money to disappear and get as far away from Kiko as possible. If she succeeds at harvesting my heart, she'll have all the power. The Romans will be the least of his concerns."

I stood up and stared at him from across the table. "Can we leave now?"

"That depends. Whose side are you on? And don't bother to lie to me. I'll know."

"I'm on my own side. As far as I'm concerned, the case is dead. Kiko and Blade can fight over you themselves."

I grabbed my jacket and followed him when he got up to show us the door. As we were about to leave, he offered me some advice. "Don't betray me, Ms. Ames. If you do, I will come after you. I may not look threatening, but trust me, you don't want that."

Great. Kiko was after me, Blade still had his leverage, and now I was on a faery's shit list. What a way to start the weekend.

"Forgive me," he said when I reached for the door handle. "I'm afraid you'll have to leave the same way you came."

Before either of us could process what he meant by that, that same fine powder suddenly filled the air. The rest was a blur.

19

WE WAITED UNTIL TEN P.M., WHEN SANGUINE WOULD BE good and busy, to pay Blade a visit. That way he wouldn't make as much of a scene when I walked in there to give him a hefty piece of my mind. The bastard had been lying to me all along, and as I've reiterated a thousand times, I don't work with liars.

We were less than ten steps into the place when I heard a ruckus. It was so loud I wondered if they were throwing a private party for a bunch of linebackers.

"Jesse!" Gabriel yelled.

Something crashed into me before I could turn around, and I slammed into a wall. All I saw was a blur of fur as Thor rolled over me and kept going. A bunch of vampires almost trampled me trying to get to him, their fangs fully extended.

Gabriel grabbed my arm and yanked me up a moment before the wolf came running back toward us with the herd of bloodsuckers right behind him.

"Thor!"

Distracted by my voice, he stumbled and slid, digging his paws into the floor as he put the brakes on. One of the vampires lunged at him and the two went at it, sending fur and blood flying everywhere. The sound coming out of the brawl made my skin crawl.

When Gabriel leaned against the wall and crossed his arms, I wanted to smack him. "Will you do something!"

"Like what? It's Thor's fight. Let him finish it."

A few more vampires jumped into the mix, so I took off my jacket and handed it to him. "Hold this."

"What do you think you're doing?"

"It's not a fair fight. They'll kill him."

He practically growled at me. "I swear, woman, you have a death wish."

I don't know what I planned to do, but I wasn't going to just stand back and let a bunch of vampires rip Thor to pieces.

Gabriel groaned and walked toward the commotion. He placed two fingers in his mouth and let out a high-pitched whistle. Thor yiped as it pierced his ears, and the vampires stopped and turned.

Blade appeared a moment later and put an end to it. "That's enough. Get him back in the basement." Beaten down, they grabbed Thor by his scruff and dragged him down the hallway. "Come on." He headed back to his office. "I assume you're here to see me."

I rushed the bastard when I walked inside. I wasn't sure where I got the guts to clock him, but I had a good idea. "Give me my wolf!" How was I going to explain to the head of the vampire cartel that it wasn't me who'd just smashed my fist into his jaw? It was Uncle Ames, who also happened to be dead.

One of the vampires came at me, but Blade stopped him. After running his fingers over the small cut at the corner of his mouth, he lifted his brows. "You're starting to annoy me, Jesse."

"Good. We'll get to Thor in a minute, but first I have something to say to you." I didn't want to lose the momentum from my anger because it was the only thing feeding my bravado. "You've been lying through your teeth all along. I know what Charles Fraser is, and I also know you gave him that money."

I think I actually managed to shock him, but he quickly sucked it up and smiled. "So you found him?"

"Oh, we found him all right. Had an illuminating conversation over breakfast this morning. And by the way, why are a bunch of faeries hanging out at a blood lounge? Isn't the business of blood your territory?" I'd said a little too much, but I was pretty hot under the collar.

"Fae have to make a living too, and a blood lounge is profitable." He must have read the surprise in my eyes. "You thought I didn't know about that little side hustle of theirs? It's part of the alliance. We throw them a little business and they reciprocate."

Which explained why Six could troll Sanguine for new business without getting herself in a world of hurt. Maybe Charles was a regular at Sanguine for the same reason. It was all one big happy bloodsucking network.

His face suddenly hardened as he started to lose patience. "Where is he, Jesse?"

"Since you know all about that side business of theirs, why don't you start by asking around yourself? Seriously," I said when he looked like he wanted to beat it out of me, "I couldn't tell you if I wanted to."

"Meaning?"

"Meaning he and his fae buddies went to great lengths to make sure we didn't know where we were when we found him. We started at the blood lounge, but they knocked us out cold with some kind of powder. We woke up on his sister's kitchen floor. I have no idea where Charles is." After being sent to la-la land again by that funny stuff, Gabriel and I had woken up in a deserted parking lot. "So don't worry. We won't be handing him over to Kiko either. And by the way, I'm done."

I ramped up my courage and walked toward the door leading to the basement. "I'm taking Thor out of here. If you try to stop me, I'll blow your fucking world up." I yanked at the handle, but it wouldn't budge. Blade was sitting on the edge of his desk, looking amused, when I turned around, so I pulled my gun from my jacket and pointed it at the door. "Open it or I will."

He had me against the wall in a heartbeat. "You're forgetting what I am, Jesse." His face was an inch from mine, and the tips of his fangs were protruding from his mouth. "I don't take orders from anyone."

Before I could come up with a witty reply, he was on the other side of the room and Gabriel was standing between us. "And you're forgetting what I am," he said to Blade. "I've let Jesse handle this her way until now." He wagged his finger. "But you just crossed a line. Hands off. Capisce?"

Blade straightened his jacket. "You and I have managed to get along for a long time, Gabriel. Don't push your luck."

It was time to lighten it up before they were at each other's throats. "Why did you lie to me?" I asked Blade. "You could have told me about Charles. I probably would have worked with you just to spite that crazy bitch."

"*Probably* wasn't good enough. I needed a guarantee. Some insurance."

"Speaking of which, what the hell happened with Thor tonight?"

He groaned and rubbed the bridge of his nose. "What do you think? Destiny took him something to eat, and he convinced her to open the door instead of sliding it under the bars. I think you can guess the rest."

"Yeah, Thor's a real charmer. But hey, it was your idea to keep him locked up in that basement."

With the tension taken down a notch, Gabriel stepped aside. Blade took a seat and swung his feet up on top of the desk, lacing his fingers together. "So where do we go from here?"

"You let Thor out of that cell, and we work together to bring Kiko down."

He studied me for a few seconds and took a deep breath. "Taking Kiko down isn't enough. She needs to die. It's the only way to stop her."

I shrugged. "No argument here. Got any ideas about how to do it? Because I've been racking my brain and can't seem to think of a good way to kill a dragon." My eyes slid to Gabriel. "Although I do know one." We knew a dragon in Savannah who could do the job easily. And Katie Bishop owed me.

Gabriel shook his head. "Don't even suggest it."

"Why not?"

"Because I said so. We'll handle Kiko on our own. We just have to find her kryptonite."

"Really?" I huffed. "Like you handled those fae?" I'd only known of Gabriel being incapacitated twice—once by that vampire in New Orleans who tricked him into her bed, and then by those faeries last night. It was a little unnerving to realize he wasn't invincible after all.

Blade seemed to be losing patience. "If anyone has any ideas, let's hear them."

I glanced at all the big bad vampires in the room. "You've got a pretty big army here. With fangs to boot. Can't you just go in there and take her out the old-fashioned way? With brute force?"

He laughed mockingly. "You really don't have a clue who your client really is, do you?"

"Ex-client. And as a matter of fact, Charles told us all about Dragon Enterprises' dirty little business of selling body parts." His cocky smirk went south, and I caught a flash of anger in his eyes. "What's the matter? You afraid Kiko's planning to sell your fangs to the highest bidder? I bet a vampire's heart would fetch a pretty penny on the black market."

"Jesse...," Gabriel warned. "Try not to provoke our new partner."

"Partner? How many times do I have to say it?" I leaned over the desk to look Blade in the eye. "I don't work with people who lie to me." Before I could say something I'd really regret, I turned around to leave, but one of his thugs stepped in front of me before I reached the door.

You're not getting out of this one, Jesse. Cooperate with the bloodsucker.

"Cooperate? Are you nuts?"

Blade glanced at Gabriel. "Who's she talking to?"

Gabriel just shook his head. "Don't ask."

I decided to do as Uncle Ames suggested. What else was I going to do? Go after an army of serpent shifters myself? Even Gabriel wouldn't go up against that alone. "I'll work with you, but if you lie to me again..."

"I wouldn't dream of it, darlin'."

He would have enjoyed it way too much if I'd taken the bait. Instead, I put my hands on the desk and leaned over it again, giving him a good look at my girls, something he'd have to admire from afar. "I'm glad we understand each other. Sweetheart."

I straightened back up and got down to business before he got too excited. "So what do we do now? Storm the palace and take her head as a trophy?"

"If it was that easy to kill her, we would have done it a long time ago." He swung his feet off the desk and stood up, walking around to take his favorite seat on the edge.

"Then how *do* we do it?"

Gabriel chimed in. "Charles said the corpse is the mother

lode, so it seems like the best way to kill the Red Widow is to destroy that tomb and everything in it."

"Then what are we waiting for?" My adrenaline was spiking from the thought of going into that basement, but I feared the alternative even more. "How do we get in there?"

Blade nodded to one of his men, giving him the floor.

"The place is crawling with snakes," the vampire said. "We won't get past the first floor without a major distraction."

Blade turned back to me. "So much for storming the basement."

"Then I guess we'll have to create a distraction. Maybe give Kiko what she wants."

"You mean Charlie."

I nodded. "And the stones."

He hopped off the desk and looked at me like I was crazy. "You sure those faeries didn't hit you over the head?"

Gabriel knew exactly where I was going. "A Trojan horse. We give them what they want and we're in."

Blade shook his head. "You two really are delusional, you know that?"

"So I've been told." No risk, no gain was my motto.

"But aren't you forgetting something? You don't know where Charlie is. Or do you?" He sat back down and gave me a chastising look. "Now who's the liar?"

"I didn't lie to you. We just need to find him again and convince him to help us."

Blade snickered. "Convince him to hand himself over to the woman who wants to cut out his heart? Good luck with that."

Smug bastard. I kept that to myself in order to keep the peace. "I'll convince him it's the only way to guarantee he won't be on the run for the rest of his life. That's a very long time for a fae. All he has to do is be the bait and trust us to do the rest."

"And the rest is?"

I hadn't gotten that far yet. But after hunting some pretty dangerous criminals for over a decade, I could guarantee this—if we walked into that building with Charles Fraser and those stones, all eyes would be on us. Kiko would be salivating. The perfect distraction while the Bastians raided the basement. Now all I had to do was find that blood lounge again and wait for Charles Fraser to find me.

20

GABRIEL WASN'T HAPPY WHEN I TOLD HIM I WAS GOING alone, but I pointed out that if things went bad, I'd need him to find me and get me out of there. No sense having both of us unconscious on Sylvia's kitchen floor. Reluctantly, he agreed. Shocker.

On my way over to Zeb's studio, I kept running the words through my head. My pitch to convince Charles to be the bait. Charles and those stones were a package deal. It was all or none. This would be my last chance to get him on board. To trust us to get that tomb destroyed before Kiko got her hands on him. It was the only way any of us were getting out of the Walden alive, because if she got ahold of that ring and the emerald first, there'd be no stopping her.

When I pulled up, I noticed how dark the place was. Zeb usually worked late, and his old Volkswagen was parked on the side of the building. The hair on the back of my neck immediately stood up.

I checked the front door. As usual, it was unlocked. After pushing it open carefully to make sure the hinges didn't squeal, I went inside and looked around the dim room. When the dogs didn't greet me, my alarm bells immediately went off.

A sound came from the other room, and I silently moved against the wall, pressing my back to it as I slid toward the doorway. With my gun gripped in my hand, I peered into the studio and saw a shadow move quickly out of view.

Something hit the window on the other side of the room, followed by a bark. It was Lula. She was outside, standing on her hind legs with her paws pressed against the glass.

What the hell?

I moved toward the window to get a closer look. To make sure I wasn't seeing things. Those dogs were Zeb's babies. No way would he have left them outside.

As I turned back to the studio to get this over with and find the intruder, a strangled cry filled the room. The shadow I'd seen earlier charged through the doorway. I stumbled back when I saw a glimmer of metal come down toward me, falling and rolling as a long pole slammed into the floor by my head.

I jumped to my feet and pointed the muzzle at the intruder when he raised the pole again. "Drop it!"

The metal rod hit the floor. I stepped back to the wall and flipped the lights on. Dizzy was standing in the middle of the room, wide-eyed and shaking. His mouth was hanging open as he glanced back and forth between my face and the gun.

"Please don't kill me!"

I gave him a confounded look. "What are you doing here?"

"I stopped by to see Zeb, and the place was like this." He motioned around the room. "I thought you were the one who did it."

I kept my gun pointed at him. "Got any of that powder on you? Empty your pockets."

He turned them inside out. "It wasn't me—it was the fae."

"Yeah, but you didn't seem to have any problem using it on us."

He grumbled, "You try saying no to a faery."

Convinced I wasn't about to get powdered by him, I surveyed the room and got a good look at the damage. Zeb kept the place sparse, but what little furniture he had was turned over. I glanced through the doorway of the studio and saw several of his sculptures lying sideways on the floor. Someone had gone through the place like a bull.

Dizzy nodded to the window. "He wouldn't leave them outside either."

The dogs!

I was relieved when they both came trotting inside after I opened the door. They bolted past me, nearly knocking me over as they ran into the studio and started sniffing around, looking for Zeb.

"You didn't see anyone?"

He shook his head. "I just got here and found all this." His fangs had descended. The palpable adrenaline coming off him probably triggered them automatically.

My phone suddenly buzzed, alerting me to a text message. A message from Kiko. After reading it, I looked back up at Dizzy. "We're going back to that blood lounge, and this time you can forget about the blindfold." He opened his mouth to argue, but I put the kibosh on his bitching. "Zeb's in a world of trouble. Unless you want him to die, you'll take me there."

He wasn't having it. "What about me? I already got a warning for taking you there last night. I could get killed for showing up with you again."

I wasn't having it either, so I pointed my gun at him again. "Die now or die later helping a friend. Which is it gonna be?"

"You can follow me, but I ain't going in." He let out a steady hiss and started grumbling again. "If anyone asks, I didn't take you there. Deal?"

"Sounds fair."

Kiko's message had said she had Zeb, and he was a dead man if I didn't produce Charles and those stones within the next twenty-four hours, which was exactly what I planned to do. Zeb getting caught in the cross fire added a layer of complication we didn't need. But it was what it was, and the more I thought about it, the more I realized it might buy me some leverage when I tried to convince Charles to help us. An innocent bystander caught in the middle might sway him. The man had to have a conscience.

After getting the dogs settled in and securing the place, we headed out. I followed Dizzy closely just in case he tried to lose me, which he did twice, but it just made me tail him even closer. No way was that heap of junk outmaneuvering my bike.

We turned on a street in a seedy warehouse district. Dizzy slowed his car in front of a run-down building and flashed his lights once. Then he took off. I recognized the street from last night, so I knew he'd taken me to the right place. Smart man.

I parked my bike on the sidewalk directly in front of the door, dreading leaving it unattended in the middle of shitsville, as usual. After steeling myself for a bumpy ride on that magic dust, I tried the door. Like the night before, it was open.

The bouncer got up from his stool and stepped in front of me, eyeing me suspiciously. I'm sure strangers walking in off the street was frowned upon. After scrutinizing me for a moment, he nodded. "You were here last night."

"Yeah." I was in luck. He recognized me.

He held out his hand. "Fifty."

Fuck! I'd forgotten about the cover. I still had the two twenties in my pocket, but something told me he wasn't the type to spot me for the rest. "All I have is forty."

"Fifty or you don't get in."

Leaving wasn't an option, and even Uncle Ames wasn't getting me past this guy without stirring up a hornet's nest. "Look. I'm not here for that. I'm just looking for someone."

He shot me a smart-ass grin. "Everyone in here is looking for someone."

Asshole.

"It's all right, Melvin. She's with me."

Melvin?

I glanced around his enormous frame and saw Six standing behind him. "Yeah, Melvin. I'm with her."

He sneered and stepped aside. I don't think I was getting a Christmas card from him this year.

Six beckoned me to follow her, but before I did, I pointed over my shoulder toward the front door. "My bike's parked out front. What are the chances it'll still be there when I leave?"

She laughed. "You're at a blood lounge, Ms. Ames. Only a fool would dare to touch it."

The fools were the ones I was afraid of.

I followed her down the hallway to a door at the other end. It led to a descending staircase. "Where are we going?"

"You're here to see Charles, aren't you?"

"He's in the basement?"

She started down the stairs without a reply. When we got to the bottom, we entered a long corridor that reminded me of Blade's dungeon, only instead of cells, it was lined with rooms. The doors were all open.

The first room we passed gave me a real show. It looked more like a torture chamber than a place for hooking up. A guy was strapped to a wheel, naked of course, with leather manacles around his wrists and ankles. There was a woman standing next to him holding a whip and a wooden goblet. She was using it to catch the blood running down his groin.

The guy caught me looking at him, and I swear his erection

twitched. But it was his partner who made me uneasy. The vampire ran her tongue along the rim of the goblet and crooked her finger at me.

"Ms. Ames."

I snapped out of it and turned back to Six. "What?"

"Focus or we'll never make it to the end of the corridor."

Suddenly realizing I was standing in the doorway with one foot inside the room, I quickly stepped back and shook off the allure.

As we continued, I kept my eyes on Six's backside, but I couldn't block everything from my periphery. It was too compelling. The grunts and moans didn't make it any easier, and I had this warm sensation traveling down my torso, working its way between my thighs. It was like a mind fuck.

We reached the last room, and she motioned for me to go inside. I was hesitant, but my only other option was to go back the way I came, and I wasn't too confident I'd make it.

There was a chair and a bed inside. "Where is he?"

"Patience, Ms. Ames." She smiled and closed the door. "All in good time."

The games were starting to get to me, and my bike was calling my name. Then there was the foreboding feeling creeping up my throat that I'd made a big mistake by coming here. "You know what? I think we're done." I headed for the door, but my legs suddenly stopped.

"Have a seat, Ms. Ames."

Six's voice filled my head, and I sat down in the chair without questioning it. She walked behind me and put her hands on my shoulders, bringing her mouth to my ear. "Tell me, Jesse. What's the worst experience you can remember?" Her voice was like a purr.

"The worst—?" She was playing with me, but I found myself shaking my head as a memory started to surface. I tried to stand up, but her hands were like lead weights on my shoulders.

I closed my eyes as a wave of grief washed over me. The room disappeared, and all I could see was the windshield of our old pickup with my bare feet up on the dashboard. We were on our way home, and my father was singing. My mother hated camping. Couldn't stand being in the woods. It was just me and him that weekend.

We were on our way home from the lake with a cooler full of fish when I saw it coming around the hairpin turn. A truck carrying a load of rocks took the curve too fast and veered into our lane.

I stood up, shaking off the memory. "Fuck you," I said to Six with tears threatening to fill my eyes. No way was I doing this.

Halfway to the door, I suddenly found myself back in that chair. The truck blew its horn, and the pickup swerved. We veered off the road onto the narrow shoulder when the left front tire blew. We sat there for a moment, laughing nervously until our hearts stopped pounding.

My father got out to change the tire. Noticing the tailgate had come open, he pointed to the cooler half a dozen yards back on the side of the road.

Get the fish.

I jumped out and ran toward it, my bare feet burning against the asphalt. I hopped to the right as a car was coming up the hill. It swerved to avoid me and—

Breathe, Jesse. Look at the sky.

It was Sam.

I looked up at the bright sun above me, and the sound of crashing metal faded away. It was just me and the empty road as she took my hand and walked me to the edge of the steep embankment. Then we were falling.

My eyes flew open, and I stood up and glared at Six. My

hands were around her neck a second later. "Stay out of my head!"

She gasped for breath as I squeezed tighter, but the shocked look in her eyes suddenly turned to amusement. When I glanced down, my hands were no longer wrapped around her throat and I was reaching into my pocket. I pulled my gun out and fought the urge to point in at my own head.

"You did this to yourself, Ms. Ames. All you had to do was walk away."

The revolver flew from my hand and hit the floor. Six watched it slide to the other end of the room and then looked at me with anger building in her eyes. "You'll pay for coming back here!"

I'd be lying if I said the rage in her eyes wasn't scary. She focused them on me intently, and a high-pitched sound filled my ears. It felt like a needle was slowly piercing my brain.

I slammed against the wall and gripped my head, falling to the floor as I prayed for backup. Uncle Ames. Sam. Anyone. But the pain intensified.

The ringing suddenly stopped, and I opened my eyes. Charles was talking to Six on the other side of the room, or was he yelling at her? I couldn't hear a thing.

My hearing came rushing back when Charles barked at me to get up. After climbing to my feet, I steadied myself against the wall and waited for the two of them to stop arguing.

"We have to make an example of her!" said Six.

Charles shook his head. "She's human!" Then he shot me a disdainful look. "Why are you so stubborn!"

"Because we need your help," I said.

"My help? We'll see about that."

He snapped his fingers, and Seven and Nine appeared. It was a real reunion. Then the room filled with that sparkly powder and it all faded away.

21

WHEN I CAME TO THIS TIME, I WAS LYING ON THE FLOOR IN a strange room, the only illumination coming from the street-lights filtering through a gauzy curtain covering a large picture window.

I propped myself up and blinked a few times to clear my eyes. At least my head didn't feel like it was about to explode. It was more like a hammer tapping away at my temples. There were shelves lining the walls, and a few feet away I saw a glass display case that spanned half the length of the room. A pair of eyes was staring down at me from the counter. The Green Man. The thick smell of patchouli confirmed I was in Sylvia's shop.

The veil of beads hanging from the doorway rustled as Sylvia came through it and flipped on the lights. Charles was right behind her. Six was nowhere in sight, which made me happy. We had a tumultuous relationship, and I wasn't interested in seeing her reaction to the request I was about to make.

Sylvia walked over to the door and pulled the shade down. Then she flipped the sign to CLOSED. If I recalled, it was pretty late, so I doubted they were open for business anyway. But this wasn't your average establishment.

I climbed to my feet and brushed some dirt from my jeans. My hair was everywhere, but there was no helping my appearance after being thrown to the wind by that powder. "Don't tell me you dragged me back to New Orleans." My hands were full enough without having to deal with the Romans, and Gabriel would shit if I called him to come collect me again.

Charles took a seat at the table by the window. "Don't worry. Nothing can get to you in here."

"Are you a mind reader too?"

He just smiled at me. "Have a seat, Ms. Ames."

"For Christ's sake, will you drop the formality? It's Jesse."

"All right. Have a seat, Jesse."

Unlike some of his friends, he seemed like a pleasant enough guy. But I had a feeling I hadn't met the real Charles Fraser yet.

With the curtains obstructing my view, I sat down and glanced out the window. It was dark outside. "Tell me it's still Friday." If it was Saturday night, Zeb was as good as dead.

"Don't worry, you haven't lost much time. You've only been out for about twenty minutes."

"Is that all? Time flies when you're being assaulted and kidnapped." He didn't find the humor in my comment, so I figured I'd go ahead and lay my cards on the table. If I screwed it up and couldn't convince him to help us, we'd all be looking over our shoulders for the rest of our lives.

Sylvia went back through the beads and returned with a tray. "Tea?"

I grabbed one of the dainty cups. "Why not." After sniffing it, I took a sip and almost spit it back out. "What is this?" I probably should have asked before sampling a drink offered by the faeries who'd just tried to kill me.

"Mugwort. It should help with the headache." She took a seat on the opposite side of the table and stared at me.

Trying to appear confident, I set the cup down while I held her steady gaze.

Never let a predator see you sweat.

"You said you need my help," Charles said. "Let me guess. It has something to do with my wife."

Sylvia bristled. "Don't use that word. The thought of you tied to that monster in holy matrimony is disturbing."

There was nothing holy about matrimony. At least not in my limited experience. I chuckled nervously. "I think I know how to rectify that problem."

"Get to the point," he said.

"We're going to destroy the tomb."

He stared at me like I had a screw loose. "And how do you plan to do that? Now that Kiko knows it's been breached, she'll have it surrounded twenty-four seven."

"We're planning to create a diversion. Entice her with something even more precious to her."

Sylvia was slowly shaking her head as her eyes filled with contempt. "You mean Charles." She stood up and let out a curt laugh. "We should have let Six take care of you, but it's not too late to send you back to the blood lounge."

When she reached into her pocket for that handy powder box, I blurted out, "You haven't even heard me out yet!"

"That's right, and I have no intention of listening to any more of your stupid ideas. You should have stayed away, Ms. Ames. I'm afraid you've become a liability that has to be disposed of now."

I glanced at Charles, hoping he'd be the voice of reason in the family, but he said nothing. "Now wait a minute. This isn't just about Charles. Innocent people will die if we don't stop her. She kidnapped a friend of mine." I figured a personal connection might spark a little compassion. "He's an artist. The guy who created those dinosaur sculptures all over Cabbagetown."

She pulled the box out of her pocket. "That's not our problem."

But Charles seemed a little more interested. "The wizard?"

It was common knowledge to Zeb's friends, but I didn't expect to hear the word come out of Charles's mouth. I guess it shouldn't have surprised me that the fae knew about the local wizard in the neighborhood. "You know Zeb?" And I hoped it worked to my advantage.

"Not personally, but we all know of the wizard of Cabbagetown."

The wizard of Cabbagetown? If I got Zeb out of this mess alive, he was going to get a kick out of that.

I pulled out my phone and showed him the text message. "Kiko sent this to me right before I came to the blood lounge tonight. We have twenty-four hours or he's a dead man."

"If it comes down to my brother or that wizard, I'm afraid—"

Charles threw his hand up to keep her quiet. "I'm assuming you have a plan?"

Sylvia huffed. "Have you lost your mind? I won't let you do this."

"This is my fault. If I hadn't fallen for that monster, none of this would be happening. And I'm tired of hiding. She'll come for us all next."

I hurried with the plan before he lost interest in hearing me out. A plan I was making up as I went. Funny how that happens. "If we walk into the penthouse with you and those stones, Kiko and her snakes will be so excited they'll let their guard down long enough for the Bastians to get into the basement."

He leaned closer to look me in the eye. "You seem like a smart woman, Jesse. You don't really believe they'll leave that tomb unguarded while we all congregate upstairs."

"Of course not, but we're just trying to get into the building. I'm betting that Kiko will have most of her men in the penthouse while we make the exchange, so Blade and his vampires can slip in and take care of the tomb. They can handle the guards down there. Once it's destroyed, Kiko and her army will fold and hopefully die on the spot. Or at least weaken enough so we can get out of there. If we time it perfectly, it'll work."

Sylvia narrowed her eyes. "And if you're wrong and the vampires are stopped?"

"Then we fight like hell. Vampires and fae against a bunch of snakes and a Komodo dragon? Sounds pretty even to me."

"And a wizard," Charles added.

I didn't have the heart to tell him Zeb wasn't exactly Merlin. He was more skilled with a welding torch than a magic staff. Nor would it help me to convince him.

"And don't forget about Gabriel." In my book, a demigod was even better than a wizard. "So what do you say?" My leg was shaking under the table as I waited for his answer. "Kill the monster and her den of snakes or spend the rest of your life running from her?"

He got up and started to pace, mumbling under his breath. He finally stopped and looked at me. "I get to keep the stones."

Faeries and their fascination with shiny objects.

I got up and offered him my hand. "They're all yours."

He shook it but didn't let go when I tried to pull it away. Instead, he looked me deep in the eyes. "You're an interesting woman, Jesse. I'm pleased that we don't have to kill you."

"Yeah, me too." He still wasn't letting go of my hand. "Can I leave now?"

He smiled and finally let go of me. "So when do we storm the castle?"

It was a little after midnight, and we had less than twenty-four hours before Kiko started taking her frustrations out on Zeb. The poor guy was probably more worried about his dogs than himself.

"Tomorrow night. I'll head over to Sanguine now and tell Blade you're in so we can set up a meeting." I took two steps toward the door and looked back at him. "How am I supposed to get in touch with you?"

"My number is in your phone."

I pulled it out, and sure enough, there it was.

As I grabbed the door handle, another pressing question came to mind. I was in Sylvia's shop, and the last time I was here, I was in New Orleans. I let go and turned around. "Mind telling me where I am?"

And then there was the matter of my bike.

Charles smiled when he saw the confusion on my face. "You'll know when you get outside."

I pushed the door open and stepped out to the street. My bike was parked right out front. After giving it a brief inspection and declaring it unscathed, I looked around and recognized the street. In fact, my house was just a few blocks south. I climbed on and grabbed my phone to call Blade and let him know I was on my way over.

"We're fucked!" he said without a greeting.

"Well, hello to you too," I replied. "Is there a problem?"

I heard him take a deep breath on the other end and let it out slowly. "You could say that. It's gone."

"What's gone?"

"The tomb! They moved the fucking tomb!"

I stared at the street for a moment, trying to comprehend what he'd said. "How do you know that?" I don't know where he was getting his information from, but I wasn't about to believe it unless he had a damn good source.

"Just get over here!"

"I'm on my way."

After hanging up, I considered walking back inside to tell

Charles the news but decided to wait until after I was convinced Blade knew what he was talking about.

I was about to pull away from the curb when I glanced back at the shop, but all I saw was the side of a building. No door. No signage of any kind. No windows. Just a wall attached to an old factory at the end of the block that looked like it hadn't been open for business in years. Once again, Sylvia's mysterious shop had vanished.

Shaking my head, I drove off, questioning what was real in this town and what wasn't.

22

I COULD HEAR SHOUTING ALL THE WAY DOWN THE HALL AS I approached Blade's office. The door was shut, and two of his vampires stepped in front of me when I went for the doorknob.

"Get out of my way," I said to the taller one with black hair, but he shook his head.

The vampire with the silver hair was a little more polite. "No one goes in."

"He's expecting me."

When neither of them budged, I announced myself the old-school way. "Blade!" The silver-haired one rolled his eyes. "By the way," I said to him. "You got a name?" I figured since we were practically coworkers, we might as well be on a first-name basis. Ignoring me, he held his ground. I glanced at the other one. "How about you?"

The door swung open. Gabriel was standing on the other side. "Let her through."

They stepped aside, and I walked into the office just in time to see Digger throwing a left hook at his brother. Blade ducked and returned the love, snapping Digger's head sideways with a gruesome crunch.

"Jesus!" I said to Gabriel. "What the hell's going on?"

"Blade isn't happy with his brother's level of detail."

"You want to break that down in English please?"

Hilli swiveled around in Blade's desk chair, her right leg draped over the side while she watched the show. "My brother dropped the ball. Like I said the other night when we met, we call him Digger for a reason."

With Digger sprawled on the floor, Blade caught his breath and turned around, smoothing his disheveled hair. "Jesse! You've met my siblings, haven't you?"

I pointed my thumb over my shoulder. "Should I leave and come back after all the testosterone wears off?"

With a satisfied grin, he strolled over to the desk. "Sorry you had to see that, but Digger here earned a good ass-kicking." He looked at his brother, who was climbing to his feet. "Didn't you?"

Evan was standing in the corner, quiet as a mouse with his hands shoved in his pockets. He glared at me when I looked at him. Blade caught it. "Is there a problem?"

I glared back at Evan. "No problem at all." I could take care of the vampire myself the next time he got ugly with me. And I had a feeling there would be a next time.

Blade grabbed a bottle of whiskey on the desk and held it out to me. "Drink?"

I shook my head, "Let's just get to this problem with the tomb. What happened?"

He laughed as he poured himself a double. "My brother over there lost it."

Gabriel shrugged when I looked at him. "Don't ask me. I just got here myself."

Blade elaborated. "Those two geniuses over there"—he nodded to Digger and Evan—"were supposed to be watching the building but let that tomb slip out from under their *fucking* noses!"

I think I saw Evan flinch.

"Can we back up and start at the beginning?" That mugwort tea was shit, because my head was starting to hurt again. "Why were they watching the building?"

"Why?" He winced as he downed half his drink. "Why do you think? That tomb is the only thing standing in the way of destroying those serpents. I wasn't going to let Kiko just walk away with it." He turned around and flung his glass, barely missing his brother as it shattered against the wall. *"Fuck!"*

Digger's fangs came out. "Calm the hell down! We'll find it!"

I'd never seen Blade so wired. But I knew what was at stake if Kiko won and got her hands on Charles and those stones. The alliance with the fae would be history. The Bastians would be on their own to stave off the Romans, and Kiko would be unstoppable. Not to mention what she'd do to me if I didn't skip town first.

"Kiko has Zeb."

That got Gabriel's attention. "What?"

"Who's Zeb?" Hilli asked.

Blade seemed equally surprised. "What makes you think that?"

"I stopped by his studio tonight. The place was trashed. While I was there, Kiko sent me a text message. We have twenty-four hours to deliver Charles and the stones or she'll kill him."

He chuckled humorlessly. "Then I guess we're all fucked."

I still didn't know what was going on with the tomb. "Back up. What happened to the tomb?"

"Let him tell you." He pointed to Digger.

Digger straightened up and wiped his mouth with his sleeve. "We were watching the building tonight, and a truck pulled around to the loading dock."

I shrugged. "So? Maybe it was a moving truck."

Evan snickered from the corner he was still cowering in. "Yeah, it was a moving truck all right."

Blade glared at him. "Shut the fuck up, or you're next!"

"We saw a bunch of those snakes in suits moving it out," Digger said. "A wooden crate big enough to hold a sports car."

"How do you know it was the tomb?"

"Because we saw the damn thing!" When he caught the warning look in Blade's eyes, he took it down a notch. "One of the idiots slipped off the side of the dock and dropped it. The crate came down so hard the side popped off. We saw it plain as day."

Evan laughed from the safety of his corner. "You should have seen their faces. They grabbed the guy and practically dragged him away. I bet we'll never see him again."

"Let me guess." I glanced back and forth between them. "You didn't bother to follow the truck."

"Of course we followed it," Digger said. "We lost it a few miles down the road when it pulled into an underground garage. We parked down the street and went inside. The tomb was in the back of the truck, but the sarcophagus containing the corpse was gone."

"Or they moved it into the building. Did anyone bother to check?"

Blade looked like he was ready to explode again. "We *borrowed* the surveillance footage. They ditched the truck for another one and went out the back entrance. No tags on the thing."

Gabriel looked like he wanted to tear Digger's head off. "So we have nothing. They must have known we had plans for that corpse. That's why they moved it. We'll need a psychic bloodhound to find it now."

"Not exactly." I locked eyes with him, and he seemed to catch on to what I was thinking. "What we need is a tracker."

By the time I looked at Blade, he was starting to catch on too. "You need to release Thor."

He shook his head and bounced his finger at me. "I know what you're up to."

"It's the only way we're going to find that corpse. If you have a better idea, by all means, speak."

After giving it some thought, he took a steady breath and pinned me with his eyes. "If you betray me, Jesse, I'll kill you both. Don't make me do that."

"Why would I? I want Kiko dead as much as you do. And don't forget about Zeb."

He looked at the vampire with the silver hair. "Bring him up, Luke."

So he did have a name. The taller one with the nasty disposition would forever be known to me as Asshole.

While we waited, we heard a commotion coming up from the basement. A few minutes later, the door burst open and Thor came stumbling through it.

He growled, "Touch me again and I'll chew your hands off!"

"Fucking psycho," Luke growled back at him before walking over to his post by the office door.

Thor was his old self. Tart as ever. He glanced at all the faces staring at him and zeroed in on Hilli, who was still lounging in Blade's chair.

Her strawberry blond hair draped over her left shoulder in a perfect swirl as she settled her green eyes on his. "Well, hello there, Mr. Wolf."

Suddenly forgetting about everyone else in the room, he walked over and gave her a thorough once-over. "And who might you be?"

She smiled, revealing her fangs. "Your new boss."

He lost his randy grin and took a step back. Noticing me from the corner of his eye, he cleared his throat and managed to pull his eyes away from hers. "Jesse? What's happening here?"

"You're free, that's what's happening."

"Took you long enough." He looked a little nervous with all the vampires staring at him. "Can we go now?"

"Not yet. Your freedom is contingent on finding something, so you need to get your radar up and running and start tracking." We had a lot of catching up to do. At the time he was thrown into that cell in the basement, we were just getting acquainted with the Bastians, and Charles Fraser was nothing but a missing person wanted by both Kiko and Blade.

"You mean you haven't found Charles yet?"

"I found him, but I'll get to that later. How hard do you think it'll be to find a corpse?"

The look he gave me spoke volumes. "A corpse? Anyone in particular?"

"Get the emerald," I said to Blade.

He pulled the box from the desk drawer. After removing the lid, he shoved the emerald under Thor's nose. "Get a good whiff. You're gonna find the other one and its owner."

Thor glanced at the stone, his nose crinkling. "What do you mean by owner?"

"It's an eye." I snatched the box from Blade's hand. "Calm down," I said when he tried to grab it back. "We're all on the same team here." I gave it to Thor so he could take a proper look at it and feel it in his hand. "Think you can find the matching one?"

He sniffed it again. "There's a familiar smell to it."

"There should be. Kiko's had her hands on it, and you got a good taste of her, didn't you?"

A light seemed to go off in his head. "Aha! I knew it smelled familiar." He squinted. "Tell me more about this eye."

I handed the box back to Blade. "I'll fill you in after we

leave." Right now I just wanted to get him out of that office before he said or did something stupid that landed him back in that basement.

Thor leaned into me. "Come on, baby, let's get out of here."

He recoiled when he saw the glare in my eyes. "Call me that again, and you'll be chewing your food with your asshole."

Grappling with the mental image, he got a puzzled look on his face.

"Grow up," I said to Blade when I saw his satisfied grin. We didn't have time for a testosterone contest. Zeb's head was on the line, and my house wasn't big enough for a couple of canine moose to move in.

Since my brain was basically mush, I decided to rely on Gabriel to make the call on where to start. "What do you think? The Walden or that garage where they made the switch?" He was staring at me, but I don't think he was actually seeing me. "Are you okay, Gabriel?"

Finally snapping out of it, he focused his eyes on mine. "I think we have a problem."

"Really? Who would have thought? What's wrong now?"

His brows pulled together. "I don't think they moved that corpse because they suspected an attack." The man had instincts like no other. A direct line to another plane. He locked eyes with Blade, and the two of them seemed to be having a silent conversation.

Blade got a disturbed look on his face and slowly shook his head. "I hope you're wrong, Gabriel."

I stepped between them, interrupting the conference. "One of you better start talking."

Gabriel finally filled the rest of us in. "They didn't move that corpse to hide it. I think they're planning to wake it up."

"Wake it up? How? The thing must be petrified by now."

"It's also an enormous source of power."

"She needs the stones to complete the ritual," Blade said, his face going blank. "The emeralds and that ring. Son of a—" He grabbed the lamp from his desk and threw it across the room.

Digger ducked before it could nail him in the head. He lunged, slamming Blade into the wall. The two vampires went at it, both flashing their fangs as the brawl escalated.

I glanced at Luke and Asshole. "You gonna stop them?"

Luke shrugged. "They're brothers. They'll work it out."

Blade turned the tables and pinned Digger against the wall. "You fucking moron! You had one job to do!"

Hilli jump into the mix and shoved Blade off Digger. "You're both idiots! Grow up!"

"They knew you were watching the building," Gabriel said. "That switch in the parking garage was carefully planned, so save your energy for finding that corpse."

Watching the three of them fight, I was curious if they were genetic siblings from their human days or if they just shared the same maker. But after what I'd just witnessed, I was leaning toward genetic.

Blade backed off first and wiped some spittle from the corner of his mouth. He offered his hand in a truce, but Digger just looked at it and walked away.

I got back down to business before they could start up again. "Why would they move it if they plan to wake it up? It's a *her* by the way. Charles said she's the mother of them all." I got a disturbing image of those men in black being birthed out of the ass of some giant lizard. "It's dark, cold, and damp in that basement. What better place to resurrect the unholy dead?"

The wheels in Gabriel's head were turning again. "That's a very good question, but think about it. What do Komodo dragons like?"

Blade got a sly grin on his face. "Warm and dry."

Gabriel nodded. "They moved her to a more suitable environment. All they need now are the stones."

The thought of it gave me the creeps on a whole new level. "By the way," I said. "Charles has agreed to help us. But now that they've moved it, we'll have to come up with another plan. Let's focus on finding it first."

Thor let out an exaggerated sigh. "I'm not hunting down anything without my lucky tooth and a full stomach."

Gabriel rolled his eyes. "Not that again."

"What? It's my lucky megalodon tooth. The biggest, meanest shark that ever lived. It gives me an edge."

"That tooth is made of wood." I wondered how I'd ever seen intelligence in the man. "It's fake."

"Well, I'm not tracking anything until I have it hanging around my neck. And then you can buy me a good meal."

I glanced at Blade. "Haven't you been feeding him?"

"Are you kidding me? That wolf has been an expensive guest. He owes me for half a dozen rib eyes."

"Rib eyes?" Maybe I needed to stay in that basement for a while. "That's mighty generous of you."

He huffed. "It's the only thing that would shut him up."

Gabriel headed for the door. "Let's go. The sooner we fetch Thor's toy, the sooner we can find that corpse."

"I'd be careful if I were you." Blade leaned against the desk and winked at me. "Kiko's probably itching for you to go home. Wouldn't want you to walk into an ambush."

I'd already considered that, but I figured they'd turned the place upside down the night of her party, after we foiled their attempt to pluck us off the highway. By now she knew we were gone. I also knew Uncle Ames would warn me if we were walking into a trap. At least I hoped he would.

As we were leaving, I glanced back at them. If the vampire cartel, a demigod, and a bunch of fae couldn't put an end to Kiko and her dirty little business, the city didn't stand a chance.

23

"Looks quiet to me." I climbed off my bike and opened my jacket to let Thor out.

He walked straight over to the building to relieve himself. After shifting, he stretched his legs. "Ah… that's better. I don't ever want to see a bucket again."

"If Ma catches you pissing against her wall, you'll be peeing sitting down for the rest of your life."

Gabriel, who was watching the house from the corner, glanced over his shoulder at Thor's naked body. "You better hope no one walks around the corner and sees you like that."

Thor turned to give Gabriel a full-frontal view. "Maybe you should have grabbed my clothes before we sped off."

"I'm not your clothes caddy."

That was my job, but no one expected Thor to gain his freedom tonight, so I didn't come equipped with a backpack. I guess I needed to get used to driving around with a saddlebag at all times.

Gabriel had insisted on riding on the back of the bike. I think he just wanted to stick it to Thor for being so insistent on getting that stupid tooth. But Thor wasn't just interested in fetching his lucky charm. I think he wanted to check on his stuff. Despite his shallow demeanor, Thor was a sucker for sentiment. He had an entire drawer full of memorabilia, and if those snakes had touched any of it, it would fuel his will to find that petrified carcass and shred it with his own teeth. Besides, I wanted to check in with Ma in person. If things got ugly, it might be the last time I ever saw her.

"Let's go." I headed across the street with Gabriel and my naked partner right behind me. When we got to the door, I reached for my gun and took a deep breath. I was pretty sure I would have known it if anyone was in there, but why get careless now?

The door slowly creaked open. I slipped in with my back against the wall and made my way to the kitchen. There wasn't a shadow or a set of glowing eyes in sight, so I flipped the lights on. The kitchen and living room were empty. The place was just as neat and tidy as we'd left it. Well, as neat as it was ever going to be. The only thing out of the ordinary was the midcentury sunburst clock on the wall—it had come with the place. It was turned upside down with the number 6 at the top.

Gabriel came back down the hallway. "The back bedroom is clear."

I pointed to the clock. "Either the house has a poltergeist, or company's been here."

At first he didn't notice it, but then he did a double take. "When's the last time you actually looked at it?"

"You think I'm one of those Gen Zs who can't read a wall clock? I look at the damn thing every day."

"Jesse!" Thor bellowed. "I think you should see this!"

When Gabriel and I walked into the main bedroom, Thor was standing by the dresser where he kept that tooth. There was a box on top of it.

Thor peeked inside and winced. "Have a look."

"Is there something alive in there?"

He shook his head. "Doesn't appear to be."

As much as my gut was telling me not to, I stepped closer and looked inside. There was a lump of dark red flesh a little bigger than my fist in the box.

Thor swallowed hard and took a step back. "Is that what I think it is?"

I shook off the shivers racing up my arms. "I'm no expert on anatomy, but that looks like a heart."

Gabriel gave it a gander next. "It's human."

"Who do you think it belongs to?" Thor asked.

Demented fucks usually didn't just send random body parts to people, but Kiko was in the business of organs, so she might have had an extra one lying around. "She's trying to intimidate me." And it was working.

Thor waved his hand at the box. "Get it out of here."

A sick feeling suddenly came over me. "Get your tooth, Thor." Without another word, I grabbed my backpack and ran out the door. My heart was beating wildly as I headed for Speaks. Gabriel caught up when I walked inside and frantically looked around the place.

Randy spotted me immediately. "Well, hey there, Jesse."

I threw my hand up when he walked toward me. "Not now, Randy. Where's Ma?"

"I don't know. I haven't seen her." He gave Gabriel a snide glance. "I just got here a few minutes ago."

"Ma!" My heart was about to come out of my chest as I walked toward the bar, glancing at the tidy area behind it. I was about to check the kitchen—the forbidden zone—when the doors swung open. Tommy nearly collided with me. The tray in his hand tipped sideways as he tried to move out of the way.

I grabbed the edge of it to help him avoid disaster. "Where's Ma?"

He eyed me sternly. "Where do you think you're going?" He glanced back at the kitchen. "You know the rules." No one was allowed back there but employees.

"Where is she?" I asked again, ready to rip that tray out of his hands to get his undivided attention.

Without answering, he walked past me and set some bowls down on one of the tables. After serving his customers, he swung the tray at his side and walked back over to me. "What's wrong with you? You look like you've eaten a bad batch of something."

Realizing I was trembling, I grabbed the edge of the bar. "I need to find Ma."

Gabriel glanced over my shoulder. "There she is."

Ma came out of the kitchen with her hands on her hips and a chastising look in her eyes. "Where the hell have you been, Jesse?"

I finally released the pent-up breath I'd been holding. She was a sight for sore eyes, and as far as I could tell, she was intact. "I'm sorry. I should have called you."

"You're damn right you should have. When you didn't answer your phone, I was about to go across the street and use my spare key to make sure you weren't dead inside the house."

She'd left a couple of messages, but with everything happening, I'd forgotten to call her back. God, I was a shit sometimes. Just the thought of her walking in on Kiko's men delivering that box made me queasy.

"Don't panic, Ma, but I need you to stay away from the house until I tell you it's safe."

She crossed her arms, which was never a good sign. "And why would that be?"

"I don't have time to explain, but that ex-client of mine is a lot more dangerous than I thought. She might send her men looking for me, so you need to stay clear of the place until this is over."

She eyed me closely. "What is *this*?"

"Look, Ma, you need to trust me."

Before we could get into it, Thor came through the door with that giant tooth hanging around his neck. "Smells good in here. What's the special tonight, Tommy?"

I glared at him, praying he didn't open his mouth and get everyone worked up with the news about what was in that box.

"Kitchen just closed." Tommy glanced down at Thor's bare feet and pointed to the sign over the door that said No SHIRT AND SHOES, NO SERVICE. "Where do you think you are?"

Shirts and pants were easy to stuff in a backpack on nights when Thor would be shifting, but shoes were bulky, inconvenient, and expensive. He'd lost more pairs than he could count.

"Sorry about that," I said before he could open his smart mouth and piss off Tommy even more. "We've got a long night of tracking ahead of us."

Ma nodded, knowing exactly what that meant. "It's all right. Get the man something to eat."

Tommy narrowed his eye at Thor. "I guess I can scrape up a bowl of stew."

"And some bread?" Thor was pushing his luck.

Tommy muttered and walked back into the kitchen, swinging that tray at his side like a weapon.

"Thanks, Tommy," I said as he disappeared through the swinging doors. Then I looked back at Ma. "Zeb's in trouble."

"What kind of trouble?"

"My ex-client abducted him. If I don't produce her husband and the ring he stole from her by tomorrow night, Zeb's a dead man."

Thor took a seat at the bar when his stew arrived. "How about that bread?"

Tommy scowled. "I have a good mind to yank that bowl out from under your nose if you say another word." He reached under the bar and grabbed a few packs of crackers and slid them to Thor. "Finish eating before I'm done with the dishes."

Thor wisely shut his mouth and dug in, inhaling his food while Gabriel and I had a talk with Ma. "This is going to sound strange," I said to her, "but we're looking for a sarcophagus."

"You mean like a coffin."

Being a witch in a town full of the strange and unusual, not to mention having a shifter for a waitress, I figured she could handle the truth. "Turns out my ex-client is a shifter." I decided to start with the basics and work my way up to the part about Kiko dealing in supernatural body parts. "You sure you want to hear this?"

She leaned in closer. "Well, you better not stop now."

"They worship some dead lizard they've been keeping entombed in the basement of the Walden."

"You mean that fancy condominium downtown?"

"That's the one. Here's the fun part. The ring her husband stole is part of the key to resurrecting the thing. If that happens, we might all be serving a new master."

She straightened back up and shook her head. "You got yourself mixed up in a real mess, didn't you? And now you've dragged Zeb into it."

Way to make me feel like dirt. "I'll fix it. I just need you to be careful until I do. Just stay away from the house and watch out for men in dark suits."

"Well, you better fix it!" She took it down a notch. "I take it you're planning to destroy this thing?"

"We have to find it first," Gabriel said, grabbing a handful of peanuts from a bowl on the bar.

Ma scrunched her forehead. "You just said it's in a tomb in that building."

I chuckled nervously. "It was. They moved it. Loaded it on a truck tonight and disappeared with it. The Bastians were following it, but Kiko's men pulled a fast one and lost them."

"Oh, for Christ's sake! You're still messing with those vampires too? Have you lost your mind?"

"Believe me, Ma, I don't like it either. But the Bastians want Kiko gone as much as we do. When this is over, we part ways. I never have to lay eyes on those vampires again."

She snickered, clearly not as confident as I was. "You worked for the FBI for all those years, so you know better than that, Jesse. Once you get mixed up with the cartel, you never get out. They'll own you." She shook her head. "I bet your uncle is turning in his grave."

My ancestors had been coming in handy lately. If it hadn't been for Sam, Sylvia would have killed me back in her kitchen. Or Six might have turned me into a basket case back at that blood lounge, serving up the memories of the worst experience of my life.

After Ma was through reading me the riot act, she did was she does best. "Is there anything I can do to help?"

"Can you find that corpse? We don't have a clue where it is now."

Thor swallowed the last bite of his stew and patted his stomach. "No worries. I'm fueled up and ready to find it now."

Ma leaned on the bar and pointed her thumb at him. "You're relying on him?"

"You got a better idea? We've got a corpse to find in a city of half a million. Where would you take a lizard if you were trying to revive it?"

She shrugged. "I don't know. The zoo?"

Gabriel cocked his brows. "Sneak a rotting corpse into a public zoo?"

"Yeah," I said. "The zoo is a long shot. My guess is the ritual will be performed tomorrow night after we hand over those stones, and they'll do it outside."

Gabriel gave me a curious look. "Why outside?"

"Because tomorrow night is the full moon. They'd be stupid not to take advantage of it."

"Mm-hmm," Ma said in agreement.

Magic is at its peak during the full moon. A ritual performed directly under it could amplify the magic even more. I'd learned that little trick while living in New Orleans for years. The place was Witch Central.

"You're right." Gabriel looked confounded. "How the hell did I miss that?"

And the man lived with a witch.

"Let's just hope it's not in someone's private backyard," I said. "In the meantime, they need to store that corpse someplace warm and dry, preferably aboveground, and we have less than twenty hours to sniff it out."

"How about a cemetery?"

We all turned and looked at the man sitting three stools down from Thor. One of Speaks's regulars. A man with a mighty powerful set of ears.

Ma shot him a look. "You're too nosy for your own good, Micky. Go about your business and forget what you heard."

Thor's eye shifted sideways to the man. "He's drunk. Cemetery," he scoffed, wiping his mouth with a napkin.

The guy had a drink in his hand, and it looked like it wasn't his first one of the night. He'd probably forget all the talk about corpses by morning.

"Hold on," Gabriel said. "He might be right."

Thor muttered something under his breath and got a sour look on his face. He had an aversion to cemeteries that I'd never understood. Something about a bad experience during a shift.

Gabriel continued with his theory. "They'll need an open space to wake that thing up. Where they won't have bystanders."

I blurted a laugh. "That narrows it down to about ten thousand places."

"Think about it. A warm, dry place. Other than the dead, there aren't a lot of spectators at night in a cemetery, and they come with their own tombs. Doesn't get any more convenient than that."

"You think they'll store that sarcophagus in someone else's tomb?"

"Better yet," Ma said. "A mausoleum. Plenty of space in one of those."

It was perfectly logical, but it still only narrowed it down to about a hundred possibilities, and that didn't include the area outside the city limits.

I gave Thor a sideways glance. "Hope your fear of cemeteries isn't a deal breaker because you'll be sniffing around a lot of them tonight."

He looked horrified. "You're joking."

"You're overlooking the obvious," Ma said. "We've got nearly fifty acres of prime cemetery half a mile east of here at Oakland."

"What's Oakland?" It rang a bell somewhere in the back of my mind.

She gave me an incredulous look. "You live in Atlanta and you don't know what Oakland Cemetery is? Sheesh! It's the resting place of Margaret Mitchell and Bobby Jones, for God's sake!"

Who the hell was Bobby Jones?

Did I have to remind her I wasn't a native? And I hadn't lived in the city that long. Cemeteries weren't exactly on my list of day trips, although they were about to be.

"The place is loaded with tombs and mausoleums. Some of them are nicer than my own house."

"Then I guess we found a place to start." I grinned at Thor. "And it's right next door."

He grumbled a few expletives. "Don't you think you should confer with your friend *Blain* to devise a plan first?"

"We're just trying to find them tonight, not burst in there and get ourselves killed."

After letting it sink in for a moment, Thor stood up. "Well? Let's go before I change my mind."

Gabriel got up next. "All right then. Let's go find a corpse."

I pulled some money from my pocket and laid it on the bar. "For the food."

Ma slid it back to me. "It'll be payment enough if you bring your ass back to me in one piece by morning."

"I'll see what I can do." I shoved it back in my pocket and followed Thor to the door. "When we get to Oakland, you can tell me about this graveyard phobia of yours. You're not going to puke when we get there, are you?"

"That depends. Do you have any Xanax on you?"

"If I did, I would have taken it already." I could have used something to chill my nerves other than alcohol.

He shifted into the wolf the second we walked out the door. A moment later, he was a tiny poodle taking his time while he relieved himself halfway over the edge of the sidewalk.

"Quit fucking around. And shake it off before I pick you up. I don't want any piss in my pocket."

His fluffy little body shook like a vibrator on high speed. I picked him up and stuck him inside my jacket. After stuffing his clothes and that damn tooth in my backpack, I swung it over my shoulders and gave Gabriel a solemn look. "Do me a favor. If I die tonight, promise me you'll get Zeb out of this alive."

He continued toward the bike, glancing back at me with an annoyed look. "No one's dying tonight. Just shut up and drive."

24

I DROVE STRAIGHT UP TO THE GIANT ARCH AT THE entrance of the cemetery, and Gabriel and I climbed the gates to get inside. The place was huge, so we had our work cut out for us.

Thor jumped from my pocket and let out a fierce growl that resonated in the darkness in an eerie way that was hard to describe. Must have been the wolf itching to come out.

The city lights glowed on the horizon, giving us enough light to make our way around without flashlights, which weren't an option for obvious reasons. Even the smokestacks of the old mill in Cabbagetown were visible over the trees.

"How have I lived right next door to this place for over a year and never been here?"

Gabriel pulled a cigarette out of his pocket and rolled it between his fingers. "It's a cemetery, Jesse."

Yeah, but it was an interesting one. There were tombs and mausoleums everywhere. The perfect place to stash a rotting corpse.

Thor was getting antsy, running ahead of us on the path to

pick up a scent. He raced around one of the graves and stopped at the headstone. After inspecting it with his nose for a few seconds, he ran back over to us and shifted. "This place stinks of death."

"What did you expect it would smell like?" I glanced around and listened, hearing nothing but distant traffic in the background. "Are you picking up on anything?"

His nose wrinkled. "There's a fresh one around somewhere."

Gabriel snickered. "What we're looking for is the complete opposite of fresh." Glancing up and down the main path, he nodded toward the distance. "I see some larger tombs down that way. Probably mausoleums. I'd suggest we stay close to the graves and work our way around to them. If they're in here somewhere, they'll be watching the paths like a hawk."

"Right." I pointed to a line of graves several rows back from the main path. "That way."

"We should probably split up," Gabriel said.

Thor's eyes widened. "Split up? Why?"

Here we go.

"What are you?" I said. "A wolf or a chicken?" This graveyard thing of his was starting to annoy me. "Get it together."

Before I could continue with the pep talk, he flashed a set of amber eyes and dropped down on all fours, shifting into the wolf. Then he took off and disappeared into the bushes.

"So much for that." I nodded to my left. "I'll go that way and meet you down by the mausoleums."

We parted ways, and I had to admit the place did feel creepy without anyone to lurk through the graves beside me. But I definitely wasn't alone. One of the grave markers I passed had an old photo on it. It was sealed in plastic or resin attached to the stone. A woman wearing a dress that looked like a lacy bedspread. Morbid if you asked me.

Careful, Jesse! You got a crowd watching. The one on the left will jump you!

My toe caught the concrete border of a plot when Uncle Ames's warning startled me, sending me tumbling into a headstone. I rolled onto my knees and looked up, coming face-to-face with the wolf's amber eyes.

Thor shifted, and suddenly I was face-to-face with his dangling penis. "Jesus, Thor!"

"You need to be more respectful of the graves." He helped me to my feet and gave me a firm nod. "Wake up the dead like that and you'll be bringing one home with you."

"Yeah, Uncle Ames just warned me."

"He's right." Thor shuddered. "They're everywhere."

I glanced around, expecting to see a bunch of eyes staring at me. I didn't see a thing, but I could sure as hell feel them. "Let's just keep moving."

As we crept closer to the mausoleums, I decided to explore his phobia some more. "What happened? Did you get left in a cemetery on a dare when you were a kid?"

"I shifted for the first time in a graveyard when I was fourteen. Had no idea what was happening to me." He seemed to muse over the memory for a few seconds and then snapped out of it. "It was also the night I murdered my uncle."

"Wait. What?" I stopped and turned to look at him. "How come you never mentioned that before?"

"You never asked."

"Asked if you murdered your uncle?" This was getting weird.

He started walking again. "Asked why I left my family."

He'd told me they'd disowned him, but he never mentioned the reason. I grabbed his arm to stop him. "Okay. Why?"

Glancing over my shoulder, he nodded. "Oh look. There's Gabriel." Then he walked past me, leaving the details of his sordid past to my imagination.

"This conversation isn't over," I said when I caught up to him. Gabriel looked back and forth at the two of us. "So much for splitting up." His eyes roamed around the vicinity. "Not a snake in sight."

My eyes wandered over to a rather large mausoleum on my right. "Christ!" It looked like a mini replica of a Gothic church, complete with bat-winged gargoyles at the top. "The front door on this thing probably costs more than the house I'm renting."

Gabriel let out a quiet chuckle. "Only the finest for the dead."

"Seriously, this is insane." There were other mausoleums around us. Not as ostentatious as the one I couldn't take my eyes off, but they were still impressive.

Thor cleared his throat. "Can we get back to the plan please?"

"You tell me," I said. "You haven't picked up on anything here, so we might as well move on to the next one." The next mega cemetery on the list was east of here with a mere five hundred acres to investigate.

Without warning, Thor dropped down on all fours and took off. Not a word or anything.

"Did I miss something?" I asked Gabriel.

He had an odd look on his face as he looked down at the ground. "You feel that?"

I shook my head. "Feel what?" I must have been losing my touch, because I seemed to be the only one not reacting. Thor had taken off like lightning, and now Gabriel was looking at his feet like the earth was about to split open.

He stepped back and lifted his right foot. Then he dropped to the ground and placed his ear to the grass. "Take your boots off."

"Come on, Gabriel."

"Do it!"

"Easy, tiger." He didn't bark at me very often, so I kicked off a boot and set my foot on the grass. "And?"

He held his hand up. "Just wait."

Feeling a little foolish, I shut up and did as he asked, but the only thing I felt was the cold grass against my sock. I was about to tell him he was getting on my nerves when a vibration traveled underneath my foot. More like a pulse. "What is that?"

He climbed back to his feet and shook his head. "I don't know, but it's getting stronger."

We stood there for a moment, both listening for the slightest sound. After a minute or two, it picked up, only now the pattern was obvious. It was the unmistakable rhythm of a heartbeat. A heartbeat coming from the earth.

I slowly pulled my eyes away from the ground and looked up at him. "They did it, didn't they?"

He shook his head. "Not until they get their hands on those stones."

"Then what the hell is that?"

"It's the beast all right. Remember, Kiko has one of those emeralds in her possession. Just enough to stir the corpse. The real fun begins when she gets the rest of them tomorrow night."

"Where the hell is it coming from?" My head shot in every direction, looking for signs of a pillaged tomb.

Gabriel scanned the cemetery and pointed north. "Thor ran that way."

"He must have found it." I took the backpack off and started rooting through it. "We have to find him before he does something stupid like charge in there."

He nodded to the shark-tooth pendant dangling from my hand. "What do you plan to do with that?"

"I'm gonna make it squeal."

He frowned. "I thought you said it was fake."

"It is, but he's had it for over a century, so he's formed a pretty powerful connection to the thing. Believe me, he'll feel it and come running." I patted my pockets. "Got a light?" Gabriel gave up cigarettes for Emmaline, but he carried a pack like I did and snuck one now and then. He always had a lighter on him.

"You really do know how to make things difficult." When he stuck two fingers in his mouth, I thought he was about to whistle loud enough to wake the dead—and bring Kiko's men running— but I heard nothing.

My head snapped in the direction of a low growl in the distance. It got louder when Gabriel did it again, only this time he didn't let up. Thor burst through the bushes, leaping over graves as he charged.

Gabriel finally cut off the high-pitched whistle and nodded to the shark tooth still dangling from my hand. "You can put that away now."

Thor kept coming.

"Ah… Gabriel."

By the time he looked up, Thor came down on top of him, tearing at his limbs with his razor-sharp teeth. They rolled onto to dirt path, stirring up a dense cloud of dust. When it cleared, Gabriel was gone and Thor was snapping at the air, covered in Gabriel's blood.

"Damn it!" I stalked over to him but stopped when he rolled over on his back and started to wiggle in the dirt. A strange whimpering sound was coming from his mouth. "Thor? Are you hurt?"

"He's high."

Gabriel was standing behind me when I spun around. "What?"

Most of his wounds were already gone, but he showed me a particularly gruesome one that was still healing. "The bastard bit me."

"Well, sober him up so he can tell us where they are."

Gabriel sighed, nudging Thor with the tip of his boot. "Get up, you fleabag."

"That's it?"

He looked at me over his shoulder. "What would you like me to do? Administer Narcan?"

"I don't care what you do, but we're losing our window of opportunity."

As Thor thrashed around in the dirt, he shifted. His euphoric grin vanished when his eyes popped open and he saw us standing over him.

"Get up." I wanted to knock his lights out, but he had valuable information.

After climbing to his feet, he glared at Gabriel. "*That* was unnecessary! You could have destroyed my eardrums!"

"You're being dramatic. I was just trying to get your attention."

"Will the two of you shut up?" I pointed toward the trees. "What's that light?" It was faint and coming from the direction where Thor had just been.

He held his hand out. "My clothes please."

I threw him the backpack. "We don't have all night."

As he got dressed, his words were music to my ears. "It's the golden ring. There's a rather large tomb over there, off the beaten path, where they've set up shop." He snorted a laugh. "You should see the size of that corpse, and it's breathing."

"We heard it," I said. "How many are there?"

He let out a heavy sigh and seemed to be counting in his head. "Maybe ten. Kiko isn't with them and neither is Zeb. Just a bunch of her henchmen."

"She'll have a lot more tomorrow night when we make the exchange. A whole army. And I doubt she plans to let us walk away after it's done." I gave Thor a once-over. "You're standing here, so I assume they didn't see you."

"They were too preoccupied to notice anything."

"What does that mean?"

He took a seat on a tombstone before continuing. "They were standing around the open sarcophagus like a bunch of witches circling a cauldron." A shudder ran through him. "Their eyes were closed while they moaned like they were about to explode with pleasure. About to peak if you know what I mean."

Gabriel nodded like he knew exactly what Thor was describing. "They're feeding off the corpse. Recharging. We need to get out of here before they finish."

"Wait," I said. "Shouldn't you and I at least take a look?"

"Not unless you have a death wish. Thor can fill us in when we get to Sanguine."

"Sanguine?" Thor looked like he was about to bolt. "So those bloodsuckers can lock me in that cell again? No, thank you."

"No one's putting you back in that basement," I said. "We're going back there to come up with a plan to kill that thing. Then I need to have a talk with a faery."

25

"WE FOUND IT," I SAID THE MOMENT WE WALKED INTO Blade's office. "Well, Thor did."

Thor squinted at the vampire. "That's right, and if you want details, you won't even think about putting me back in that basement."

Blade was sitting with his feet up on the desk, tossing a baseball between his hands. "And disturb the peace around here? I wouldn't dream of it." He got up and threw the ball across the room, stepping closer to me. "Where is it?"

"Whoa." I took a step back. I wasn't about to lay all my cards on the table without some reassurance we were square when this was over. Thor and I were done after that corpse was destroyed and Kiko was dead. We were out of the Bastians' business for good. No *I have one more job for you to do, and then we're even* bullshit. Ma was right about no one getting out of the mob once you'd dipped your toes into their dirty business. "Let me make something very clear. We help you destroy Kiko, and our temporary partnership is dissolved. We all go our separate ways after tomorrow night. Got it?"

An amused grin crossed his face. "I see. You think I'm gonna come after you and force you to work for me?" He chuckled. "You've been watching too many movies, Jesse."

"And you're forgetting what I used to do for a living. I know exactly how cartels operate, so I'd suggest we come to an agreement right now." I held my hand out to shake on it. Not that criminals had any honor, but there were witnesses in the room, and his word had to mean something.

After thinking it over, he took my hand and squeezed it slightly. As he let go, he kept his sky-blue eyes trained on mine. "Am I allowed to call you? If I need to hire a good investigator," he quickly added.

"I'll think about it."

Thor let out a groan. "Now that we've settled that, can we get on with the plan?"

"Yes," Blade said, still gazing at me. "What is this plan?"

"Same as before. We're going to deliver Charles and the stones to Kiko while you and your vampires are destroying that corpse."

He squinted at me. "And where is this all supposed to take place?"

"They moved the sarcophagus to Oakland Cemetery and conveniently hijacked a tomb."

A look of surprise appeared on his face, followed by a laugh. "Damn. How perfect is that?" Then he stifled the humor and looked at me with a straight face. "Where is this exchange supposed to take place?"

Kiko's message hadn't actually specified a location. "She hasn't told me yet. Said she'd be in touch." There was that laugh again. "You think this is funny?"

He was suddenly in my face. "Not at all. I think it's absurd." His eyes bored into mine as he came even closer, his bourbon-laced breath all over me. "I like to win, Jesse. If this plan of yours fails, you'll owe me."

Was he trying to gaslight me? How the hell did I become indebted to him? If anyone owed anyone, he owed me. But with a room full of vampires, he had the upper hand here.

I poked my index finger in the center of his chest and gently pushed. "Back off."

After he gave me a little breathing room, I proceeded with the plan. "I'll convince her to meet somewhere nearby, but I doubt she'll stray too far away from that corpse. As soon as I leave with Charles—another variable I need to deal with—you guys head for the tomb." I motioned to Thor. "He'll take you there."

"Me?" He looked like he wanted to bolt again.

"Would you rather make the exchange?"

He clammed up tight, allowing me to continue. "We're gonna stall like hell until we get a signal that the deed is done, so you've got to get in there fast. If she gets her hands on those stones first, it's over. No mistakes, Blade. None."

He still seemed skeptical. "And if she insists on making the exchange at the tomb? We could just drop a load of dynamite on it and call it a day. Nothing could survive that."

"Including Zeb."

He raised a brow. "Is he a *good* friend?"

"Fuck off! Besides, you're giving Kiko too much credit." I knew the mindset of desperation. Another handy little skill I'd picked up at the bureau. "She's desperate. If she wants those stones, she'll compromise and meet where I say."

"You said Charlie has agreed to help us."

"Yeah. He gave me his number to set up a meeting." I pulled my phone out to give him a call.

Blade glanced at it. "Give me that phone!"

It rang as I yanked it out of reach. "It's Kiko." The room fell silent as I stared at her name on the screen.

"Answer it," Gabriel said when I just stood there.

I held the phone to my ear. "Hello." After listening to her instructions without saying a word, I hung up and looked at Blade. "We're making the exchange tomorrow night at eleven o'clock, and we couldn't have asked for a better place."

CHARLES WALKED into Sanguine two hours before we were to make the exchange. But instead of heading for the office, he walked over to the bar.

"Son of a bitch!" Blade pulled his eyes away from the security monitors and stood up. "That idiot doesn't know what's good for him. I told him to come alone."

I looked at the screen and spotted Sylvia standing next to him at the bar. Six and Nine walked up behind them a moment later. After the bartender handed him a drink, he walked toward the hallway.

Blade swung the door open and waited. "What the fuck is this?" he demanded when they approached his office.

"You're looking well, Blade." Charles walked past him and headed straight for me with the others on his heels. "Hello, Jesse."

"You don't listen, do you?"

He smiled pleasantly. "You expect me to walk into a lion's den without backup?"

"We're your backup!" Blade growled.

"Funny. Last I heard, you had a bounty on my head."

Gabriel was a little more pragmatic about the situation. "We can use as many hands as we can get. A few fae in our court will increase our chances of success tonight."

Blade finally calmed down but wagged his finger at Charles.

"You double-crossed me. You were supposed to get out of town, not disappear off the face of the earth."

"Yes, but it was safer for me to disappear."

I'd had enough of them. "If you two are done, we need to get down to business. We have less than two hours."

"By all means, speak," Blade said, giving me the floor.

"Charles and I will show up on that rooftop at eleven o'clock sharp. Not a second earlier or later." Unbeknownst to Kiko, she'd given us a gift. The perfect location to make the exchange. An abandoned building on the street opposite the cemetery. We'd checked it out this morning. It was literally across the street from where they'd stashed the corpse, and she'd instructed us to meet her on the roof. The perfect place where she could keep an eye on the tomb and so could we. We couldn't have asked for a better location.

"I'm going with you," Six said.

I scoffed. "Like hell. Her instructions were clear. The two of us. That's it. If she sees you, the game's over."

Charles gave her a firm look. "You'll stay with the others."

Six shot her eyes to me. "Fuck the roof! I don't understand why we can't just go in there and slaughter them all!"

Was she stupid? "Because she'll kill Zeb, you idiot!" I stood eye to eye with her, not forgetting about that mind fuck she'd given me. "Are you gonna be a problem?"

Gabriel broke it up before it could get any hairier. "Jesse's right. We won't sacrifice Zeb."

I continued with the plan. "When the clock strikes eleven, you go in there and kill them all and destroy that corpse." I looked at Six. "Is that enough slaughtering for you?"

The look she gave me made the hair on the back of my neck stand up. No one should ever have a faery look at them like that.

Blade brought up the one thing that could shoot the whole

plan to hell. "You better hope it's that easy and we don't run into a delay."

"Like I said last night—we'll stall like hell until it's done. By the way, how *will* we know?"

He had a wicked grin on his face. "Oh, you'll know."

26

We parked a few blocks down from the entrance because why chance it? I had a feeling they wouldn't be as preoccupied tonight. Kiko's whole damn army was probably charged off that corpse and ready for the big resurrection, so the sound of a Harley pulling up to the gates was a risk we couldn't afford to take.

One of the side gates was open when we walked up, but Blade and his crew were nowhere in sight.

"Someone's here." I checked the time. It was ten thirty, and there were no vampires to be seen.

Right on cue, vampires started stepping out from the surrounding graves. It was like watching a bad horror movie.

"Thought we bailed, eh?" Blade grinned as he walked over to me. "Wouldn't miss it for the world. Let's go kill some snakes."

"Where's Thor?" He'd caught a ride with Blade because I wasn't lugging around a backpack full of his clothes tonight, and no one needed to see his naked ass when he shifted.

"He's around here somewhere. Probably taking a piss on a grave."

He was probably right. "What about Charles?"

He motioned for me to follow him. For the sake of avoiding a confrontation and drawing attention to us, I headed into the cemetery with him. The fae were conspicuously absent, and the mission would be over before it even started if Charles didn't show up with that ring. I was about to panic when I saw someone sitting on a tombstone up ahead of us.

Six stood up as we approached. "Charles has a few questions before you go." She nodded to a row of shrubs.

"Is he behind the bushes or what?" We didn't have time for games. If he was having second thoughts, I was going to drag him up to that rooftop. When I looked back to the bushes, he was standing in front of them.

"Tell me again why I should do this," he said when I walked up to him.

"Because it's the only way to stay alive. You know that better than anyone." He seemed a little fidgety. "Look. We go up there, they blow that tomb to smithereens, then we get the hell out of there while Kiko melts like the Wicked Witch of the West. She'll fold the second her power source is cut off."

He bit the edge of his lip and started to pace. "I don't know. It's risky."

"Hell yeah, it's risky. But if you have a better idea, please enlighten me." I played the guilt card next. "Don't forget there's an innocent man on that roof who wouldn't be in this situation if it wasn't for you."

"All right." He reached into his pocket and pulled out the ring. The pink stone reflected the moonlight like a fine diamond. "A jeweler would value this as a novelty stone, but it's worth a fortune to those serpents. It's the final key." After stuffing it back in his pocket, he took a deep breath. "I'm ready."

We went back over to the others so we could spend our last five minutes walking through the plan for the hundredth time.

But first I needed the emerald. The thought of getting up to the roof and realizing it was still in Blade's pocket made me shiver.

I held my hand out. "Give me the emerald."

A startled look appeared on his face as he patted his jacket, followed by a grin as he pulled the small box from his pocket.

I grabbed it from him as my heart stopped racing. Why did people think shit like that was funny?

Gabriel glanced at the time and moved the conversation along. "You walk onto that roof at eleven sharp. We'll take care of the tomb, so you do whatever you have to do to stall until you see fireworks over the cemetery." He turned to Blade. "Where's the device?"

Aka the bomb.

"Don't worry. It's right where it needs to be."

"Make sure Zeb isn't in there before you do it." I doubted Kiko would be stupid enough to show up on the roof without him, but I didn't want to take any chances and get the man blown up.

A headstone to the left of me shook and tumbled over as that beating vibration we'd felt last night started up again, only now it was much stronger.

Blade's eyes darted to the ground. "What the fuck is that?"

"It's the corpse," Gabriel said. "It's waking up. Probably senses the stones." He gave me a commiserative look. "It's time to go. I wish I could go up there with you."

"That makes two of us."

Charles got a wary look on his face, and Six just had to open her damn mouth. "You don't have to do this, Charles. Just say the word and we're gone."

Sylvia grabbed Six's arm when she started walking toward him. "Let it go! He's tired of running. We settle this tonight."

"Don't worry about me." He glanced around at the vampires

and fae standing in the shadows. "Worry about yourselves getting that corpse destroyed."

Couldn't have put it better myself.

As we were leaving, I looked back at Blade. "Don't fuck this up."

"Not on your life, darlin'."

We left the cemetery and crossed the street to the building. After going inside, we took the stairs up four flights. When we reached the door to the roof, I checked the time and held up two fingers. I was so nervous I wanted to puke.

Charles leaned against the wall as we waited for the exact moment to walk out. A minute too soon, we'd be stalling and saying a prayer at the same time. A minute too late, we might miss the fireworks and give them the chance to kill Zeb before they died along with their queen.

At exactly eleven o'clock, I braced myself and pushed the door open. The night air hit me as a rush of adrenaline raced through my veins. All sound seemed to cease except for the blood rushing through my ears as I stepped onto the roof and glanced around.

Where is everyone?

I spotted Kiko standing near the three-foot wall overlooking the front of the building, in the perfect position to keep an eye on the cemetery. Zeb was right in front of her. Her arm was wrapped around his chest, pulling him tightly against her. He looked okay, but I noted the fear in his eyes. What I didn't see were any of her men. It was just the two of them.

Fuck!

The cocky bitch was so confident she could handle me and Charles that she'd come alone. All her men were down in the cemetery, creating a fortress around that tomb.

I glanced at Charles. "She fucked us."

"Just stall," he muttered back.

We made our way across the roof and stopped about ten feet away from them. Kiko wasn't looking so good. Her pale skin had a bluish cast, and the whites of her eyes were bloodshot. Even her hair, which was usually impeccable, looked dull. Faded and lacking its usual shine.

"I see you found my husband." She had a strange grin on her face as she gazed at him. Like she wanted to eat him or something. God help the man if the plan went south and she got her hands on him. But that wasn't going to happen while I was still alive.

The stalling commenced. "You hired me to do a job, and I did it. But I haven't decided yet if I'm going to hand him over to you. Why don't you convince me."

Her grin turned into a sneer. "Give me the ring and the emerald and your friend goes free." She smiled at her husband. "Charles can bring them to me."

The clock kept ticking but still no boom. "Wait a minute. I have terms."

"You have nothing! Give me the stones, or I'll slit his throat and throw him over the side of the building!" A knife appeared in her other hand as she positioned it over Zeb's neck. "Five seconds!"

I glanced across the street but didn't see so much as a plume of smoke rising up from the cemetery. Five seconds wasn't going to do it. "Hand Zeb over first."

If blood could boil, hers was roiling. I could practically feel it. Kiko Orochi wasn't accustomed to people defying her. She was also desperate, like a junky about to come apart.

She gripped Zeb tighter and ran the blade slowly across his neck, barely cutting deep enough to leave a thin trail of blood on his skin. His teeth gritted, but it was probably more from fear. It was a bluff. She needed him alive to get me to hand over those stones.

I pulled the box from my pocket and opened it to show her the emerald. Her eyes lit up as a gasp came out of her mouth.

"I'll give you this, but you don't get the ring until I get Zeb." I tossed it toward her, and she dropped the knife and let go of him. It was pathetic, watching her scramble to catch it. The emerald came to life in her hands, giving off an intense glow. You'd think it was the Hope Diamond the way she cradled it with both hands.

The rooftop suddenly rumbled. I braced myself and looked down at my feet. There was a crack starting to form between them. A few seconds later, the rumble came again. Kiko was vibrating when I looked back up at her. She appeared to be absorbing the emerald's light as her entire body started to glow from the inside out.

I glanced at Zeb, who was standing a few feet away from her, in a perfect position to run while she was distracted. But he just stood there.

"Give me the ring!" It was no longer Kiko's voice. It was deep and raspy.

Something caught my eye in the distance. A flash. There was a swarm of commotion below in the cemetery.

Kiko looked over the edge. "What have you done!"

"Got any of that powder on you?" I muttered to Charles. "Maybe I can get close enough to her."

His eyes were fixed on the woman he'd married. "No, but I don't think it would have any effect on *that* anyway." He nodded to her.

When I looked back at Kiko, she was vibrating again, fading in and out. "Take Zeb and get out of here."

Charles shook his head. "I can't help him. He's moving in the wrong direction."

Zeb had finally gotten control of his feet, but he was inching toward the other side of the roof instead of the door. The man was his own worst enemy at times.

"Then take the ring and run."

"She'll kill both of you."

I still had faith that the explosion was coming, and I wasn't leaving Zeb behind.

Charles took my advice and backed up toward the door. "I'll send help."

"Yeah, you do that. Now get out of here before she gets her hands on that ring."

He made a run for it when Kiko went into a spin. She sped up, becoming a blur and dropping to the roof floor. When she finally came to a stop, the dragon was staring back at me. A Komodo dragon with a two-foot-long forked tongue that swept the ground as it swung its head around toward Zeb.

"Your precious ring just walked out the door," I said to distract it.

The beast lost interest in Zeb and focused on me, swinging its massive tail sideways as it approached. A hiss filled the air as it crossed the roof so fast I barely had time to stumble back against the wall separating me from the street below.

I reached for my gun and fired, hitting it between the eyes. The tiny hole oozed with rosé-colored blood but healed within seconds as the dragon shook it off and kept coming toward me, the stench from its mouth making me cringe. Its head swung back and forth, and then it was close enough to flick its tongue over my face and neck.

A loud pop came from below, and the dragon stepped back and turned its eyes toward the cemetery.

It looked back at me and lunged. I rolled, losing my grip on the gun. The dragon lashed out, clipping me with its powerful claws, dragging me forward as it crawled on top of me with its considerable weight. When its teeth sank into my shoulder, I nearly passed out.

The eyes, Jesse! Take out the eyes!

My hand took on a life of its own as I jammed my fist, index and middle fingers first, into the dragon's right eye. I slammed my fingers into the socket over and over until the beast let out a cringeworthy sound and slithered backward.

Zeb was in its direct path, but he didn't move as it backed up toward him.

"Run!" I yelled.

He just stood there, making strange sounds and moving his arms as if he were conducting the whole thing.

I backpedaled and hit the wall, looking for my gun to buy some time before the dragon was on top of me again. I grabbed it, but my body started to shake as I took aim.

The poison.

Damn it, Jesse! Get to Zeb!

I shoved the gun in my pocket when the rooftop started to shift. As I crawled toward Zeb, the whole building started to shake violently. In a commanding voice, Zeb yelled at the sky, and the crack in the roof started to split wider, leaving a large gap running directly under the dragon. It swung its head from left to right as the crack threatened to swallow it up. Then it let out a deep growl that culminated in an ear-piercing hiss and took off toward the door.

Zeb ran over and looked at the wound on my shoulder. "You got bitten!"

"Sure did," I said with a faint laugh. "Damn, Zeb. Did you do all that?"

"I surprise myself sometimes, but now isn't the time to talk about it. I need to get you off this roof."

He pulled me to my feet and practically dragged me to the door. Then we took the stairs the hard way.

27

ZEB NEARLY FINISHED ME OFF BY ROUGHLY DRAGGING ME down four flights of stairs, but he was no spring chicken, and I wasn't exactly a twig. Lucky for me, Gabriel was already on his way across the street when we staggered outside.

"That lizard took a bite out of her," Zeb said as he lowered me to the ground.

Without hesitating, Gabriel pulled a knife out of his pocket and slit his wrist, holding the cut to my mouth. After getting a good dose of his blood, I sat up and gripped his arm tighter, practically digging my teeth into his skin.

"That's enough, Jesse!" He pulled his arm away, looking relieved.

I licked my lips and slowly climbed to my feet, steadying myself against him as the rush hit me. "Whoa!" Then I stepped back and glared at him. "What the hell happened? Kiko almost had us both for lunch."

"Her army. That's what happened. We walked right into an ambush."

"Where's Charles?" He seemed uneasy about the question, so I grabbed his jacket and pulled him closer. "Where is he?"

Before he could answer, the vibrations traveled under my feet. The heartbeat coming from the ground. My eyes shot to the cemetery when the sky lit up.

"Kiko has him," Gabriel finally said. "He walked right into their waiting arms when he ran out of that building. When Kiko showed up next, I knew you were in trouble."

As it sank in, I looked at Zeb. "Go home. And lock your damn doors this time."

He looked at me like I was crazy. "How am I supposed to get there?"

"Walk!" We were less than a mile from his studio.

"All right, but you be careful. If I don't hear from you by morning, I'm coming back."

If he didn't hear from me by morning, it was because I was dead. "Okay, now get going."

I watched him disappear down the sidewalk, and then I ran across the street.

"Jesse, wait!"

There was no time to wait. As soon as I entered the cemetery, I spotted Six walking toward me. Her fist landed on the right side of my jaw, sending me stumbling backward.

"You were supposed to protect him!" she growled.

I could respect the sucker punch, but her finger pointed dangerously close to my face was a no-no. I rubbed my jaw and returned the love, clocking her square in the face and sending her back against a tree. After spitting blood on the ground next to her, I wiped my mouth with my sleeve. "Now that that's settled, let's go get him back."

Blade came through the graves and looked at the two of us. "Did I miss something?"

Glaring, I walked past him toward the tomb, watching the light in the sky grow brighter.

"Jesse!" Gabriel called out.

I kept moving because every second mattered and I'd just wasted precious time on a woman who for some reason couldn't get past her hostility for me. The closer I got, the more remnants of Red Dragons I spotted on the ground. It was littered with shriveled serpents. The vampires must have had a field day taking them out. But there was still an inner line of defense guarding that corpse. I came to an abrupt stop when I realized why. Beyond the Dragons circling the tomb, there was something else guarding it. Something big.

I started to move closer but was blindsided and knocked to the ground. Thor rolled me back a good ten feet, finally straddling me with all fours as the wolf's amber eyes stared down at me. He bared his teeth, and for a second I thought he'd lost his mind and planned to take a bite out of me.

"What the hell's wrong with you?" I tried to shove him off, but he wouldn't budge.

A moment later, he shifted. "You're going to get yourself killed, Jesse!"

Gabriel and Blade caught up to us, both raising a brow when they saw Thor straddling me naked.

Thor finally climbed off me and stood up. "She was about to go gung ho at that tomb." He didn't seem the slightest bit concerned about his genitals being spotlighted by the light of the full moon. The man was a classic exhibitionist.

I climbed to my feet and looked at the creature. It had to be at least ten feet tall. It stood on two legs and had shiny scales up to its shoulders where it transitioned to porcelain-white skin. But that wasn't the creepiest part. Its hair hung down in stringy black strands, and its eyes were cloudy white without pupils. I couldn't tell if the thing was awake or if it was caught up in some kind of trance.

"That thing is Kiko, isn't it?" I said.

Blade nodded. "Went straight from the dragon to this. She's been standing like that ever since."

Gabriel let out a frustrated sigh. "That's what I've been trying to tell you, but you don't listen."

"Yeah, I need to work on that. How do we kill her?"

"The same way we planned. We blow up the corpse inside that tomb. But we have two problems—Charles is in there, and we have to get past Kiko and the rest of her Dragons to set the explosives."

We were close enough to hurl that bomb over their heads. But even if we were lucky enough to hit the target, we'd kill Charles in the process.

Gabriel took a deep breath and exhaled slowly. "We've killed most of them, so taking the rest out is doable. But…"

"You mean we need to distract Kiko to get Charles out," I said, finishing his thought.

Thor stepped up. "I'll do it."

"Like hell. I didn't agree to work with a bunch of vampires just to see you get yourself killed after all."

Blade leaned in with a wolfish grin. "You're gonna miss me when this is over."

"About as much as a toothache."

"Then I'll have to make myself memorable. I'll distract her."

I was about to volunteer myself when the pulsing of the ground picked up. Something big was happening, and I suspected the ritual was moving along nicely. If we didn't get the lead out and make a decision about who was going to take one for the team, it wouldn't matter.

An owl suddenly called out from the trees, followed by the caw of a crow. But crows generally weren't vocal at night unless there was danger. A war cry followed, and figures started raining down from the oak trees all around us and headed for the tomb.

My hopes for a well-executed attack faded. "You've got to be kidding me."

"Is that who I think it is?" Gabriel asked, watching the last one land and take off.

Blade's playful demeanor shifted on a dime. "The fae. They're going in for Charlie."

Six led the charge, followed by her entourage of mostly females, including Sylvia and Nine. She shot me a vicious glare before taking off. A fae with a grudge. If we got out of this alive, something told me I'd be looking over my shoulder for a very long time.

"Change of plans." Gabriel looked at Blade. "Start slaughtering. Jesse and I will handle Kiko."

"What about me?" Thor said.

"Do what a wolf does best. Bite."

Blade gave a signal, and the cemetery came alive. Vampires emerged from the shadows and ran into the fight. Thor shifted and followed them while Gabriel and I waited for that she-reptile to show signs of movement. But Kiko just stood there, motionless, with all the carnage taking place around her and the moon shining down and illuminating her ghostly blank eyes.

I glanced at Gabriel. "What are the odds she's conscious?"

He studied her for a few seconds, stroking his chin. "I don't know, but we're about to find out. Ladies first."

I countered. "Age before beauty."

On the count of three, we headed in together. Up ahead, I spotted Six coming out of the tomb with Charles. He was walking on his own, but he looked shaken.

I nudged Gabriel and pointed to them. "We just got the green light."

With Charles out of danger and a path quickly being cleared for us, we took off to blow up that corpse.

Halfway to the tomb, my foot caught something. A casualty. It was a woman with two large bite marks to her neck. One of the fae. We kept moving, dodging bodies. Dragons that would shrivel to almost nothing within minutes. Blade had underestimated the power of his team, but none of us had anticipated the fae showing up in force either. I doubted they would have put themselves at risk if Charles's head hadn't been on the line.

We approached the tomb, both of us dumbfounded by Kiko's lack of consciousness. Not even the slaughter taking place a few yards away had stirred the beast.

Gabriel pulled the device from his inside pocket as gently as possible as we crept past her catatonic form standing at the entrance of the tomb. I expected her to wake up and focus her eyes on us at any moment, forcing us to pull off a miracle.

Once inside, I got a good look at the woman at the center of all the fuss. The lid of the sarcophagus had been removed, and the rotted, petrified corpse was on full display. The emeralds had been placed in her eye sockets, and her chest was moving up and down. The only thing missing was the ring.

"What's that?" I pointed to a light coming from the foot of the sarcophagus.

Gabriel followed its path with his eyes. "I have no idea, but it can't be good."

We followed the light out the door and watched it trail across the ground and radiate into Kiko's body. With each breath, both the light coming from the corpse and the moon above grew brighter. Then I noticed that the missing ring was on Kiko's finger and the rosé-colored stone was swirling like it was made of liquid.

"Here's a thought," I said to Gabriel, pointing my thumb at the corpse inside. "What if they're not trying to resurrect that thing? What if Kiko is becoming it?"

We both turned to look at the sarcophagus. The corpse let

out a raspy sound and appeared to shrivel a little more with each breath that Kiko's sleeping giant took.

"Shouldn't they be trying to *unshrivel* that thing?"

Without wasting another second, Gabriel went back into the tomb and placed the device inside the sarcophagus. His foot brushed through the stream of light as he turned to leave, and a screech that I could only describe as what a pterodactyl might sound like filled my ears.

He looked up at Kiko's fluttering eyes. "Run!"

I took off, yelling for anyone within earshot to take cover. Glancing back, I saw her hair come to life, twisting and turning with snakes trailing down her head and past her shoulders. The cloudiness of her eyes had cleared, revealing black slits and emerald irises. Medusa in the flesh.

She took a single step, and everything exploded, the impact sending me hurtling into the darkness. I felt myself floating, and a ringing sound filled my ears as the light from the moon dimmed. And then everything was gone.

GABRIEL WAS SLAPPING my face when the world came back into focus.

"Come on, Jesse, wake up!"

It took me a second to remember where I was, but the ground shaking underneath me quickly brought it all back. "What happened?"

He yanked me to my feet as Kiko came toward us, her skin shriveling as her bright green eyes lost their glow. That nest of snakes on top of her head was as alive as ever though.

One of them dropped to the ground and slithered toward us. I grabbed my gun and took aim, but before I could pull the trigger, it stopped and started to smoke. A moment later it was nothing but a piece of dried-up leather. The rest of the serpents slid from her head and combusted before hitting the ground. Kiko herself seemed to be withering.

I glanced at the spot where the tomb had been a few minutes earlier. "She's dying."

"No," Gabriel said. "She's losing her immortality."

I took a step closer and got a good look at her face. Her right eye was sunken in. The one I'd jammed my fingers into up on the roof. And her skin wasn't just shriveling, it was aging.

Her mouth suddenly opened and she lurched, sending a river of something black spilling out of it. It looked like motor oil. The woman was cooked.

Blade pulled a knife from his boot and started to walk toward her. "I've been wanting to do this for a long time."

Gabriel grabbed his arm to stop him. "Let her go. She needs to live with herself for a while."

I agreed. Karma was a bitch, and Kiko Orochi was about to feel it with a vengeance. I had no idea how old she actually was, but without her immortality, her days were numbered. The woman looked like she was one step away from the grave.

"Do whatever you want with her," I said. "I'm going home."

Blade gave it some thought. "You're right." He stuck the knife back in his boot and looked at Kiko. "Have a nice life."

Her eyes flew wide as her new reality started to sink in. "You can't leave me like this!" Then she dropped to her knees. "Kill me!"

Gabriel caught up to me as I headed for the gate, and Thor came stumbling out of the bushes next, naked but intact.

I glanced around for the fae. "What happened to Charles?"

Gabriel quietly chuckled. "As soon as the fae got him out of that tomb, they disappeared."

Those faeries were smart. They knew damn well we'd finish the job without them. I wondered what this all meant for the alliance, and since Thor and I benefited from keeping the Romans out of Atlanta, I was praying for that relationship to continue.

"Jesse!"

I turned around to look back at Blade. "What?"

"I'll see you soon." He grinned before disappearing into the graves.

As I walk through the gate, Ma's words ran through my head. But a deal was a deal, and I didn't work for anyone but myself. I just hoped I wouldn't have to convince Blade of that.

28

MA SET MY PLATE DOWN AND LEANED OVER THE BAR. "SO it's over?"

"God willing." I took a bite of my sandwich and thought about it for a minute. The corpse and the Red Dragons were history, but Kiko was another story. We'd left the cemetery last night with the Red Widow on her knees and begging for death, but there was no mercy. She was on her own, mortal, and on her last leg. I'd actually felt a tad guilty leaving her out there—for about five seconds. But I'd learned from my years at the bureau that a dangerous criminal wasn't really dealt with until he or she was dead, and I was starting to regret not letting Blade finish the job.

Gabriel and Thor walked into Speaks as I was finishing up my lunch. Thor had slept in after our night of fun, and Gabriel had gone to have a word with Blade before returning to Savannah. He said it was to tie up some old business with the vampires, but I had a feeling that business involved me.

Whatever got the Bastians off my ass.

"How's Zeb?" Gabriel asked.

I'd stopped by the studio early that morning to let Zeb know

I was still alive and kicking. After helping him clean up the mess from Kiko's thugs ravaging the place, we had a little talk about what he'd done on top of that building. Zeb wasn't your average wizard, and contrary to his reputation, he said he'd never been very good at magic. But something changed last night. Said it was like the hand of Merlin entered him on that rooftop. Personally, I thought it was just his latent powers waking up when faced with death.

Anyway… he'd decided to dedicate more time to developing his wizardly skills. I worried for the safety of Cabbagetown if it became the center of his experimental incubator.

"Zeb's fine. In fact, he's better than fine. I think last night gave him a whole new perspective on his mission in life."

Thor snickered. "Mission, eh? Please don't tell me he's decided to run for mayor of Cabbagetown."

"We don't have a mayor, but there's always city council."

I got up to walk Gabriel out. "I hate to say goodbye to you, but I know you want to get home to Emmaline. She's probably ready to hunt me down for keeping you here so long."

He laughed. "I think it's me in the doghouse, not you."

When we got outside, I stuffed my hands in my pockets and let out a long breath. I hated goodbyes. But the two of us always seemed to be crossing paths, so it was just a matter of time before he showed up in Atlanta again or I ended up in Savannah.

I gave him a hug and shoved him. "Go on. Get out of here. Give Emmaline my best."

"I will. And stay out of trouble."

"Yeah, right." As he was about to make his dramatic exit, I stopped him. "Gabriel."

He turned. "Is something wrong?"

I shook my head. "Thanks for always having my back. I love you, man."

A wide grin crossed his face. "I love you too, kid." Then he was gone.

As I was walking back inside, my phone rang. The call was from a number I didn't recognize so I almost let it go to voice mail. I answered it anyway.

After a brief conversation, I hung up and continued to the bar.

"Who was that?" Thor asked when he saw the smile on my face.

My grin grew wider. "Our new client. Looks like we're going to Hollywood. Hollywood of the South that is."

COMING SOON!

Book 2 of the Chronicles of Jesse Ames

The Katie Bishop Universe

The Jesse Ames series is part of the Katie Bishop universe. If you want to know more about Jesse and Gabriel, read their backstories in the Katie Bishop series. Gabriel is introduced in Dark Nightingale and Jesse in Conjure Queen. But do yourself a favor and start at the beginning and get to know them all! You'll be seeing more of Katie and crew in Jesse's world!

THANK YOU

A book means nothing without someone to read it. Thank you for that. I hope you'll consider taking a few minutes to leave a brief review, even if it's just a sentence or two. And if you don't have time for a review, Amazon allows you to leave a simple rating. Five seconds and it's done!

Sign up to become and Insider at:

LuanneBennett.com

ABOUT THE AUTHOR

LUANNE BENNETT is an author of fantasy and the supernatural. Born in Chicago, she lives in Georgia these days where she writes full time and doesn't miss a thing about the cubicles and conference rooms of her old life. When she isn't writing or dreaming up new stories, she's usually cooking or tending a herd of felines.

I love to hear from readers. Contact me at:
www.luannebennett.com
books@luannebennett.com
facebook.com/LuanneBennettBooks

Printed in Great Britain
by Amazon

13378524R00154